Amazon in Exile

Amazons of Themyscira Book One

Elizabeth Salo

EBOOK ISBN: 978-1-962460-00-2

PRINT ISBN: 978-1-962460-01-9

To Chris for always believing in me, to Jessi for getting me started, and to Heather, Pru, and Glori for your endless encouragement.

Chapter One

K ALLIOPE JAMES SHOT OUT of her desk chair and into the front hallway as soon as the first shout penetrated her office door. Vanessa Paine—her best friend, assistant, and all-around go-to person—was using her bulk to block someone from entering the front door of the women's shelter. The man on the other side wasn't particularly happy about it.

"You bitch! Let me in now!" The man's voice was slurred and laced with anger. The stench of bourbon rolled off him in waves. "Sharon! Sharon, you get out here right now! And bring those girls too. I know you're in there. I tracked your phone!"

Not good. This had the potential to go south very quickly.

"Sir," Kalli said, trying to interrupt his ranting. "Sir, I'm going to have to ask you to leave."

"I'm not leaving. Not without my wife and daughters. You can't keep us apart. We're married," he explained drunkenly.

Like a piece of paper made much difference when your wife's face was black and blue.

"Be that as it may, you aren't welcome here. You need to leave before I call the police," Kalli said, readying herself in case he pushed past Vanessa.

"You can't do that. Sharon's my wife. I'm allowed to be with my wife."

"You're not allowed to be with your wife if she doesn't want you around," Kalli said.

"Carl." The whispered name and a small sob behind her whipped Kalli's head around. Sharon, a tiny blonde woman with a black eye and a split lip, was shaking in fear at the bottom of the staircase leading to the bedrooms on the second floor. Her two young daughters cowered a few steps behind their mother.

The terror in their eyes hardened Kalli's resolve. "Carl, you need to leave. I'm calling the police."

Kalli picked up the phone from the desk behind her and dialed 911. "I'm calling to report a disturbance at the Safe Haven women's shelter. There's a man trying to break into our building," she said just loud enough for him to overhear.

"Fine. I'm going," he said and stormed off.

"Yes, thank you," Kalli said to the police dispatcher, who offered to send over a unit. They would come around to take statements and get a description of the man. It was nothing that hadn't happened before and would likely happen again.

Vanessa pushed the door shut and slid the dead bolt home, collapsing against the wood. "Phew. He was a strong one."

"You did well, thanks," Kalli said, before turning and facing the three scared faces staring back at her. Now her real job began.

·»»»⟩ ⟨«««·

Collapsing into her desk chair felt like heaven. Despite it being a regular occurrence, dealing with threatening husbands and rookie police officers who barely knew how to take statements was always draining. Her eyes drifted closed, and Kalli was tempted to take a nap, but before she drifted off, Vanessa shoved open her office door and pushed her way inside.

"Oh no you don't," Vanessa said.

Kalli eased one eye open and glanced at her friend. "Oh no I don't what?" she asked innocently.

Vanessa plopped her heavyset frame into one of the soft armchairs facing Kalli's desk. "You're not going to stay here tonight." Vanessa's narrowed gaze drilled into her.

Kalli's second eye popped opened as she swiveled her chair to face Vanessa. "I wasn't going to do that," she lied.

Vanessa just cocked her head, her chin-length black hair falling away from her face. "Don't give me that line of crap. I've known you too long."

Kalli stared at her longtime friend and coworker and sighed. It was true. She'd known Vanessa for almost fifteen years. Very little escaped the eagle eyes of Vanessa Paine. Kalli had only one major secret she'd been keeping from the other woman, and while Vanessa didn't know what it was, she definitely knew there was something Kalli wasn't telling her.

Unfortunately, Kalli could never share. It wasn't exactly easy to tell your best friend that you were a four-thousand-year-old Amazon warrior. Even someone as open-minded as Vanessa would have trouble swallowing that one. Plus, Kalli had distanced herself from that part of her life a long time ago. This was her life now, and she loved having the opportunity to help people in a way that didn't involve swords and armor.

"I just like being around after a situation like that." Kalli rolled her shoulders, attempting to relieve the knots that were forming.

"I get it. But that's why we have Ben," Vanessa said.

Kalli could handle anything that happened during the day, but she'd hired Ben Fields to watch over the place at night. The man was six feet four inches and the size of a small boulder. His shaved head, nose ring, and arms full of tattoos made most unwanted visitors think twice about trying something. Ben would do anything to protect "his girls." The fact that he was gay and had a soft spot for kids helped many women feel more comfortable around him, and they were grateful to have him at the shelter in case anyone came knocking.

Kalli knew it too. She really did. After all, she was the one who'd hired Ben. She'd done a more thorough background check on him than even the FBI would have done. She wasn't about to risk the safety of her charges. They came to her for safety and security, and she was going to make sure they got it. Ben was more than capable of dealing with whatever unpleasantness might come their way.

With a long-suffering sigh, Kalli stood and reached into her desk drawer to grab her purse. Vanessa watched her and smiled. "Good. You need a night out on the town."

Kalli almost winced. "I don't do those."

Vanessa rolled her eyes. "Why not? Go out somewhere. Kick up your heels. Take your sexy ass to a bar and make men buy you drinks."

The image of Sharon's black eye and split lip came rushing back. "How can you say that? After everything you've been through and everything you see here day in and day out."

Vanessa shrugged. "I don't believe every man is like my Stan was. I still believe there are good people left in the world, and some of those good people happen to have penises."

That startled a laugh out of her. She could always count on Vanessa to cheer her up. "I wish I had your optimism. I've seen enough in my life to wonder how much good is in the average person."

"Girl, you are too young to be talking like that," Vanessa said with a grimace.

If she only knew the truth.

"You're still in your prime. Go out. Have fun for once."

Kalli just shook her head. "A good book and a hot bath for me. If I'm feeling wild, there might even be bubbles." She waggled her eyebrows suggestively.

Vanessa gently shoved her out of her own office and practically forced her toward the door with a shooing motion. "At least pick up a bottle of wine or some dinner."

Kalli stepped out into the dark streets of downtown Washington DC. Most of the businesses near the shelter were already closed for the night, so she didn't have to contend with crowds of people. She pulled out her phone and scrolled to find the number of a pizza place near her house. Before she could dial, someone smacked her wrist and sent her phone flying into the street, where it was promptly run over by a car speeding down the road.

Kalli whipped her head around, looking for the person who'd hit her, and immediately ducked sideways as a fist came flying at her. She took a rapid step back, her fists instinctively rising to protect her face. A movement caught her eye, and Sharon's husband Carl emerged from the shadows.

"You bitch," he said, this time with no evidence of an alcohol-induced slur. "It's your fault she left me. You're filling her head with lies. It's time she comes home. With me."

Kalli held her palms out toward him as he advanced on her. "Carl, you don't want to do this."

He took a step closer, looming over her, his eyes tinged with hatred. He stepped into the glow from the streetlamp, the angle of the light making it difficult to see his face. "I think I do." He licked his lips lecherously, his eyes skimming up and down her body, making her shudder.

She tried for diplomacy. "You should know that we've contacted the police. Your wife has filed a restraining order against you. You can no longer be within three hundred yards of her."

"Then it's a good thing she's inside, isn't it?" he asked with a sneer, taking another step toward her.

Kalli considered her options. She could try to duck back inside Safe Haven, but that wouldn't make the situation go away. Her phone was now in a thousand little pieces in the middle of the road, so she couldn't call the police. There was only one option left, and it wasn't one she took lightly. "Go home, Carl. Leave Sharon alone."

She shouldn't have mentioned Sharon's name. As soon as he heard it, Carl screamed and charged at her, arms outstretched toward her throat.

She sidestepped again, dodging his grip. She used her right hand like a blade, chopping down on his neck. Carl dropped to his knees with a groan. Before he had time to react, she pivoted behind him, formed her fingers into a point, and jabbed right behind his collarbone, hitting the nerve cluster.

He screamed and bent forward, leaning away from her. She ground her fingers deeper, just to make her point. The whole encounter was over in seconds. She wasn't even breathing hard, but Carl was cursing up a storm.

The door to Safe Haven opened, and Vanessa walked out, stopping short as she saw what was going on. She let out a long-suffering sigh and pulled out her cell phone, dialing 911. "Another one?" she asked Kalli.

Kalli shrugged. "Nope. Same one as earlier."

"Let go of me, you bitch!" Carl snarled. She ignored him and dug her fingers in again, making him whimper and keeping him frozen in place.

Vanessa stayed with her, on the phone with the dispatcher, until the police came. When the cops arrived and got out of their car, Kalli released Carl and backed away slowly, arms raised by her ears. The same officer who'd taken the report earlier was back, and this time he'd brought his partner.

Carl barely glanced at the flashing blue lights or the cops. As soon as Kalli released him, he lunged to his feet and tried to tackle her. The police officers caught him before he made contact.

"You all right, miss?" the younger officer said as he struggled to get a pair of handcuffs on Carl.

"Just dandy, thanks," she said without a hint of sarcasm.

"I like it when they make it easier to press charges," Vanessa chimed in, gesturing as the two police officers loaded Carl in the back of their cruiser. "What did he think he was doing, attacking you right in front of them?"

Kalli shrugged. "I'm just glad it was me and not Sharon. I can take care of myself." Centuries of combat training had ensured that.

"Yes, you can." Vanessa hummed in agreement.

Kalli rolled her shoulders, trying to ease the tension that had settled between them. "Well, that made for an unfortunate start to my night."

"You need to unwind, seriously. If you don't, you'll explode one of these days. And that probably won't be good for anyone, especially not the next Carl."

Vanessa was probably right, but unwinding was against Kalli's nature. She enjoyed action and didn't know how to do the whole "relax on the beach with a drink" thing. "What would I even do?"

Vanessa's hands perched on her considerable hips as her eyes narrowed. "Something, anything. Start by not coming into work for a while. Get out of the house and don't darken the door of Safe Haven. I mean that." She waggled a finger under Kalli's nose.

Kalli smiled, love for her friend filling her heart. Even though she could clearly take care of herself, Vanessa was always trying to mother her. It was a nice feeling, and something she hadn't felt in a long time. "Yes, ma'am!" she said with a cocky little salute.

"Go, get out of here. And don't come back for at least two days."

Kalli waved goodbye and started down the block toward the train station. Two days. What on earth was she going to do for two full days?

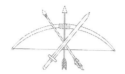

Chapter Two

KALLI WOKE UP THE next morning and stared at the ceiling. Her internal body clock told her it wasn't yet dawn, and when she glanced at the glowing red numbers on her bedside table, they agreed. It was five forty-five. She was awake and had nowhere to go.

She tried rolling over and going back to sleep, but her body refused to cooperate. After rolling around and tangling herself in the sheets for half an hour, she finally gave up and put on sweats. She might as well get in a good workout.

She spent an hour whaling away at her punching bag, picturing Carl's face each time she whacked it. The exercise soothed her, giving her tension a sorely needed escape valve.

There wasn't much food in her house, but she scrounged up just enough to call breakfast as she tried to figure out what to do with her suddenly empty Saturday. She grabbed the newspaper off her front porch and took it into the living room to read. Most of it was covered in the usual political arguments and celebrity gossip, which she didn't care about, considering she hadn't heard of any of the people the newspaper considered famous. She dropped the front section on the floor and grabbed the local section.

The first article she saw revealed that today was the opening day of a new exhibit at the Smithsonian National Museum of Natural History. That alone would have been enough to get her attention—she'd always loved the Smithsonian—but the subject made her jaw drop.

It was all about Amazons.

As much as she'd distanced herself from that part of her life, she was still tempted to go. She was curious how much a museum could know about a race of women that most people in academia would deny ever existed.

Her curiosity won out. A trip to the museum would get her out of the house before she got too antsy, especially since her own employee had barred her from work. She dashed upstairs to her bedroom, changed into an outfit acceptable to wear in public, and donned her shoes. She was out the door in less than ten minutes.

She popped out of the underground Metro station on the National Mall and glanced around. The cherry blossoms bloomed brightly, their pink and white petals coating the trees and dropping like snowflakes onto the grass below.

She loved this time of year. The beauty of the trees and the warm spring air made her forget about the darker parts of life and instead focus on the wonderful ones. Nature's glory made it easier to forget about abusive husbands and terrified wives. Vanessa was right. She definitely needed to get out more.

She crossed the Mall to the Natural History Museum, whose gold-tinged dome and huge columns stood out from hundreds of yards away. Inside she was confronted by a giant elephant rearing its huge trunk in her direction. Looking at magnificent creatures like this one was another reminder that not everything in the world revolved around her current problems.

She found the Amazon exhibit easily. Right outside the entrance hung a large banner with a depiction of what was clearly supposed to be an Amazon warrior but looked more like a Princess Leia wannabe in a leather bikini. The image was striking, to be sure, but not particularly realistic. The woman's ample breasts were almost pouring out of the skimpy leather outfit, which didn't cover enough to be considered armor. She carried a small knife strapped to her leg and a shield so tiny it didn't even cover her torso. Clearly whoever had drawn the picture had never actually seen a battlefield.

In the lower portion of the banner, small text stated that the exhibit was being put on jointly by the Smithsonian and Georgetown University. Apparently an anthropology professor named Dr. Samuel Treadwell of Georgetown had headed up the research team. Kalli pictured some doddering old man with gray hair and a tweed jacket to go with his multiple degrees.

With one final eye roll at the banner, Kalli entered the hall.

The exhibit was huge. She didn't know what she'd been expecting, but she definitely hadn't pictured something as big as this, especially about a culture most people knew about only because of a cheesy TV show or a comic book character. The dim lighting made it difficult to see, but she approached the first display case with curiosity.

Inside the case was a series of placards along with photographs of an archaeological dig site. In one photo five people stood around, grinning, each holding a small shovel or a brush. In front of them was a pit revealing a skeleton with a damaged sword by its side. Kalli's stomach rolled at the sight. The caption of the image read, "The first proof of Amazons."

The next case contained the sword from the photograph. It was blackened and falling apart, but Kalli's heart kicked into high gear, the sound echoing in her ears. The sword was amazing, even in its damaged state, but it was the barely visible symbol etched into the metal that caught her eye. It depicted a bow crossed with an arrow, a spear, and a sword. The familiar icon practically jumped out at her—the symbol of the Amazons.

The crowds and noise faded into the background as Kalli moved from one display case to another. The research team had found bows, spears, the remains of leather armor, and shields, all etched with the same symbol. Each item had a carefully documented information card next to it, aisle after aisle of evidence pointing to one inevitable conclusion.

Amazons were real.

For the first time in recorded history, there was documented evidence that her culture actually existed. She wasn't sure if she should be excited or terrified. No one was supposed to know about them, yet here she stood amid proof that they were real.

In the far corner of the exhibit she came across a vase with an image of a warrior woman painted on its side. Her heart stuttered before it started beating again. Proof of her past life was staring back at her, a version of herself she hadn't seen in thousands of years. Unconsciously she lifted her hand toward the glass, as if she could reach out and touch the cool clay.

"She looks a bit like you."

The masculine voice startled her, making Kalli's hand freeze halfway to the glass. She glanced around for its source, and her eyes collided with a pair of gorgeous brown ones tucked away behind geeky but adorable rectangular glasses. The man was taller than her by about two inches, which would have put him at around six one. His dark-blond hair was groomed neatly, and his suit perfectly fit his toned body. Definitely hot.

"Is that a compliment?" she finally asked. She gestured toward the vase and pointed out, "She looks a little terrifying, like she wants to hurt you for looking at her."

The man smiled. "And perhaps she did. That vase depicts an Amazon queen, one known for her skill in battle."

"A queen, huh? I can guarantee you that I'm no queen." Not anymore, at least. A twinge of sadness shot through her heart.

"A tragedy, to be sure." He smiled, offering his hand. "I'm Sam Treadwell."

She took a startled step back. "You're the one behind all of this?" she asked skeptically, her head tilting to the side as she looked at him more closely. He didn't look at all like what she'd been picturing. She glanced at his outstretched hand and contemplated turning and leaving but shoved the thought away. She was being irrational. He might know more than most people about Amazons, but there was no way he would figure out that she was one of them. "I'm Kalli," she said and finally shook his hand.

His warm hand enclosed hers, feeling more comfortable than it should have. She quickly tugged her hand back. He smiled again. "Kalli, hmm? What a coincidence. The name of the queen that you admired so much was believed to be Kalliope. You have something else in common, it seems."

Kalli sucked in a quick breath. She had to play it cool. She retreated a step, dropping her gaze. "It was lovely to meet you," she said, trying not to sound too rushed. He opened his mouth as if to reply, but she didn't give him the chance. Kalli darted around him and headed for the exit.

Before she'd made it a handful of steps, her eye caught a quick flash of pale skin, gray eyes, and a red ponytail. Kalli's eyes locked with the cold gray ones for an instant before the other woman ducked around a corner. *No way.* Her stomach soured.

Kalli reached the doorway where she'd spotted the movement just in time to see the woman leave out the exit at the far end of the room. Even more convinced she was right about who it was, Kalli hurried after her, tracking the woman through the length of the museum and catching up to her as they exited the building onto the National Mall.

"Eris," Kalli said, a slight catch in her throat.

The redhead spun around, revealing her tiny leather miniskirt, matching leather vest, and frosty gray eyes. She sported bright-red lipstick and a tattoo of barbed wire that wrapped around her right biceps. Eris glanced at Kalli's slim-fit jeans and short-sleeved polo shirt and sneered. "If it isn't Kalliope, after all these years. Oh, how the mighty have fallen."

Kalli shifted her stance, straightening her shoulders and lifting her chin. "I see you haven't changed much, Eris."

Eris threw her head back and laughed loudly, drawing the attention of several nearby people. "Change? Why would I change? It's only been, what, twenty-five hundred years give or take?"

Kalli looked around, not liking the curious glances from the small crowd outside the museum. The men in particular eyed Eris's short skirt and deeply plunging vest with interest. Kalli took a step closer, attempting to speak quietly. "You can't say stuff like that. Not here."

Eris laughed again, spinning around in a circle with her arms outstretched. "Why not? Do you honestly think these people care? Do you think they would believe me if I told the truth?" She winked provocatively at a man who stood with his wife and two kids. His wife gave Eris a death glare. Eris blew her a taunting kiss in return.

Kalli wasn't sure how to respond. Eris was probably right that most people wouldn't believe a word she said, but Kalli still saw no reason to call attention to themselves. "Let's not find out," she said.

"Hey, everyone!" Eris yelled, waving her arms to make sure everyone in the vicinity was looking in her direction. She gestured to Kalli, then to herself. "We're Amazons! That's right, we're immortal women warriors. What do you think about that?" She threw her head back and laughed maniacally.

Kalli grabbed Eris by the right elbow, jabbed her thumb into the pressure point near the joint, and dragged her around the side of the museum. "I can't believe you did that. You exposed us to anyone who would listen," Kalli hissed under her breath.

Eris snatched her arm back from Kalli's grasp, the corner of her lips turned up in a sneer. "I guess I was wrong. You really haven't changed. You're still as high and mighty as you were back then."

That shouldn't have hurt, but it did, scratching at a wound that had never quite healed. "That may be, but I'm the high and mighty one that kept us alive."

Eris's eyes narrowed, and she crossed her arms across her chest. "And what kind of existence was that? We could have ruled this world, and you had us hiding from it, cowering in fear."

Kalli's gut twisted. She knew Eris wasn't the only Amazon who thought that way, but to Kalli the idea of the their people as some sort of superior race designed to rule over humans had always felt like a betrayal of their very purpose.

"Well, at least I no longer have to put up with your meddling anymore. It's high time I get what's coming to me." Eris was practically raging. "Plus, are you even sure that the rest of our sisters are still alive? It would be a shame if someone found them and something happened to them." Eris spun around and stomped off, her red ponytail bobbing through the crowds.

Kalli's stomach bottomed out as she watched Eris leave. The redhead had always been power hungry, but now she seemed almost mad with it. Her thinly veiled threat against their people left Kalli queasy. Kalli was kept from panicking only by the knowledge that if she didn't know how to get back to Themyscira, then neither did Eris. With a sigh, she headed back toward the front of the museum.

She debated going back inside to finish the rest of the exhibit. The yummy Dr. Samuel Treadwell had discovered more about the Amazon race than any other researcher in her very long existence. Looking at the images he'd captured and the jewelry and weapons his team had uncovered had made her homesick.

Through the years, she'd tried not to think too much about Themyscira. The pain was still fresh after all these centuries. The Amazon homeland was lost to her, and it didn't do any good to dwell on it.

Unfortunately, now that the Band-Aid had been ripped off, her memories were forcing their way back in piece by piece. She remembered flashes of what had happened all those years ago, the sisters she had lost on her long journey through Greece and the ancient world.

She'd seen those images of the excavated graves and wished she could remember who they belonged to. Was the one with the sword Chara? Or had it been Aster? After all this time, she had forgotten, and it pained her that she couldn't remember.

It probably wasn't a good idea to go back inside. Who knew, she might lose control and try to break through the glass to get to that silly vase with her picture on it. No, it was probably a much better idea to go home and curl up with a good book. Maybe something by Stephen King or James Patterson. Feeling slightly more settled, she turned to head to the Metro.

"Leaving so soon?" She froze in her tracks on hearing the familiar voice. She spun around and saw Sam standing at the top of the steps, smiling in her direction.

Crap. How long had he been standing there? Had he overheard Eris's outburst? She stood paralyzed, unsure if she should try to avoid him with an impolite brush-off or if it would be less awkward if she just talked to him.

Her innate politeness won out. *Damn it.* "Sorry I left so abruptly. I thought I saw someone I used to know." She tucked a lock of hair behind her ear.

He descended several steps in her direction, watching her every move. "And was it her?"

She nodded. "Yes, it was."

He came closer still, only stopping when he was right in front of her. "Did you enjoy catching up?"

Kalli's eyes narrowed. She couldn't see why he would be interested in Eris and her unless he'd overheard their conversation. "Not particularly." No need to elaborate.

Sam's eyebrows lifted. He waited for her to continue, but she had no intention of doing so. After an awkward silence, he spoke, "Can I show you around the rest of the exhibit?"

She wanted to say no. It wasn't a good idea to go anywhere with him. If this man had heard her conversation with Eris, he already knew too much. She had a feeling the good professor was more astute than most.

Her heart won out. It had been so long since she'd allowed herself to think about home and the people she'd lost or left behind. Even though she knew she could never go home, she had wondrous memories of her time there. She would never have believed that someone would be able to discover as much as he had, and she was curious to see what else he'd found.

She just couldn't let her guard slip. He might be sinfully attractive, in a bookish sort of way, but his knowledge about Amazons could prove dangerous.

Plus, she didn't get involved with men. It was her hard-and-fast rule. Men had spent countless centuries intimidating women and treating them as inferior. It was sad how little had changed through the years. Kalli might allow herself a one-night stand once in a while, but she didn't do relationships. She'd seen where that path led. Safe Haven was full of women who had been attacked by men who were supposed to love them. Just because Kalli could take care of herself didn't mean she wanted to open herself up to that.

She glanced at Sam's gentle face. It wasn't like he was proposing or anything. It was just a tour of the museum. Everything would be fine.

"Sure, that would be nice." She smiled slightly and took a few steps away from him and toward the museum. He didn't comment, just gestured with his arm for her to take the lead.

Chapter Three

S AM WASN'T SURE WHAT to make of the woman in front of him. She was gorgeous, in a very nonchalant sort of way, but she had an air about her—something that said stay back or I might bite you. Normally he wouldn't consider himself a glutton for punishment, but she intrigued him. It could be her lithe body, which was long and lean and just muscled enough to make it interesting. Or it could be her strong yet elfin face, which was framed by shoulder-length shiny brown hair.

No, it was more than that. She'd caught his eye all the way across the room, and it hadn't been her beauty that had ensnared him. It had been her longing. The way she'd looked at each piece in the room as if it was the most precious thing in the world to her. He'd never met anyone outside of academia who cared that much about a bunch of old and crumbling artifacts from halfway around the world.

He'd been watching her the moment the vase had caught her eye. She'd been transported, as if she was no longer in a modern-day museum in Washington, DC, but rather watching the artisan who had crafted the vase thousands of years before. He'd needed to know more about her, about what made her so fascinated by the Amazon culture.

Sam escorted her back to the second-floor wing and past the ridiculous depiction of the Barbie-like Amazon. He'd fought hard against the image, not liking what it conveyed, but he'd been over-ruled. What the Smithsonian wanted, it got.

Once inside, however, it was all his realm. He'd overseen the careful discovery and preservation of every piece in the collection.

"This exhibit is the culmination of my life's work," he said, gesturing toward the glass showcases and descriptive signs on the walls.

Kalli smiled. "You make it sound like you're ancient."

He sometimes felt that way, but for an academic he was rather young. At thirty-two, he was one of the youngest professors ever to get an exhibit of this size in the Smithsonian. He dropped his chin and glanced at her sideways. "I just meant that this is what I've been working on for as long as I can remember. I've always been fascinated by the Amazons. Unlike most, I never thought they were a myth." He stopped in front of a photograph of him and his crew at a dig site in what was now modern Türkiye.

She gave him an odd look he couldn't quite discern. "Why not? Everyone else clearly does."

He was about to give his standard canned answer—that if there was that much lore about a subject, it generally turned out to have some basis in fact—but he stopped himself. Something about her made him want to admit the truth. "I think I wanted to believe they were real. Invincible women warriors who could defend their homeland and hold off invaders. It was like G.I. Joe, but cooler."

That got a smile out of her. "You must have been a very odd child."

He laughed. "My brothers used to think so."

"And yet here we are." She walked up to another display and stared at the jewelry inside.

"Here we are." He was at a loss for what to say, but he didn't want to stop talking to her. He wanted to impress her with his knowledge about the Amazon culture, both what was displayed in the museum and what he believed but for which he had no proof. He wanted to show off, but he felt uncharacteristically awkward. She wasn't like the women he normally went for.

"Your friend was looking over here, if it helps." He gestured to a case to their left.

Kalli turned and scanned the map he was pointing to. "The location of Themyscira?" Her voice rose several octaves.

He nodded, waving his hand back and forth. "More or less. The exact location of the city was never known, but this is what I've been able to put together from bits and pieces I've found in all sorts of obscure references."

If he'd thought his academic prowess would impress her, he was sorely mistaken.

"I have to go." She whipped around and made a beeline for the door.

What was going on? This was the second time she'd taken off on him. A rational man would have let her go, but apparently he wasn't that man. "Wait!" He dashed after her.

"I can't stay here any longer. I have to go," she tossed over her shoulder, giving him an annoyed look.

"I get that," he said, finally catching up to her on the staircase, "but can you at least explain why? Did I offend you?" He was really hoping that wasn't the case.

"No." She glanced at her watch impatiently. "It isn't that. I just need to see if I can catch up with my friend."

His brows knit together. "The friend from earlier? The one you said you didn't particularly enjoy talking to?"

"Yes, that would be the one. Now if you'll excuse me." She tried to turn away again and head downstairs, but he touched her shoulder. She took several steps back and gave him a glare that instantly reminded him of the picture on the vase.

"You mean the one who claimed you were both Amazon warriors?" He meant the question jokingly, hoping to get her to laugh, but the panic in her eyes had him backing off a step. He didn't understand where her alarm was coming from, but the last thing he wanted to do was frighten her.

"You eavesdropped on a private conversation?" Her eyes narrowed.

"Sorry to burst your bubble, but nothing was private the way that woman was yelling." Even if she had been spewing nonsense, she'd been doing it at the top of her lungs. She'd also referred to the gorgeous brunette in front of him as Kalliope.

"So you believe everything some random person on the street tells you?"

The question gave him pause. He'd never actually said he believed what the redhead had been yelling, but it was odd that she would assume he had.

A small, easily overlooked factoid floated to the top of his mind. It was something he'd dismissed out of hand as pure myth and fantasy, like much of what the Greek legends mentioned. Something about her tense stance and the dismay he could see on her face had him rethinking.

The legends claimed that the Amazons were immortal.

It seemed preposterous, but he had no problems picturing the woman in front of him holding a sword and charging into battle. She had an air of power surrounding her that drew him in and made him want to explore further.

There was only one way to find out if he was right. "You can't really be her, can you?" He hadn't planned on being that blunt, but he'd panicked.

She froze, turning slowly and meeting his gaze, her blue eyes searing into him. "Excuse me?" Her eyes burned like blue fire. Her fear flared to life again, but she masked it quickly, irritation taking its place.

He guessed he had only a few seconds before she either took off running or beat him to a bloody pulp, and he couldn't tell which was more likely. "You're Kalliope. The queen from the vase." It seemed impossible but somehow also inevitable.

She took several measured steps back in his direction, stalking him like a leopard. "Let me get this straight. You think I'm the woman portrayed on a vase made over three thousand years ago? How has Georgetown not revoked your academic credentials by now?"

She had a point. It was a ridiculous notion but one he couldn't shake.

Tension fairly radiated off her. Her arms were tight by her side, her legs primed as if ready to spring. He'd touched a nerve; he was certain of it.

Whether or not it was a smart idea, he poked the bear even further. Taking a step closer to her, he lowered his voice to a near whisper. "My research indicates that the Amazons were special in more ways than one. They weren't just incredibly strong and fast. They were also immortal." The legends and myths surrounding the immortality of the Amazons were one of the hardest parts of his research for him to swallow. He was a modern scientific researcher, not some member of a primitive culture trying to explain away the amazing. Yet here she was, not five feet away from him, and his Spidey senses were tingling.

He looked at the woman standing in front of him, taking in her defensive stance and wary eyes. There was something about her that radiated power in a way he'd never experienced with any other person.

"Now I know you're crazy," she said, but she didn't move.

He smiled inside but didn't let it show on his face. He had her. Now he had to reel her in. "If I asked your friend Eris, would she say the same thing?"

She swore under her breath and turned away from him, her hand coming up to pinch the bridge of her nose. Thankfully she didn't immediately leave. "Damn it," she finally muttered.

He'd felt a bit guilty about eavesdropping on their conversation, but at the moment he was glad he had.

She muttered something unintelligible under her breath, then spun back around to face him. "So what's your plan now, huh? You want to stick me in a lab somewhere and run tests on me? I'd like to see you try."

He held his hands up in surrender, offended at the thought. "Whoa. I never said anything about running tests on you." She hadn't exactly admitted to being an Amazon, but even if she had, that wouldn't have been his intention. He had no desire to expose her to the world. Now he had to make her believe that.

"Then what?" she shot back. "What's your interest in me now that you know—or at least think you know—who and what I am?"

Again, it wasn't a denial.

He smiled sheepishly. He really hadn't intended to put her on the defensive. His original goal had been to work up to asking her out on a date, but he had a feeling he'd blown that opportunity completely. Now he just had to get to a point where she didn't plan to kill him in his sleep. "I wouldn't mind sitting down and having a conversation. Perhaps with the hot beverage of your choice." He licked his lips nervously.

She scoffed and took a few steps down the staircase away from him. Turning back, she eyed him. "Yeah, right. You'd be satisfied with a conversation."

Taking a calculated risk, he took two steps closer to her. "For now. I mean, how many opportunities am I ever going to get to interview an Amazon warrior queen?" It felt strange to say that. Even if he was right, this was going to take a bit of getting used to.

Her face blanched, and she dropped her gaze to the cold stone of the staircase. "I told you. I'm not a queen."

"All right, suit yourself. How about just an Amazon?" He held his breath, afraid to move while he waited for her response.

She sighed, tucking her hair behind her ear. "I really don't have time for this. I need to leave." She turned around again and headed back down the steps until she finally reached the bottom. Sam followed her, making sure not to get within an arm's distance of her lest she decide to swat him down like a fly.

"So, Eris is immortal, too, right?" he asked as she pushed her way through the museum's outer doors.

"Are you ever going to leave me alone?" she tossed over her shoulder, marching toward the Mall.

"Probably not. I'm incurably nosy. It's part of being a researcher for a living." It may have been slightly twisted of him, but he enjoyed the pissed-off glare she gave him.

"Don't you have an exhibit to curate?" She kept walking, not bothering to look at him.

"Nope," he said, savoring their verbal sparring. "The museum is curating it. I was only there for opening day to give it a formal send-off."

She headed toward the Smithsonian Metro stop, then stepped on the escalators and headed underground. He followed a step behind.

"You realize I could call the cops on you for stalking me," she said, exasperation leaking through.

He smiled at the back of her head. "Yes, but you won't. You don't exactly need the cops to handle your dirty work for you, now do you?"

She growled under her breath, sending an amused shiver through him. Part of his brain registered that he shouldn't be poking so hard at a woman who could probably kill him with her pinkie finger, but he couldn't seem to resist. As much as she was clearly well honed and trained in combat, she was also buttoned up tight. She obviously didn't view him as an actual threat, because if she did, he had a feeling he wouldn't have made it out of the museum.

"So where are you headed?" he asked as he waved his Metro card at the machine and followed her down to the tracks.

"That's none of your business."

"That's certainly true."

She finally stopped walking as she reached the platform, forced to wait for a train to arrive. He stopped next to her. She glared at him out of the corner of her eye but didn't say anything else.

The train arrived a few minutes later, and they both boarded, still not talking. He took a seat across from her, studying her closely while she made it a point to not look in his direction. When she transferred trains, he followed her again, a move she obviously saw and just as obviously tried to ignore. She got off at the Cleveland Park stop, and he followed her out of the station.

It was probably a terrible idea to be stalking her across all of DC. Sure, he had an academic interest in her—and his libido certainly enjoyed watching her rear as she'd stalked away from him—but objectively he was being creepy. Never in his life had he chased a woman through the city after she'd made it abundantly clear she wanted nothing to do with him.

He couldn't seem to make himself stop. He felt drawn to this woman in a way he'd never been drawn to anyone in his life. He felt like he was supposed to be there and—despite her outward anger and obvious ability to take care of herself—he knew without question she'd never hurt him.

He followed her for several blocks, through a neighborhood he could have afforded to live in only if he won the lottery. It was a pleasant stroll past well-kept yards the size of postage stamps and houses that were much larger than average for the DC area.

Finally, after several minutes of silent walking, she turned to face him, her eyes burning fire. "This puppy dog thing was cute for a while, but you really need to stop following me." Her hands curled into fists, her knuckles going white.

He stopped. "This isn't a puppy dog thing, I promise you. I mean, you're gorgeous and all, but I'm not some creepy psycho stalker." Yeah. Like a stalker wouldn't say the same thing. He glanced uneasily around. They were now alone on the street. His pulse kicked up a notch, his hands suddenly damp. Had he been wrong about her?

"Go home, Dr. Treadwell. Trust me, I'm not what you're looking for." Her fists relaxed, her body slumping slightly.

Her words made him pause, but it was the sadness in her tone that hit home. He hadn't intended to upset her. He'd let his obsessive researcher loose, and it had distressed the beautiful woman in front of him. He needed to let her go, despite how much his brain would complain about not getting the answers he'd been seeking for years. He couldn't force her to want to talk to him.

"All right," he finally said as he pulled a business card out of his wallet and handed it to her. "If you ever change your mind, look me up."

She nodded ever so slightly, just a quick head jerk, then walked away.

He watched her go, her long strides eating up the sidewalk as she got farther and farther away. With a sigh, he turned to head back to the Metro.

A car screeched to a halt next to him, and one of the rear doors flew open. A dude who would have looked perfectly comfortable in a WWE ring lurched out of the car, catching Sam off guard. Before it even occurred to Sam that the guy was after him, the wrestler already had his arm around Sam's neck and was tugging him back toward the car.

"What the hell?" Sam choked out as he kicked and flailed at his attacker. Sam managed to land a solid elbow jab to the guy's stomach, forcing the air out of his lungs with a whoosh.

"My boss wants to see you," the man grunted.

The guy spun him around, trying to toss Sam into the car head-first, but Sam brought his legs up and braced them against the rear quarter panel of the car. He gave a huge push and sent the wrestler stumbling back several steps. Unfortunately, he dragged Sam with him.

Sam's vision was starting to go spotty as the larger man cut off his air. He could feel the fight draining out of him, his limbs weighing more by the second. He tried to fight it. If he blacked out, there was nothing more he could do for himself.

Suddenly the pressure on his neck was gone. He stumbled until he found a wall to brace himself against as he gasped for breath. At first he couldn't make sense of what he was seeing. The huge muscly dude was being thrown across the pavement, and Kalli hovered over him like an avenging angel. The man fell hard, barely stopping his head from cracking into the curb.

"Who do you work for?" Kalli asked, her voice laced with icy calm.

The man on the ground looked around frantically, but the car he'd gotten out of took off, tires chirping and the rear door slamming shut with the force of the acceleration.

Kalli put her foot on the man's chest, pinning him in place. "I said, who do you work for?"

"A chick named Eris," the wrestler finally spat out.

Kalli's foot inched closer to the dude's neck. "And what does Eris want with the good doctor here?" Kalli's head jerked in Sam's direction.

"I don't know. I just heard something about a map."

Kalli's eyes flew to Sam's before she focused once again on the man she had trapped beneath her. "I don't suppose I have to tell you not to come back here." The toe of her shoe was now firmly pressing against the wrestler's neck.

He shook his head twice and grabbed Kalli's foot, but it wasn't budging.

Kalli nodded once and lifted her leg. The guy scrambled to his feet and immediately took off. Kalli turned to Sam and stared at him, watching him as he gently rubbed his throat. "Do you have a death wish?" she finally asked, throwing her hands up in defeat.

"Not usually," he answered, his voice raspier than usual. "Thanks for that," he said as he waved his hand vaguely in the direction of the man who had fled.

"You're welcome," she said with seeming reluctance. She took a deep breath, then asked, "What, exactly, do you want from me?" Her hands went to her hips, making her look like an angry wood nymph.

He took a step closer, positive she wouldn't hurt him. "I only want to talk to you. I've spent my entire life researching Amazon warriors. I can't believe I actually found one." After the strength she'd shown, there was no longer any doubt in his mind. She could never have taken that guy out if she hadn't been supernaturally strong.

If only his younger self could see him now. He'd meant what he'd said about his fascination with Amazons. His parents had thought he was ridiculous, but he'd always known they were real. He'd certainly proved his parents wrong.

She rolled her eyes. "Because we're so fascinating." She crossed her arms, doing interesting things to her breasts that he tried to ignore.

He smiled. "So you admit it. You really are an Amazon." Excitement shot through him. He'd been right about her.

Her mouth dropped open. "You tricked me," she accused.

He held his hands up. "No. Or at least not intentionally." He didn't want to piss her off any more than he already had.

With a huff, she turned around and walked away again. Not quite willing to give up his chance to interview an Amazon, he followed her.

Her house fit her perfectly. It wasn't showy, like so many of the McMansions they'd passed along the way, but it was stately and obviously well taken care of. It was smaller than the ones around it, but it didn't lack for charm. The brick exterior was wonderfully complemented by several small gardens in riotous bloom. The porch was painted a crisp white, a utilitarian swing hanging on one end.

She stomped up the steps, ramming her key into the lock and clicking it home with more force than necessary. He hesitated on the porch, but as she went inside, she paused in the doorway, holding the door open. "You coming?" she asked.

He didn't hesitate.

He closed the door quietly as she stalked down the central hallway toward the back of the house. He'd never believed he would get this far, so he had no idea what to do with himself.

Glancing around, he took in his surroundings. Just like the outside of her house, she kept the inside neat and tidy. Classical paintings hung on the walls, but they appeared to be prints, not originals. She kept her house in order—as if she was always expecting company—even though she'd had no way to know he would follow her home.

Wandering into her living room, he scoped out her entertainment center. She was seriously hooked up, with more screen real estate than he could dream of. She also had a wall covered top to bottom with Blu-rays, which told him she spent an awful lot of time at home. Out of the corner of his eye, he spotted her punching bag, treadmill, and free weights in an adjoining room. She was serious about keeping in shape. It appeared she was a "punch first, ask questions later" kind of woman. The thought made him smile.

"What on earth are you doing out there?" he heard her call from the back of the house. Following the sound of her voice, he wound up in the kitchen. She had poured herself a large glass of wine and was sipping it slowly. Almost as an afterthought, she held the bottle out in his direction and gave it a shake.

He shook his head. "I'm good, thanks."

"Suit yourself," she said, taking another sip. "You want some lunch?"

Was it only lunchtime? So much had happened he would have assumed it was practically time for bed, or at least time for dinner. It was hard to imagine that it was only noon. "Sure, what do you have?"

She took another sip. "Take-out menus."

He laughed. She probably hadn't even intended to be funny, but he couldn't help himself. There was something so unbelievable about standing across the kitchen from an immortal woman who was holding out a menu for Chinese food. "I'm easy. Whatever you want." He hadn't meant the double entendre, but her raised eyebrows showed that she'd read more into it than he'd intended. Oh well, it wasn't like he wouldn't go for that too.

He listened to her call the restaurant and, to his surprise, order in Mandarin. As it fluidly rolled off her tongue, even his untrained ear could tell she was perfect at it. Yet another unexplored part of this fascinating woman. He had no idea what sort of food they were getting, but he didn't much care. He would eat anything if he got to keep spending time with her. There were so many questions he was dying to ask.

She turned around and caught him staring at her. Instead of glancing away in embarrassment, he smiled. She certainly was easy on the eyes. "What are you staring at?" she asked, an annoyed lilt changing the tenor of her voice.

"You're even more fascinating than I realized. You speak Mandarin."

Her eyes narrowed. "So?"

He crossed his arms over his chest and studied her, leaning back against her kitchen counter. "I'm just trying to figure out what someone would do with their time if they knew they had an infinite amount of it. Clearly one answer is learning languages. How many do you know?"

A slight pink flush crept up her cheeks. "Over a hundred."

His jaw dropped. "Seriously? You can converse fluently in over a hundred languages?"

She put her phone down on the granite countertop and paced around her kitchen. "Not exactly."

"What do you mean?"

"Well, a few of them are extinct."

She covered the same six feet of tile over and over again. Kalli kept glancing at him but never let her gaze stay for long.

"Extinct? Like no one else in the world speaks them?"

She growled slightly under her breath. "Yeah, that's exactly what I mean. The people who spoke them are no longer around."

He whistled. What must it be like to have lived for so long that entire cultures had come and gone during your lifetime? "What about other Amazons? Are there more of you out there in the world?"

Kalli shrugged. "Apart from Eris? No idea."

"Do you ever get lonely?" he asked softly.

She went rigid, slowly spinning on her heel to look at him. "Why would you ask that?"

Maybe the question had been out of line, but it was too late to take it back. He shrugged. "It seems like a very hard way to go through life. You've been around since . . . what year were you born, exactly?"

"2021 BCE." She said it so quietly he wasn't even sure he'd heard her right. It felt rude to ask her to repeat herself, however.

He swallowed thickly to process that little gem, then cleared his throat and continued. "You've been around for over four thousand years. You've seen whole civilizations come and go. You've seen thousands upon thousands of people be born and then die. Apart from someone who's more of an enemy than a friend, you have no one else like you. It has to be painful to watch everyone you know leave you eventually."

Moisture gathered in the corners of her beautiful blue eyes. He mentally cursed himself for delving too deeply. He'd wanted to pick her brain about everything she'd seen and experienced over the years, but he hadn't meant to upset her. He reached for her arm, but she pulled away. "I'm sorry. That's none of my business. I should never have asked." He pushed away from the counter. "I'll leave. I didn't intend to hurt you." He couldn't believe he'd blown it so quickly. He cursed his own stupidity.

He was halfway to the door when she said, "You don't have to go. Those guys might come back."

Holding his breath, he slowly turned around. The tears were gone from her eyes, and her expression was once again a combination of annoyed and angry. He much preferred this Kalli to the other one. At least with this Kalli he knew what he was getting.

"The food's almost here anyway," she said, shoving past him as if he'd imagined whatever bit of vulnerability she'd let him see.

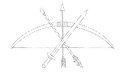

Chapter Four

K ALLI HAD NO CLUE what she was doing. She had rescued him from his attacker because it was the right thing to do, but she didn't really believe that Eris's men were waiting outside her house for Sam to emerge. She'd put the fear of God into the man who'd tried to kidnap him, so it was unlikely that they would go after him again anytime soon. It was undoubtedly safe for him to go home. However, her protective instincts had flared up, and she felt responsible for his safety. That had to be all it was.

Or, a small part of her whispered, she was just as lonely as he'd accused her of being. Moving every twenty years made it hard to keep up any long-term relationships. Her heart could barely stand the constant ache of having to leave everyone she cared about before they figured out she wasn't aging like a normal person.

It was a terrible idea to get involved with him in any capacity. First, he was a man. If her experiences in the last four thousand years had taught her anything, it was that men couldn't be trusted. Thousands of years' worth of men trying to tell her how to live her life had left her more than a little jaded when it came to the opposite sex. She could never trust that men weren't using her for their own agenda.

Second, Sam was a nosy professor who wanted nothing more than to pick her brain about something she'd spent centuries trying to forget. No one in her life knew who or what she was. She didn't talk about it—for good reason—and yet here she was, talking to the one man on the entire planet who could blow the lid off her secret.

Still trying to figure out what to do, she paid the delivery driver—giving him an extra-large tip and thanking him in his native language. She'd ordered a ton of food, hoping to have leftovers for an extra meal or two. A cook she wasn't.

"Plates?" he asked, gesturing randomly toward her cupboards. She pointed, and he spotted the stack of paper products. To his credit, he didn't flinch as he grabbed two. He guessed the right drawer for silverware, then pulled out plastic forks and chopsticks.

The smell of the Chinese food hit her like a punch as she opened the cartons. The scrambled eggs and banana she'd had for breakfast felt like forever ago. As soon as he handed her a plate, she loaded it up with heaps of sweet-and-sour chicken and beef and broccoli. She grabbed three spring rolls, the best part about Chinese food.

Sam glanced at her plate as he loaded his own. One eyebrow went up, but he didn't comment. She was glad. No one stood between her and fried rice. He sat across from her at her scarred wooden table, tucking into his own meal.

An awkward silence settled over them. She spent most of her time at a shelter for domestic abuse victims. Most of the people she interacted with were women. She was a bloody Amazon, for crying out loud. Small talk with men was not her forte. Thankfully, he saved her the trouble of having to come up with something to say.

"So what was it that had you bolting out of my museum exhibit? My research was very thorough. I hope I didn't make a mistake." He took a bite and waited for her answer.

His first question, and she wasn't sure she wanted to answer it. She carefully used her chopsticks to select a piece of chicken and bit into it to buy herself time. "It was the diagram showing the location of Themyscira." That was true enough.

He sat up straighter in his chair, his food forgotten. "Did I get it wrong? I thought no one ever knew the true location. The map was just what I could piece together based on various texts." He paused and took a breath. "If it's wrong, I can have it taken down."

It must have cost him a great deal to offer that. He was an academic who prided himself on his research and his powers of deduction. To admit that he may have gotten something incorrect, and then offer to fix it, probably went against his nature.

"It isn't wrong." She hesitated, then blurted out, "At least, I don't think it is."

The fork that had been hovering empty in midair fell out of his hand and landed atop a pile of noodles. "You don't think?"

She nodded, taking a bite of rice and chewing it. "Yes, that's what I said. The location on the map in the museum might be the location of Themyscira."

"But you don't know for sure? How is that possible?"

Here was one of those tricky questions she probably shouldn't answer and wasn't sure he would believe anyway. She hedged around the truth. "The location of Themyscira is obscured. Amazons didn't allow outsiders to know where it was."

"But you lived there." He grabbed his fork and twirled a noodle around it absently.

She nodded. "Yes, I did. But once I left, I could no longer find my way back." She was telling the truth, just not all of it.

He started eating again, sucking the noodle into his mouth with a loud slurp. "You couldn't return." She nodded once. "So, Eris . . ." He didn't finish the rest of his question.

"Her either."

Kalli bit into one of her spring rolls, then coated the exposed part with duck sauce before taking another bite. As much as she'd once hoped for it, Kalli had never thought she would find Themyscira. She'd grieved over that loss thousands of years ago and thought she'd accepted that she could never go home again. Yet, even after all this time, she missed her friends, the town, and the daily rituals involved in being part of a highly trained warrior society. An ache she hadn't felt in centuries rose up to choke her.

"Were you really the queen? Just like the myth surrounding the vase portrayed you to be?"

She didn't want to answer, more out of self-pity than anything else. "At one point, yes, I was."

"So what happened?"

"Are you done eating?" Kalli stood, her plate still covered in food. Despite her hunger, her stomach wouldn't allow another morsel without violent consequences.

Sam took the hint. He swallowed one last bite of chicken before following her to the trash to dump his plate. "Thanks for the food. It was delicious."

She nodded. "I'll tell the owner you said so."

They worked in companionable silence for a few minutes, tucking the last of the food into the refrigerator and wiping down the mess on the table. As much as she appreciated the help, she had to get this man out of her house. She had things to do, and she couldn't do them with him hanging around.

Kalli turned, about to make a weak excuse to kick him out of her kitchen. "So what's our next move?" he asked, preempting her.

She opened her mouth to respond, then closed it again, uncertain what to say. It felt like she was always on the wrong foot around him. "What do you mean?"

He ran his hand through his dark-blond hair, messing it up and making him that much more adorable. She tried not to think about it and focused on his eyes.

"I mean, what's the next step to find Eris?"

Dumbfounded, Kalli took several steps back and leaned against her counter, staring him down. How could he know what she had planned?

"Come on," he said with an exasperated huff. "You flew out of the museum after you figured out what Eris had been looking at. Her brute just jumped me in the street. It wasn't hard to put together."

She crossed her arms across her chest and stared at him. He had a point. She hated being predictable.

"The only thing I haven't figured out," he continued, "is if you're trying to find her so you can both go back to Themyscira together, or if you're trying to stop her from going back at all."

Kalli waffled but ultimately decided that there wasn't any more reason to keep secrets. "Something that Eris said at the museum is bothering me. She made a snide comment about something happening to the Amazons. I didn't think much of it at the time, because I didn't think she knew how to find Themyscira any more than I did. But now . . ."

"You think that's why she tried to kidnap me. So I can help her find the way there."

A sense of urgency was building in her, almost choking her. Now that Eris had a clue where to look for their home, would she try to get back there? It seemed only logical, especially after her not-so-subtle threat and her attempt on Sam. What did Eris have planned? Whatever it was couldn't be good.

She needed to find Eris. But once she did, she had no idea what her next move would be.

Could she really do this? She'd never actually believed she'd get the chance to go home again. She'd had both the best and the worst times of her life in Themyscira. She'd loved being part of the Amazon sisterhood and fighting for what was right.

But then there was that night. That one fateful night that had rocked her world, completely upending everything she'd foreseen for herself. She'd been kicked out by her own people. That wound had never healed.

Still, sometimes in life you had to suck it up and do what needed to be done, regardless of your personal feelings. The greater good was more important than she was.

"I need to find her."

"How are you planning on doing that? Do you know where she lives?" he asked.

Kalli shook her head. A fighter she may be, but an investigator she wasn't. They didn't have a lot to go on. "Nope."

"It's too bad we don't have access to the police database. Maybe she'd show up there."

That was a brilliant idea. Eris wasn't known for subtlety, or for listening to authority figures, which made it possible she had a police record. The trick would be in getting their hands on it. "I may have an idea." It wasn't one that she relished, but the situation necessitated it. If anything was worth calling in a favor, Eris popping back into her life after all this time was it.

"Don't tell me that you've also gained the skills of a computer hacker in addition to your hundred languages." His eyebrows went up as he stared at her.

She smiled. "You wouldn't ask me that if you'd ever seen me around one of those beasts. Computers hate me."

"So you have some other magical skill tucked away in your Amazon tool belt?" he asked eagerly.

"Something like that." With a sigh, Kalli picked up her phone and dialed.

Chapter Five

A N HOUR LATER, SHE walked through the doors of the DC police headquarters, Sam still at her side. Apparently he wasn't yet bored with following her around and had decided that a nice trip to talk to some cops was a good way to spend an afternoon.

Go figure.

She explained to the guard at the front desk who she was there to see, and he waved them through security. They rode the elevator to the third floor, then wound their way to the desk in the far back corner, dodging men and women in uniform as they darted around the cubical farm, carrying case folders and escorting witnesses.

"Kalli!" The man who stood to greet her was in his fifties, with graying hair and a paunch that said he'd spent most of the last several years behind a desk.

She smiled, leaning in to give him a hug and a kiss on the cheek. "Timothy, it's good to see you." She turned around and gestured to Sam, who watched the comings and goings of the police station with interest. "This is Dr. Samuel Treadwell. Sam, this is Officer Timothy Larson."

At the mention of his name, Sam's attention snapped back and he smiled, reaching out to shake the police officer's hand. "Nice to meet you."

Officer Larson's shrewd gaze made a slow traversal of Sam, from the tip of his blond hair to his leather loafers. His eyes finally came back up and landed on Sam's. "Nice to meet you." He slowly shook Sam's hand.

Sam cleared his throat uncomfortably, and Kalli stifled a laugh. She didn't visit Larson often, but she'd never brought a man with her when she did. And since Larson was familiar with her job, she didn't blame him for giving Sam a second look. "Sam is a professor at Georgetown University," she said, hoping to ease the tension.

The suspicion left Larson's gaze, and he nodded as if Sam had passed an unwritten test. "What can I do for you?" he asked Kalli with interest as he sat down in the chair behind his desk. Sam gestured for her to take the only other chair. She wanted to refuse out of principle but decided it wasn't the time. She sat.

"What is it this time, another nuisance husband?" Larson asked.

Kalli heard Sam shift behind her but didn't acknowledge him. She hadn't told him what she did for a living, so she could only imagine what he was thinking.

"Not today, Larson. I need your help to track someone down."

Larson picked up a notebook and a pen. "Who is he?"

"It's actually a she. We had a bit of a disagreement today near the Natural History Museum. I need to find her before anything bad happens."

He tapped his pen against his notebook. "What can you tell me about her? Do you have a picture?"

"Not unless you can tap into the security cameras at the museum," Sam said eagerly.

Kalli gave him a glare. "Her name is Eris. I'm not sure what last name she's using."

Larson wrote that down. "She's one of those types, huh? Let me see what I can find." He spun his chair around to face his computer, opening a database and typing in his credentials.

"I appreciate you doing this for me, Larson. I'm aware it's not really on the up-and-up."

Larson just huffed. "For you, kiddo, anything. I've seen some of the creeps you deal with on a daily basis. Anything I can do to help stop harm from coming to those women I'll be happy to do."

Kalli glanced at Sam, who cocked his eyebrow in her direction but said nothing. He was probably storing away all sorts of facts and tidbits in the filing cabinet he had for a brain.

"You're in luck," Larson said, leaning back in his creaking desk chair. "There aren't that many Eris's in the world. This her?" He gestured to a picture on his screen.

The photo wasn't particularly flattering. It showed her—in stereotypical black leather pants and a black leather jacket—with a phone plastered to her ear. It looked like someone had captured it without her knowing about it, like someone had been following her.

Her red hair was slicked back in a high ponytail, and she was glaring at someone off the edge of the photo.

"That's her, all right," Kalli said.

Larson nodded. "She's definitely a bad one, that's for sure. She's got a file as long as my arm. Looks like she's suspected of racketeering, smuggling, and gunrunning, both in the US and in Europe."

"Suspected, not convicted?" Sam asked.

Larson hummed under his breath as he tapped at his keyboard. "Yeah, she looks like a slippery one. She's been linked to dozens of dirty deals, but no one can prove anything."

Eris had never exactly been the picture of love and harmony, but international arms dealer came as a bit of a shock. Though Kalli had to admit that Eris had always been power hungry. It probably stoked her ego to be in charge of such a dirty operation. "Any idea where we might find her?"

Larson's eyes narrowed. "Are you sure you should be poking around her? I mean, you can take care of yourself and all, but this is a whole different level."

Kalli smiled, reaching out to pat the police officer's arm. "Thanks for your concern, but trust me, I'm the only one who can get to her." She appreciated that he was looking out for her, but this was her responsibility, like it or not.

"If you say so." He shrugged and glanced at his monitor again. "It looks like she may have ties to a warehouse by the river." He scribbled the address on a Post-it and handed it to her.

"Thanks."

"You get into trouble and we never had this conversation," Larson said.

"Understood." Kalli rose, nodding in Larson's direction before turning to leave. He'd been a good ally through the years, and she appreciated his help, especially since what she'd asked of him today wasn't exactly legal. She tucked the note into the pocket of her jeans and headed for the elevator.

Sam waited until they left the building before he pelted her with questions, a new record for him. "So how do you know Larson? And what did he mean by 'nuisance husbands'?"

She shrugged and kept walking, dodging in and out of people crowding the sidewalks. "The answer to both is basically the same. I run a shelter for domestic abuse victims. Sometimes we get visited by their not-so-nice husbands. The cops are pretty familiar with our place."

He grabbed her arm and pulled her around to face him. "Wait a minute. You've been alive for four thousand years," he said, making her glance around in a panic to make sure no one overheard, "which pretty much means you're free to do anything you want to, and what you choose to do with your time is help victims of abuse?"

She yanked her arm out of his grip, tugging her shirt back into place. "Yeah, so?" It came out more defensively than she meant it to.

He smiled, which did wonders for his already attractive face. Her heart did a little pitter pat.

"You're even more amazing than I realized."

Kalli huffed, uncomfortable with the praise. She didn't do what she did for the recognition. "I'm just doing what anyone else would do," she said, trying to turn away.

"No, you're not," he replied. "You're doing far more than most have ever thought about doing. You're a genuinely good person."

Heat rose to her cheeks, and she turned to walk away. She didn't know what to do with Sam. She didn't normally allow men into her life, so her interactions with them—at least from the last few decades—had mostly been in the form of police officers or abusive husbands. Sam was neither, and it threw her for a loop. She was used to being the one in control and liked knowing the lay of the land. She felt constantly wrong-footed around him.

He caught up to her again. "So what's our next move?"

Kalli stopped, then spun to face him again. "Why are you still here?" It came out whinier than she'd intended.

She wanted nothing more than to figure out what she needed to do next, but she seemed to have gained a clingy shadow. She refused to look too closely at her own reasons for not sending him on his way.

He put on an innocent-looking smile. "Would you believe me if I said I was scared that Eris's men would come after me again?"

"Not really." She crossed her arms and stared him down.

"Well then, let me surprise you by telling the truth. I'm fascinated by you. I've spent my entire life wanting to know more about the Amazons, and here you are, right in front of me. Even better, you're about to go kick someone's ass, and I really want to see it."

He sounded like a giddy schoolboy, and she had to work to repress a smile. "You realize what I could do to you without even breaking a sweat, right?" She cocked her head sideways.

"Yep." He grinned widely, his brown eyes flashing.

She growled in frustration, but even she could tell it was half-hearted. As much as he brushed off the incident earlier with Eris's men, Kalli still felt her protective instincts going into overdrive. As nosy as he could be, she wasn't quite ready to kick him to the curb—for his own safety, of course. Obviously her best strategy was to ignore him. She spun around on her heel and stalked off. He didn't leave, but at least he shut up. Baby steps.

It wasn't quite dinnertime yet, which meant the sun wouldn't set for a few more hours. Eris probably wouldn't be conducting illegal activities in broad daylight, so it made sense to wait until dark before attempting to find the warehouse. That left her with several hours to kill and a tail she couldn't bring herself to shake.

It couldn't be loneliness—she was around people all day long. She had Vanessa and Ben, not to mention all the women at her shelter. They were her family. She enjoyed spending time with them even though it came with tons of responsibilities. The work challenged her, but it mattered—and she was uniquely qualified to do it.

She didn't know why it felt different being around Sam. Obviously he was a man, and—apart from Ben—she didn't spend much time around men. That seemed like too simple an explanation, but she didn't have a better one. Whatever the reason, she was reluctant to give him the boot, despite his constant questions. She gave up—at least for the moment—and contemplated their next move.

If they were going to sneak around a warehouse crawling with possible illegal arms smugglers, they needed to change. She wasn't exactly stealthy in her jeans, sandals, and polo shirt, but Sam was even worse. He wore a navy suit that practically screamed desk jockey. As attractive as he looked in that suit, it wouldn't fly where they were going.

Kalli switched directions midblock and headed back the way they'd come. Sam, wisely, didn't say a word. Several minutes of walking later, her destination came into view, a giant Macy's sign shining down on them. Still ignoring her gorgeous blond shadow, she went inside.

An hour later they left the store fully decked out in new clothes. Kalli had picked out a pair of black leather pants and a black long-sleeved shirt. She'd replaced her sandals with heavy boots. As much as she scoffed at Eris for looking like a biker chick, the supple leather would likely protect her skin far better than the ratty denim she'd been wearing.

Sam had changed into black jeans, a black T-shirt, and a black leather coat. She had to admit, as tasty as he'd looked in his uptight professor suit, the casual look had her mouth watering. The denim cupped him in all the right places, and the tight T-shirt showed off muscles that had come as a surprise. She had no idea how someone who spent their time reading ancient texts and digging through the dirt could be as well built as he was, but she wasn't complaining.

He'd put up a fight when she'd plunked down her credit card to pay for their new outfits. She'd just given him an exasperated look. It was a nice change that a man was being chivalrous, but she was four thousand years old. Her bank balances looked like phone numbers.

"So what do we do now?" Sam asked.

"Now we wait," Kalli said as they walked the streets of DC.

"We could go back to the museum and kill a few hours there," he offered.

"Looking like this? I don't think so." They would fit in at a biker bar but not at the Smithsonian.

"Can we at least get something to eat? We didn't exactly finish lunch," he said.

"Sure." The next block up had a greasy burger joint on the corner, and she headed inside, grabbing a booth in the corner.

"This place isn't exactly what I expected you to pick," Sam said as he slid in across from her.

The restaurant happened to be one of her favorites. The burgers were to die for, and the fries were bottomless. "Hey, no one is making you stick around."

He held up his hands in surrender. "Don't forget, I've seen where you live. I figured you would have gone for a higher-brow place than this. I happen to love burgers and fries."

The waitress came and took their orders. Kalli waited until the woman had left before turning back to Sam.

"Clearly you've made a few incorrect assumptions about me," she said.

"How so?" Sam studied her.

She popped a peanut in her mouth and chewed. "The whole five-star restaurant thing for starters."

He shrugged. "You were a queen. It seems logical."

A sharp pang shot through her heart, as it always did when she thought about her former life. She should have known his reasoning and understood the train of thought. If Eris had been the queen, she probably wouldn't have settled for burgers and fries, even twenty-five hundred years later. She probably would have had people waiting on her hand and foot. Kalli wasn't like that, for more reasons than one. "Yeah, well, I'm not so sure I was a great queen."

It escaped before she had time to stop it, the fear that had been suffocating her for centuries, the thing she'd never shared with anyone else. She didn't understand what he was doing to her. The old Kalli would never have confessed that openly. She'd had many friends over her long life, but not once had she confessed her deepest fear.

She refused to look at him, keeping her eyes trained on the Formica tabletop. After several long moments of silence, however, she gave in and glanced in his direction. He cocked his head to the side and studied her as though she were on a slide under a microscope.

"Why would you say that?" He sounded genuinely confused.

Her gaze dropped again, her finger tracing a constellation between the silver flecks embedded in the table. She wasn't sure how to respond. Her instinct was to clam up and blow off the question. She wasn't one to get personal, and sharing her innermost secrets with a man was just weird. But there was a strange pressure inside her, something that felt like it had been building for ages. She needed to unburden herself, and she had a willing audience, one that already knew her secret.

"Because it's true. I was deposed," she blurted before she could change her mind.

"Deposed? Like kicked out?" he asked, grabbing a peanut and peeling back the shell.

She sighed, her heart aching with the memory. "There was a coup. A small group of Amazons thought I wasn't fit to be the queen. They removed me."

He blanched, his mouth dropping open. "Why did they think that?"

"Do you remember me telling you Themyscira's location was hidden?" She waited for him to nod. "It wasn't always. The location is a secret because of me. I asked the gods to hide it." Which sealed her fate and kept her from her homeland forever.

His head cocked sideways, and his eyebrows winged up. "Why would you do that? You must have had a good reason."

She'd thought so, but maybe she'd been wrong. "Amazons are immortal warriors, but we're not invulnerable. It was our duty to fight and protect. We went all over, defending our own land from invaders and helping those who needed assistance. We fought—we usually won—but not without a price. Our numbers dwindled. Our way of life was in danger, and we couldn't replenish our lost warriors—we're infertile by nature." She swallowed thickly. "In a desperate act to protect my people and our way of life, I made a deal with Hermes, the god of travel and boundaries. I asked him to cloak our city so that no one from the outside could find us."

It hadn't been a decision she'd made lightly. She'd known that not everyone would be happy with her actions, but she'd had to do something. Looking back on it now, even with the centuries she'd had to rethink the decision, she believed she'd made the right choice.

Sam sat back against the shiny red bench seat, his gaze burning into the top of her head. Finally, and with great reluctance, she lifted her gaze to meet his. "An Amazon named Nyx didn't agree with my decision, so she gathered a group of her followers and staged an uprising. On the night that the boundary was supposed to form, Nyx sneaked a band of Greek soldiers into Themyscira before it happened. She and her followers separated me and a few loyal to me from the rest and restrained us. After telling me all the reasons I was no longer fit to rule, Nyx took the crown and left us to the soldiers. They drugged us and took us with them as they left."

Her voice was flat and unemotional, but deep down she was churning. She could still picture with perfect clarity Nyx's brown eyes and feral scowl as she'd taken it upon herself to tell Kalli everything she'd done wrong. Her right hand went to her left wrist, rubbing away the remembered pain of the manacles the Greek soldiers had forced on her.

By far the worst moment had been when she'd awoken from the drugs. She'd known instantly that the veil had dropped and that they were on the wrong side.

"How did you escape from the soldiers?" His hands reached out to grasp hers, stopping the rubbing movements.

Kalli sent him a bittersweet smile, enjoying the warmth of his hands on hers. "I have no idea how long we were drugged, but when we woke up, we were on a boat in the middle of the sea. It didn't take long for us to escape from our bindings and kill the Greek soldiers, but then we were at a loss. Themyscira was a coastal city, but Amazons never took to boats, preferring to ride horses. We didn't know how to sail the ship. Eventually it washed ashore, and we made camp where we landed."

"How many of you were there?"

"Eight." She paused her story while the waitress brought their food. Her burger looked delicious, but she wasn't sure she could eat it anymore. Instead, she took a sip of her shake, enjoying the delicious coldness. "Including me and Eris."

Sam took a bite of a fry and chewed. She could almost see the wheels turning in his head.

"See, that's where you lose me. You said they ousted you and your loyal followers. How on earth did Eris make the cut? I don't imagine you two were friends back in the day."

She decided that the fries looked good and doused hers with ketchup before taking a bite. "No, we weren't. She was one of Nyx's confidants. I don't know how she wound up with us, and I don't think she knows either. It probably eats her alive."

Sam took a bite of his hamburger, chewing slowly. "So that's why you're here?"

She nodded.

"It also explains why you don't know where you came from or how to get back."

"The entire purpose of the veil was that people outside of it wouldn't remember how to find the city. It would be lost to them forever." It was supposed to protect them from outside invaders, but her brilliant idea had come back to bite her in the ass.

"Which then explains why Eris is so interested in my maps. It might show her the way to get home."

She nodded again.

"Well, for whatever it's worth, I'm sorry," he said, eyes full of sympathy.

"For what?" She couldn't imagine what he had to be sorry about.

"You didn't deserve what they did to you. No matter what Nyx would have you believe. You're a good person, and I'm willing to bet my relatively moderate professor's salary you were an amazing queen."

No one had ever said that to her before.

She hadn't done her duty as the queen with the expectation of praise, and it was hard to admit, even to herself, that she'd needed to hear it. Tears gathered in the corners of her eyes. Not wanting to cry in public, she blinked rapidly until the sensation vanished.

Who would have thought that talking to a total stranger would feel this good? Sam's belief in her was like a soothing balm to her tattered confidence. Unburdening herself was like lifting a weight from her shoulders, allowing her to breathe freely for the first time in centuries. With a smile of gratitude, she dug into her hamburger.

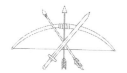

Chapter Six

S AM HAD NO CLUE why he'd thought accompanying Kalli while she broke into a building was a good idea. He was a professor, not a criminal, and he was scrupulous about following the law. He didn't even speed.

Even beyond the legalities, he had no skills for this sort of thing. No matter how fascinating his companion was, he had to admit he was in way over his head. Apparently he was a glutton for punishment.

They were crouched behind a large green dumpster that reeked of old food and possibly toxic sludge. Kalli was scoping out the warehouse. So far there was no sign of Eris, but there was far more activity than he would have expected for close to midnight. From his position behind Kalli he couldn't see much, but he could hear the beeping of forklifts and the rumbling of truck engines.

Kalli ducked back behind the dumpster and let out a huff. "I can't tell what they're doing, but if they're this blatant about illegal activity, it seems like the FBI or ATF would have been all over them already."

"Maybe there's nothing to find. Maybe Eris is involved in a legal business venture that just happens to be taking place at night." The story didn't even sound plausible to his own ears, so he wasn't surprised when Kalli rolled her eyes. Right. Not his forte.

"I think I need to get inside," she said, glancing around the edge of the green metal.

"Are you sure that's a good idea?" he asked. Now that they were actually here, he was having second thoughts. Dressing an anthropology professor in biker gear did not make him a badass. He wasn't a total wimp in the fighting department, but it wasn't exactly his specialty.

"No, but so far this place is my only lead to finding Eris. I have to find her, and the answers might be in that building."

She was right, as much as he hated to admit it. "So how do we do this?"

Her eyebrows winged up. "Are you sure you want to do this with me? Once we move, there probably won't be a chance to turn back."

Every instinct he had was telling him to run. Except one. There was one voice—sounding suspiciously like his ten-year-old self—that was urging him on. Even though he'd known the Amazons were exclusively women warriors, it hadn't stopped him from wanting to be one.

Here he was, twenty-two years later, on the verge of going into battle with one, or at least committing a felony with one. This might be his only chance.

He swallowed past the sudden thickness in his throat. It was probably a mistake, but he'd already made up his mind. "Yes."

She nodded once. "The building is shaped like a U. Most of the activity is happening on the inside of the U, probably so that it's harder to see. However, on the outer wall closest to us, there's a door and a bunch of partially broken windows. The door is likely to be locked, but if it is, I can get in through one of the windows and come back and open the door for you."

It seemed much more real now that she was actually talking through a plan to break into the building. This was so not him. It was unbelievable that he was thinking of going through with this, but something about the way she was looking at him, her pale pink lips smiling at him, her eyes searching his face, that made him want to do this with her. He just hoped this crush he was developing wasn't going to land him in jail.

"Sounds good." He mentally cursed when his voice trembled.

She nodded once more, then stepped around the corner of the dumpster and darted toward the building. It was now or never. He drew in a steadying breath and bolted after her.

By the time he'd reached the side of the building, she'd already unsuccessfully tried the door. She moved on to the window and found a broken pane that looked like it had a hole just big enough for her to squeeze through. He watched her bend and twist, carrying out feats worthy of Cirque du Soleil as she managed to maneuver her body through the window without ever coming into contact with the broken glass. She moved so silently and efficiently that she could have had an excellent second career as a cat burglar, if she wanted.

She successfully made it inside and came back around to the door. The lock clicked, and the door let out a metallic groan as she pushed it open. He glanced around, paranoid that the sound was going to be noticed, but no one came running. He slipped inside the building, closing the door as quietly as he could.

The inside of the warehouse was dark, only illuminated by whatever light from the streetlamps managed to filter its way through the filthy windows. The room they were in appeared to be unused, with hulking piles of debris slowly rotting away. The heaps were covered in tarps that had at least a half inch of dust on them. Clearly no one had been in this part of the building in some time.

Muffled noises came from a distant part of the building, but he couldn't tell what they were. Kalli was already making her way down the wing of the building. She was so quiet he wouldn't have known she was there if he hadn't seen her. His own steps were much louder, despite his best efforts to tread lightly. Not wanting to be left behind, he tried to catch up, his steps echoing uncomfortably through the open space.

When they reached the end of the hall, she sneaked a quick glance around the corner. She headed down the next hallway. Sam followed as closely as he could. The closer they got to the far side of the building, the louder the noise. He could hear shouts from men and the beeping of heavy equipment backing up. Something was either being loaded or unloaded from the warehouse.

They found an unoccupied room and slipped inside. The lights were off, but it had a window that they could use to spy on the movement on the warehouse floor. A handful of muscular men were loading large unmarked wooden crates onto a truck.

"I don't see Eris, but there's an office on the second floor," Kalli whispered. "It overlooks the loading docks. It has to be the one that she would use if she's involved in whatever they're doing here."

Sam glanced out the window and spotted the office she was talking about. It looked promising—there was a light on inside, and the door was cracked open just an inch. There was just one problem. Five burly men loading heavy equipment stood between them and the office.

"You may be right, but how on earth do we get over there?" he whispered back.

"Leave it to me," she said, then disappeared out the door and into the half-lit darkness of the warehouse.

Sam fought the urge to panic. Not only was he alone in the dark, watching what was likely an illegal trafficking operation, but his only offensive weapon had just left him. Kneeling on the ground, he peeked his head above the windowsill, squinting to track her progress. He could barely see her as she moved around the perimeter of the building, her black clothes making her melt into the shadows.

The office was on the second floor, and the only way to get there appeared to be a rickety-looking metal staircase less than ten feet from the men. Sam held his breath as she approached it, certain she would be spotted or that the metal steps would creak and telegraph her movements. To his surprise, she didn't take the steps. Instead, she grabbed on to a metal support pole for the platform above and started climbing hand over fist. She'd made it to the second floor before he had time to exhale.

The second-floor office also had a window, but the curtains were drawn. She'd be going in blind. Plus, now that she was near the door where the light was seeping out, she was far more visible than she'd been darting through the relative darkness of the floor below. He saw her hesitate, then quickly dip out of sight through the door, closing it as soon as she was inside.

Waiting for her to emerge was torture. Every time one of the workers took a step in his direction, Sam hurriedly leaned away from the window, certain he was about to be discovered. His crouched position made his knees ache, but he couldn't risk stretching them in case he accidentally made a sound and drew attention to himself. Just when he was about to chance it, the office door opened, and Kalli emerged.

She didn't go unnoticed.

"Hey! Who are you?" shouted a worker who'd been loading a wooden crate onto a forklift. The man could be a lumberjack. He was probably six foot four and solid muscle. His face looked like he spent too much time drinking and not enough time sleeping.

Kalli glanced around quickly, but there weren't any escape routes. The office was the only thing on the second floor. If she wanted to leave, she had to go right past the men.

Kalli shrugged casually, cocking her hip and crossing her arms like she didn't have a care in the world. "I'm Eris's friend. She sent me to pick up some things from her office." Sam was impressed by her quick lie. Unfortunately Lumberjack wasn't buying it.

Sam shifted position, ready to launch himself out of his hiding place. He wasn't sure how he could help her, but he wasn't about to leave her by herself.

Lumberjack took a step closer, and his biceps bulged as he crossed his arms menacingly. The rest of the guys had stopped what they were doing to watch. "I don't believe you. Eris doesn't have any friends. Though," he said with a disgusting leer as his eyes raked over Kalli's body, "if you want to come down here and convince me, I'd be okay with that." His chin jutted confidently in her direction.

Sam shuddered, trying not to let the dude's slime rub off on him. He left his hiding spot and stepped behind a large piece of dormant machinery. He moved as silently as he was capable of, almost hoping Kalli would go off on the creep.

Sam's eyes stayed riveted on the confrontation as he moved closer to the group. Kalli just sighed, and in a flash she executed a perfect forward flip off the second story, landing on the warehouse floor. Three of the warehouse workers took surprised steps back, but the cocky lumberjack didn't even move.

"Impressive." He whistled.

"You ain't seen nothing yet," Kalli said, her voice laced with fake sweetness.

"Honey, I'd like to see everything you've got." The dude grabbed his crotch.

Kalli cocked her head slightly, then pulled back her arm and let her fist fly, catching the guy by surprise and breaking his nose. Unfortunately the man seemed like he was used to getting punched. He barely flinched, despite the blood gushing down his face. He did, however, make a ton of noise. "You bitch!" he yelled.

The other four workers looked like they were coming out of a trance. They glanced at each other in confusion, then toward their friend with the bloody nose. After a slight hesitation, they went after Kalli.

Sam leapt to his feet. He wasn't about to let her get jumped by five guys, each of whom probably had a hundred pounds on her. He grunted as he darted at the man closest to him, hitting him in the back. The element of surprise was on his side, and he managed to bring the guy to his knees with the force of his lunge. Sam followed it up with a quick punch to the ribs and a right cross to the dude's jaw. The guy stayed down, but Sam no longer had the element of surprise. A second hulk of a man stepped around his buddy—who was moaning and gasping for air—and stalked toward Sam. If possible, this guy was even bigger than his friend.

Crap.

The man stared him down, feral anger narrowing his eyes. His nose had a misshapen look that hinted it had been broken more than once. The man cracked his neck and wiggled his fingers into fists. Sam sent a mental apology to his mother for refusing to take karate lessons as a kid.

Sam got a quick glimpse of Kalli—who was handily taking on the other three workmen—before the guy in front of him tried to headbutt him. Sam quickly sidestepped and managed to avoid getting creamed, but it was a narrow miss. The man bared his teeth and flexed his muscles, drawing Sam's attention to his humongous arms. "What you looking at, pretty boy?" he growled.

Sam wanted to take offense but figured it wasn't the right time to debate his looks. "Nothing, Ugly." It probably wasn't the smartest thing he could have said, but he wasn't exactly thinking straight. Sam kicked his opponent in the knee, hoping it would send him to the ground like his friend. No such luck. His foot basically bounced off the other man's extremely dirty jeans. The ugly workman lashed out and smacked Sam upside the head.

Without a way to brace himself, Sam went down. His nose came inches from smashing into the concrete, but he caught himself just in time and rolled sideways away from his attacker.

Out of the corner of his eye, he could see Kalli still fighting. She was a magnificent blur of movement. Her hand lashed out and punched one man in the throat before elbowing a different guy in the nose. She spun around, her leg catching the third man across the stomach, making him double over and grab his ribs.

Sam had just enough time to glimpse how beautiful she looked when she was kicking ass before Ugly grabbed him by the shoulder and hip and rolled him over. "I ain't done with you yet." With a huge yank, he pulled Sam upright, slamming him to his feet. Sam tried to pull away, but the other man wouldn't let go.

"You sure you want to keep this up?" Sam asked, trying to stall so he could come up with a plan, or at least get his breath back.

Ugly just smirked. "I can keep this up all night."

Sam tried a right-left combo punch to Ugly's gut, but it just made him grunt. A huge grin on his face, the other man pulled back his meaty fist and plowed it into Sam's jaw, sending him crashing to the floor. Sam's head bounced off the concrete, and blood streamed from his temple into his eye, obscuring his vision. Glancing up, he braced himself as Ugly cranked his arm back to send another punch his way.

The man's hand stopped in midair. He tried unsuccessfully to get his arm to move, but someone was holding his elbow, keeping him in place. Ugly glanced over his shoulder and saw Kalli, his mouth dropping open in shock and his skin going pale. He tried to yank his arm free, but he could barely move it. She looked like she wasn't even making an effort.

"Who are you?" he asked, his mouth gaping as he glanced behind her and saw his three coworkers laid out on the floor.

Kalli's eyebrows shot up. "I told you. I'm a friend of Eris. Now why don't you tell me where I can find her."

Ugly tried to turn around, but with her grip on his arm, he couldn't move. "I don't know where she is."

"I don't believe you." She yanked his arm behind his back and bent it toward his neck. The guy flinched sideways and practically stood on his tiptoes under the pressure.

He let out a groan and squeezed his eyes shut. "I think she left the country. Got on a plane this afternoon. That's all I heard." He panted heavily.

"You'd tell me if you knew more, right?" she asked. The overly sweet voice was back.

The guy groaned again. "I swear, that's all I know."

She let his arm drop. "Just in case you're lying to me, I'm going to give you a message. Tell Eris that Kalliope stopped by to see her."

After taking a step to the side, she spun around with blinding speed and sent a powerful kick into the side of the closest crate. The wooden panel smashed open, and assault rifles spilled out onto the floor of the warehouse. With more cool and guts than Sam could have managed, she reached into her pocket and pulled out her phone. She snapped a quick photo of the guns and, with a few swipes of her fingers, sent an email. "I have a few people who just might want to know about these. You don't mind, do you?"

Ugly put his hands up as a sign of surrender. Kalli just smiled sweetly in his direction. "We'll be going now." She spun on her heel and walked over to Sam, then grabbed him by the elbow. She tugged him in the direction they'd come from, seemingly unconcerned by the mess she was leaving behind.

Chapter Seven

I T WAS LONG AFTER midnight when they got back to Kalli's house. Her stomach soured as she thought about Sam's injuries. She hadn't felt comfortable making him head home alone to recuperate, especially since she'd been responsible for his safety and had let him down. To assuage her own guilt, she'd invited him back to her place. At least that way she could assess the damage and protect him against any backlash their attack might have drawn.

She'd left the hallway light on when they'd left, so her house was well lit and welcoming. She ushered Sam inside and sent a last glance around her property, hoping they hadn't been followed. She suddenly regretted that she'd never had an alarm system installed. She'd never felt the need for one, but now that she had Sam with her, she wasn't so sure. Violent scenarios played out in her head, each one more horrible than the last.

Kalli rummaged around in her kitchen drawers and came up with a towel. She ran it under cool water and handed it to Sam. He mopped himself up, wincing every time he moved, his breath hissing out with pain. She filled a bag with crushed ice from her freezer and set it down on the counter.

"Can I take a look at that for you?" she asked tentatively, gesturing to his head.

His eyes narrowed. "Did you pick up a medical degree in the last four thousand years too?"

She smiled. "Nope, but spending the first fifteen hundred years in constant combat situations made me an excellent field medic long before I left Themyscira."

He stared at her, then nodded slowly. She was slightly surprised by the level of trust he was willing to put in her. After all, despite everything they'd been through, they'd known each other less than a day.

She approached him slowly, then lifted her hand to the gash on his forehead. She used the damp cloth to wipe away the remaining blood. Sam hissed and muttered curses as she poked and prodded at his wound.

"Not exactly the type of language I'd expect from someone in your position," she said, trying to distract him.

"I've been around a few unsavory characters in my time."

She held in a laugh, but it was a near miss. "I'll bet you have," she said. Sam was far too well bred for her to picture him hanging out with lowlifes.

She carefully removed his glasses and set them on the counter next to him. Her experienced eyes took in his entire face, lingering on his beautiful straight nose, the sexy stubble that graced his chin, and the warm brown eyes that drew her in. She felt like she could swim in the pools of his eyes for hours. While she hadn't been lying about doing battle triage on her fellow Amazons, she had to admit none of them looked like him. She snapped out of her daze and caught his knowing grin, even as he winced.

Embarrassment flooded in, and her cheeks flamed. She shook her head and dragged her mind back to what she was supposed to be doing. The cut on his temple looked fairly shallow. Head wounds tended to bleed far more than other types of injuries, but you could never be too careful. It wouldn't require stitches, but it still needed something.

She opened her pantry and grabbed the first aid kit. She gently rubbed antibiotic cream on the injury, doing her best to ignore the warmth of his skin. She grabbed a butterfly bandage and carefully pulled the edges of the wound together, using the bandage to hold it closed.

"You'll probably have a killer headache tomorrow, but you'll be right as rain soon enough," she said as she handed him the bag of ice.

He nodded and changed the subject. "So did you find anything in the office?" He blanched as he put the ice against his head.

Kalli gave him a smug smile. "I thought you'd never ask." Reaching around her back, she lifted the hem of her shirt and grabbed the folder she'd tucked into her waistband. She dropped it onto the granite counter next to Sam.

He glanced from her to the folder and back again. "You had this in your pants the whole time?" he asked incredulously.

"Of course. Do you think I somehow magically conjured it from somewhere?" she teased, enjoying his surprise.

"You mean to tell me that you quite handily kicked the butts of three huge dudes and didn't even drop your paperwork?"

"Yep." She shrugged nonchalantly.

His eyebrows winged up, making him wince. "Will wonders never cease." He turned to the folder and flipped it open.

She'd stolen a series of shipping manifests, which were all probably faked or forged in some way—Eris wasn't likely to list her illegal cargo on a shipping bill—but it gave them a place to start. "She seems to have a bunch of different warehouses in Europe and the Middle East, but a few appear more frequently than others."

He quickly scanned through the documents she'd managed to steal. When he got to the end, he flipped the folder closed, sliding it back across the counter toward her. "Looks like we have our work cut out for us," he said, staring at her expectantly.

Kalli stared back, not sure what he was after. She'd just gotten him mixed up in an illegal gun deal and managed to get his head split open to boot. What sort of person would volunteer for round two?

An awkward silence fell between them, the only sound the clinking of the ice as he situated the bag against his temple. Trying to avoid agreeing to anything, she glanced around the room, her eyes falling on the clock on her microwave. It was almost two in the morning. He'd probably woken up early for his exhibit opening and had just gotten beat up. He looked ready to collapse.

"Bed," she blurted, then felt her cheeks heat again. That hadn't come out like she'd planned.

Sam stood up a little straighter, cocking his head in her direction. "What about bed?" he asked, his eyes sparkling wickedly.

"I have a bedroom upstairs," she tried again, shaking her head when it still didn't come out right. She wasn't normally this incoherent around men and wasn't sure why she was acting like a blithering idiot. She couldn't even use the fight as an excuse. None of the warehouse workers had managed to cause any real damage to her.

"Now, honey, I know we just met and all, but if you insist," Sam said with a teasing smile.

She shook her head and backed slowly across the kitchen. "No, that's not what I meant." She let out a frustrated huff. "Follow me." She spun around on her heel and marched down the hallway to the staircase by the front door.

Her house wasn't huge, but she'd never needed it to be. It was nice and airy, decorated in neutral shades of gray and blue. When she'd purchased it, it had seemed like the perfect place for her. Not too big, not too small, just enough room for her to spread out. She hadn't been worried about having guests over, especially not overnight guests. He'd gotten that right about her earlier. She didn't make a lot of close friends. It was too painful in the long run.

She was suddenly regretting her lack of forethought. She reached the top of the steps and turned into the first of two open doors, taking him to the only bedroom in the house. The sheets were a mess, since she hadn't made the bed before leaving. Suddenly paranoid about what he would think, she tried to surreptitiously straighten the comforter but didn't manage it in time. Sam came into the room seconds after she did and caught her in the act. She dropped the blanket like it had burned her.

"It's nice," he commented, the bag of ice still clutched to his head.

"Thanks," she said, awkwardly shifting her weight from one foot to the other. She wanted nothing more than to dart out past him into the hallway, but he was blocking the entire doorway, so she couldn't escape.

"Make yourself comfortable," she said, gesturing toward the bed.

She felt ridiculous. She'd had men over before, obviously. At over four thousand years old she wasn't a virgin. Yet she'd never been this awkward around a man and couldn't figure out why she felt so ruffled. He hadn't made a single move on her. He hadn't even hinted that he wanted to sleep with her, unless you counted her blunder downstairs. She shouldn't be thinking about him that way and needed to put it out of her mind entirely. He was a patient. He was someone she was taking care of because he'd gotten hurt on her watch.

End of story.

Sam finally moved farther into the bedroom, slowly perusing her belongings. She didn't have a lot in the way of knickknacks or decorations. Her life as an Amazon had mostly centered on training and fighting, and even though she'd been the queen, she hadn't lived a very opulent life. She'd lived in the Royal Hall, but she hadn't owned it, and she hadn't decorated it lavishly. In fact, only a few precious pieces of jewelry had set her apart from the women she'd ruled.

He paused in front of her bookshelf. Most of the books were of the self-help variety. When she wasn't working directly with her guests at Safe Haven, she was reading about ways to help them cope with everything they'd been through and get back on their feet. However, directly in the center of the top shelf was something else entirely. Before she could stop him, he reached out and picked it up.

"What's this?" He turned the ring over in his hand and inspected it closely. Kalli opened her mouth to protest but snapped it closed when she couldn't think of a valid reason why he shouldn't be allowed to see it.

She didn't need to look at it to know exactly what he was seeing. The platinum filigree band was so polished she could practically see the lights glinting off it from all the way across the room. The center of the ring contained a large sapphire, and on either side of the stone was a small carving, a bow crossed with an arrow, a spear, and a sword.

"This is the symbol for the Amazons." It wasn't a question.

"Yes," she answered anyway.

He held the ring up to the light so he could examine it more carefully. "I've never seen a piece preserved this well. All the artifacts we found during our digs, well, you saw them. They weren't in this condition."

She didn't know what to say. There was a reason for the condition of the ring, but it wasn't because she wore it. In fact, she hadn't put it on her finger since she'd removed it the day she'd been exiled. Despite the bitter memories it brought, she kept it polished and immaculate.

She couldn't do anything else.

Sam seemed to sense her reluctance to talk about it, because he didn't press the matter. He handed her the ring, which she accepted silently, tucking it into her pocket. "You take the bed. I'll go sleep on the couch." She turned and headed toward the door.

"That's not necessary. It's your bed. I can take the couch."

Kalli turned toward him and gave him a weak smile. "Believe me, I've slept in much worse conditions. Good night." She left the room, pulling the door closed quietly behind her.

She stood in the hallway, second-guessing her decision to leave. It had been longer than she cared to think about since she'd been with a man, and it would be nice to get a little bit of relief. Unless she was totally off base, Sam wouldn't say no. She couldn't imagine him turning down the chance to sleep with one of his childhood heroes.

Except she wasn't a hero.

Not anymore.

Plus, she couldn't bring herself to use him like that. She couldn't keep a man in her life. It was too painful to keep anyone around when she was destined to outlive them.

She drew in a deep breath. She was an Amazon, for crying out loud. She didn't need any man in her life.

Sam seemed to be the kind of guy who wouldn't settle for a one-night stand. He would want more, and she couldn't give him that.

She turned and went back downstairs, grabbing a blanket and pillow out of the linen closet as she passed. She set up a makeshift bed on the living room couch and lay down, not even remotely ready to sleep.

The ring in her pocket was like an anchor pulling her down while she tried to tread water. Damn the sexy Dr. Treadwell. He'd inserted himself into her life, sticking his nose into things she'd never talked about with anyone else, things she'd buried for a reason. Things she had no desire to reexamine.

With a sigh, she fished the ring out of her pocket and slipped it onto the chain around her neck.

The cool metal was a constant reminder of everything she'd lost.

Chapter Eight

S AM WOKE WITH A groan as the light from the window poured in and hit him in the eyes. He shifted to get away from the beams, immediately regretting it as his head gave a dull throb. He rolled over and glanced at the clock. It was ten in the morning.

He sat bolt upright, a knife of pain stabbing into his brain. He was supposed to be at the museum for the exhibit again today. Despite everything that had happened, he had to remind himself that he'd only met Kalli yesterday. So much had gone on during the last twenty-four hours that it felt almost impossible, but it was true. This was still the opening weekend of his exhibit, and he'd agreed that he would be there to help guide people and answer any questions.

The wicked headache reminded him that even if he'd shown up at the museum, he probably wouldn't have been able to stay for long. He took slow, even breaths and tried not to puke. He'd give up one of his PhDs for some ibuprofen. Having learned his lesson, he lay back down much more slowly than he'd sat up.

He glanced around. He was still in Kalli's house, in her bed. It was a shame she wasn't with him, but she'd clearly been giving off the "get me out of here as soon as possible" vibe the night before. A shame. He had a feeling they would be amazing together. His fertile imagination was picturing what they could have gotten up to with someone as strong and as flexible as she was.

In all the years he'd been interested in Amazons, he'd be lying if he said he hadn't thought about what it would be like to sleep with one. According to the legends, the Amazons did take lovers, but only for brief periods. They would never allow a relationship with a man to alter their way of life. They were fiercely independent and wouldn't stand for it if a man tried to do for them what they could do for themselves.

When he was younger, that had been a big turn-on. No strings, no fuss. An incredible woman and no messy relationship or breakup. Now, however, he was starting to wonder what that must have been like. It seemed like a lonely way to go through life, especially if you were going to live forever. He could understand the desire to be in charge of your own life, to not have anyone telling you what to do, but there was a strength in vulnerability as well. There was something to be said for being able to share the burdens of life and to not always have to deal with everything yourself.

He reached his arm up, mashing the pillow into a more comfortable shape behind his head. He wondered what Kalli had been like back then. The woman he knew now, despite her physical prowess and no-holds-barred attitude, didn't strike him as a queen. She was missing something, like something had been taken from her. The regal bearing was there, but it seemed like her confidence wasn't.

Of course, getting deposed would probably do that to anyone. He couldn't imagine what it must have been like for her. She'd been forcibly removed from her throne by someone who didn't sound like a good candidate to take her place. She'd been drugged, kidnapped, and removed from everything familiar. She'd been forced to find her way in a world much bigger and possibly more challenging than anything she'd known, even as a warrior.

Now he came bursting into her life, following her around like a lemming. She probably couldn't wait to get rid of him. His constant interest in the Amazon culture likely reminded her of everything she'd been forced to give up, everything she'd lost.

Then there was the situation with Eris, the Amazon turned smuggler. If Kalli was right, and she probably was, Eris was looking for a way back to Themyscira. Whatever her end goal was, if she planned to return home, it probably wasn't going to end well.

He couldn't imagine Kalli's struggle. She'd clearly made a good life for herself in DC. She had a nice home in a great neighborhood. She was doing amazing work that was clearly important to her. But it wasn't what she was trained to do, what she was born to do. Going back to Themyscira would be a painful reminder of what she'd had ripped away from her, but her conscience wouldn't allow her to do anything else. Stopping Eris was the only thing that mattered. And who knew, if she went back to Themyscira, perhaps things could be different.

Maybe she could get her throne back.

He, on the other hand, would go back to just being him, a somewhat stuffy professor living a sheltered life at a university. His heart sank at the thought of going back to his boring way of life. He'd had a few exciting moments during the research digs he'd done for the museum exhibit, but nothing like the intrigue and heart-hammering thrills of the last twenty-four hours. He wasn't sure he was ready to give it up.

There was one option he could see to keep himself in this world a little longer. His mind flashed downstairs to the folder that was probably still sitting on the kitchen counter. If he could help Kalli figure out where Eris had gone, she might let him stick around. He might even have a secret weapon or two in that department. With a smile, he carefully rolled to his side and sat up. It was time to get a move on.

Sam made his way downstairs gingerly, trying hard not to make his headache worse. He entered the kitchen and spotted the folder exactly where they'd left it. Kalli was nowhere to be found. He glanced in the dining room and didn't see her, so he tried the living room. There was a pillow on the couch, a blanket folded neatly on top, but no Kalli.

Not knowing what else to do, Sam shuffled his way back to the kitchen and rifled through her cupboards until he came up with a packet of instant coffee and a bottle of painkillers. He grabbed a mug and prepped what he was sure was going to be the worst cup of coffee he'd had in a long time. He quickly swallowed a few pills, then took the steaming hot liquid and the folder to the table, determined to find something they could use.

He was still at it twenty minutes later when he heard the front door open and close, followed by footsteps in the hall. He glanced up just in time to see Kalli jump at the sight of him, nearly dropping the bags she carried. He smiled, secretly pleased he'd caught her off guard. It probably didn't happen often.

"Morning," he said, lifting his coffee mug in a salute.

She gazed from him to the file and then to the empty coffee wrapper on the counter. "Sorry. I didn't think to buy more." She lifted a small brown bag in his direction. "Bagel?"

"You read my mind," he said, accepting the sack. He glanced inside. It was sesame, his favorite. He took a huge bite of the bagel, chewing carefully. It was still warm and tasted heavenly.

"Find anything?" she asked, gesturing toward the folder as she leaned back against the counter.

"Possibly. I'm actually waiting for . . ." His phone started to ring. He snatched it off the table and said, "Bryce, good to talk to you."

Kalli's eyes kept darting to the clock as she listened in on his half of the conversation. Eventually she crossed her arms and began tapping out a rhythm with her shoe. He watched her agitated movement with amusement, and after several minutes of back and forth, he got the information he'd been hoping for.

"What was that about?" she asked as she uncrossed her arms and stopped tapping her foot.

"That was Bryce Hancock. He works for the State Department." He leaned back in his chair and rolled his neck.

"You have contacts at the State Department?"

He nodded. "Yep. Comes in handy for doing archaeological digs in foreign countries."

"So, was he able to help?" She gestured toward the folder.

"I had him look into the places we think Eris uses for her operations. I was hoping he would know something about them, specifically if any of them were currently in use."

Kalli sat down next to him at the table, inches away from him. "And were they?"

"He was aware of activity at two of the locations from the invoices. The first one was in Germany, just outside of Munich. The second one was in Greece on the island of Lemnos."

Kalli's eyes widened, and her fingers tapped frantically at the table. "That's it, Lemnos. That's where she's going."

Taken aback, he asked, "Are you sure? How do you know?" Munich seemed like a far better option for illegal arms sales than a remote island with a small population.

Kalli leaned back in her chair, the wood squeaking in protest. "I've made several attempts over the centuries to figure out where I came from, where Themyscira was located. I've never come as close as you have, but there were a few things I did figure out. Do you remember me telling you the story about being kidnapped?" She waited for him to nod before she continued. "The Greeks brought us on their boat. As soon as we woke up, we overpowered and killed them, but that left us in the middle of the sea with no knowledge of how to sail. We drifted for several days before the boat grounded itself on an island. We made camp and eventually explored the land and found

other inhabitants. We lived peacefully side by side for some time."
Her voice had taken on a faraway, wispy tone, her eyes softening.

"That island was Lemnos?" It seemed far too coincidental.

She nodded. "I believe so. I won't know for sure until I see it,
but that's the only island that makes sense. We weren't there for
very long, at least not in the grand scheme of things. After a few
years, we'd figured out how to blend in with the local population and
decided to move to the mainland of Greece. Over the decades—after
we realized the futility of trying to get back home—we slowly drifted
apart, eventually going our separate ways." She shrugged.

"You think that Eris would go back there?"

"I bet she's going to try to retrace the path we took away from the
city. It's what I would do. The maps you had in the museum weren't
very explicit, but it's more than we've had in twenty-five hundred
years. You did a lot of work to put those together. Hermes would be
upset if he knew that someone was able to piece together what he'd
thought he'd hidden."

A crooked smile crossed her face, and it warmed his insides, at least
until the implications of her words sank in. She'd just said the name
of a Greek god like he was an old friend or a wayward uncle. Despite
having spent his entire life believing Amazons were real, it was a
whole different ball game to think in terms of the gods. According
to legend, the Amazons were the offspring of Ares, the god of war,
and Harmonia, a woodland nymph. If Amazons were real, that had
to mean the gods were, too, right?

He was starting to think he might be in way over his head. It was
one thing to accept Kalli. On paper he might believe in her immor-

tality, if only because his research hinted at it, but it was quite another to actually accept that he was staring at a four-thousand-year-old person. He could just as easily believe she was an MMA fighter as a badass Amazon warrior. Gods, however, were a totally different level of disbelief. He had never been particularly religious, but he also didn't want to take his chances. He didn't need a vengeful god angry with him.

Maybe it was time to cut and run.

Something must have shown on his face, because Kalli's eyes narrowed. "Sam? What just happened?"

He stood, the wooden chair legs scraping loudly across the floor. He retreated a few steps toward the door, wondering how he could smoothly extract himself from this bizzare situation he'd found himself in. "Well, it sounds like you have your next step to track down Eris. I wouldn't want to hold you up."

She stood slowly, her hands out in front of her like she was approaching a wild animal. "I'm not sure what just went through your head, but I can tell it freaked you out. I'm sorry if I did or said something that scared you."

"No, that's not it," he tried to protest, even though that was exactly what had happened. "I'm sure you have stuff to do. I should get out of your hair." He turned to leave.

"Please don't go."

Her soft voice froze him, his hand on the doorknob. He glanced back at her and saw unexpected vulnerability in her shining blue eyes.

"Sam, I need your help. I don't think I can do this without you. I've been looking for Themyscira for twenty-five hundred years, and I've never come as close to finding it as you have."

He knew what it had probably cost her to ask for help. Kalli was the type of person who took pride in being able to do things for herself. Admitting that she needed his help was a big step. If she was willing to step outside her comfort zone, so could he. He'd just have to deal with his freak-out later.

He nodded at her, and she smiled in return. "We need to stop by my place, though. I should grab my notes from my digs. Maybe there's a clue I've overlooked."

She bobbed her head. "Sure, but let's be quick about it. We should head out on the first flight we can get."

Chapter Nine

I T TURNED OUT THAT the first flight they could get wasn't until that evening. They used the time wisely, each packing the essentials of what they thought they would need for the trip. Sam seemed to have a lot more essentials. She'd packed one small bag of clothes. He, on the other hand, had insisted on going by his apartment to grab anything from his research he thought might come in handy.

Kalli took the time to call Safe Haven and let her employees know that she was going out of town. Vanessa practically crowed with excitement that she was finally taking some time off. Unfortunately Kalli had let it slip that she was going with a man she'd just met, not realizing exactly what she'd gotten herself into. She was then subjected to five minutes of badgering as Vanessa tried to squeeze any dirty secrets out of her about their nonexistent whirlwind romance.

She finally managed to break away after promising all the details when she returned. She wasn't sure how on earth she was going to hold up her end of the bargain, considering Vanessa didn't know what she was, but that was future Kalli's problem. Right now, they had a plane to catch.

They'd booked a flight out of Reagan Airport since it was Metro accessible. Sam had balked about her paying for his plane ticket, but she'd ignored him again. Several thousand years of saving had left her more money than she knew what to do with. First-class plane tickets were nothing.

As they were standing on the Metro, crushed in next to all the eager tourists and bored locals, a strange tingle started at the base of her neck. Her senses perked up, the hairs on the back of her neck bristling. Something was pinging her radar in a big way, but with the crush of the crowds, it was hard to tell what was causing it. She casually glanced around the train car and tried to spot anything out of the ordinary, anyone who glanced at them a moment too long or looked a bit too interested in them. Perhaps Eris's men had somehow followed them and were looking for round two.

Nothing caught her eye, but her skin was still crawling. She almost gave in to the temptation to get off the train and take a cab the rest of the way, but they were almost to the airport. It seemed silly to go to such lengths when they were almost at their stop. Hopefully whoever or whatever it was would stay on the train.

No such luck. The sensation of being watched didn't disappear.

She tucked her hand in Sam's elbow and smiled in his direction as they exited the train, earning a confused look for her trouble. She didn't want to tell him her suspicion, in case it was wrong, but it wouldn't hurt if the two of them looked just like any other normal couple off for a European vacation. With a slightly raised eyebrow, he went with it, not asking any questions.

The sensation of being followed wouldn't leave her alone. Thankfully they were about to enter a busy airport, and she would have plenty of opportunity to lose whoever was tailing them in the crowds. As soon as they were inside, she dragged Sam into the first travel shop she found, hoping to get a good look at whoever was behind them. Whoever it was, they were good, because she didn't spot them anywhere. She was half tempted to brush it off and wondered if she was being paranoid, but something wouldn't let her do that. Years of honing her instincts for battle had given her extremely keen senses.

"What is it?" Sam asked.

She grabbed a pack of gum and a candy bar and took them to the register. "I think we're being followed," she said under her breath. She grabbed his arm before he could look around suspiciously. "I got this. We're going to walk out of here toward the security checkpoint like nothing is wrong."

She tucked her purchases into her purse and grabbed his elbow again. Walking slowly, she directed him down the hallway. A large crowd was walking toward them, and, spotting her opportunity, she let go of Sam's arm and quickly darted sideways behind a pillar. She circled around behind Sam and spotted what she was looking for. A woman was eyeing him a little too closely.

The woman was wearing jeans and a navy long-sleeved shirt. Her blonde hair was in a ponytail tucked through the back of a red

Washington Nationals baseball hat. Unfortunately the hat blocked Kalli from getting a good angle on her face.

Kalli caught the exact moment when the other woman realized she was no longer with Sam. Her head whipped around frantically, and her eyes scanned the crowds. Moving quickly, Kalli approached her from behind, grabbed her wrist, and yanked it behind her. She forced her sideways down a deserted hallway. It happened so quickly no one in the area noticed what had happened.

"Why are you following me?" Kalli asked, shoving the woman face-first against the wall.

"After all this time, you're still the best I've ever met," the woman said through gritted teeth.

Startled, Kalli let her grip on the other woman's arm go slack, allowing her to yank away and turn around. Kalli saw her face for the first time, a face she hadn't seen in more than twenty-five hundred years. "Zoe?"

Kalli's heart fluttered frantically as she took a step back, drinking in the sight of the woman in front of her. Her features were almost as familiar to her as her own. Her blue eyes sparked with both mischief and relief. The nondescript outfit she was wearing did nothing to take away from her tall, muscular form or her innate beauty.

Something clenched in Kalli's heart. She'd lived a good life and had done amazing things during her exile, but she'd been lonely. She hadn't realized exactly how lonely until she saw that smirking face staring at her. Before she could think better of it, she threw herself at the other woman, yanking her into a huge hug. Zoe squeezed her back, nearly knocking the breath out of her.

"So I take it we're not killing her?" Sam asked from the end of the hall.

Pulling away, Kalli blinked a few times, making sure there was no moisture left before she turned and glanced down the hallway to where he was standing. "No, we're most certainly not."

"You going to introduce me to the hottie?" Zoe asked, a smile spreading on her face.

Kalli laughed, a sense of relief pouring through her entire body. She hadn't realized exactly how tense she'd been. "Zoe, this is Sam. He's an anthropologist with Georgetown University. Sam, this is Zoe."

"Another Amazon," he said. It wasn't a question.

"He knows about us?" Zoe asked, raising her eyebrows in Kalli's direction, her mouth dropping open.

"Yeah, well, that's sort of a long story," Kalli said with an eye roll. Explaining the last twenty-four hours would take a while.

"Our flight to Greece doesn't leave for at least another few hours. I'd say we've got time to chat," Zoe said as she checked her watch.

"You're going to Greece too?" Sam asked, coming up next to them. "Why?"

She shrugged. "I imagine I'm going for the same reason you're going. Because of Eris."

"You've been watching Eris?" Kalli asked. The whole situation seemed fishy. It was strange that they were both going after Eris at the same time.

"Only for about the last twenty-five hundred years," Zoe replied with a smile, tucking her hands into the pockets of her jeans and rocking back on her heels.

Her admission made Kalli feel even worse about tuning out everything to do with her past. If Eris had been up to something for that long, Kalli should have done something about it rather than bury her head in the sand. Just one more example of her falling down on the job.

She shook her head, trying to drive away the distracting thoughts. What mattered was that she was here now.

"Clearly we have a lot to catch up on," Kalli said. "Shall we?" She gestured with her arm toward the main terminal.

"Let's," Zoe said, taking her invitation and strolling back down the empty hall. "You really are a choice morsel, aren't you?" she asked as she passed Sam and patted him on the cheek with a wink.

A sick sensation pooled in Kalli's stomach. Her hackles were up, and she had to fight down the urge to yell at Zoe not to touch Sam again.

It wasn't possible that she was jealous. The very idea was ludicrous. She wasn't the jealous type, nor was she the relationship type. It wasn't like she had any sort of claim on Sam—they weren't involved or anything—so she shouldn't have any problem with the idea of Zoe flirting with him.

Except she did. Bile rose in her throat, and she had to swallow it back down.

Sam, thankfully, didn't seem to realize what was going on. He smiled at Zoe, then glanced in Kalli's direction and narrowed his eyes as he caught her gaze. "Everything good now?" he asked.

"Yep." She swallowed down the lie. Her strange surge of jealousy was her problem, not his.

The three of them made their way through the crowds of swarming people to security. Once on the other side, they found a cozy Italian place to grab dinner. They ordered food and a bottle of wine, Zoe flirting with the waiter the entire time.

Kalli watched her friend and the ease she seemed to have with everyone around her. She seemed happy and confident, like she was on top of the world. Kalli was having trouble figuring out how she felt. It was amazing to see Zoe again after so many centuries apart. Truthfully, she'd never expected to see any of the other Amazons again, and the fact that she'd seen two in the course of two days was unheard of. They'd gone their separate ways after they'd landed on mainland Greece, each making their way in the world in the way they saw fit. Considering what they'd been like before they'd been kidnapped, it wasn't that much of a shock she'd centered her life on helping people, especially those victimized by brutal men. It also wasn't that much of a shock that Eris had become a smuggler and black-market arms dealer.

She wondered what Zoe had become, what she'd done with herself for all these years. Every time she thought to ask, however, it seemed that Zoe was far more interested in cooing at Sam.

It was still troublesome that she was bothered by Zoe's flirtation. Kalli had decided a long time ago that she wasn't going to have a man in her life, despite Vanessa's best efforts otherwise. Sam was free to flirt with whomever he wanted.

"So, Zoe," she finally interrupted. "What have you been up to since I last saw you?" It was a question with a likely long-winded answer, and she took a petty pleasure in stopping Zoe from hitting on her anthropologist.

Zoe glanced around, as if worried she was going to be overheard. Maybe she was part of the seedy underground as well. She reached into her pocket and pulled out a leather folder, which she flipped open to reveal a brass badge. "I'm with Interpol," Zoe said, surprising her.

"Really?" Sam asked in his eager professor voice. The sour feeling was back in the pit of Kalli's stomach, but she tried to drown it with a sip of wine.

Zoe nodded, her high blonde ponytail bobbing. "It's handy. It allows me to keep an eye on some of the less savory members of society, including Eris." Zoe picked delicately at her shrimp scampi.

"So that's why you're here? You were tracking her?" Kalli asked, drawing Zoe's attention back to her.

"Yeah. I've been watching her for a while. She's into some shady stuff."

"We know. We paid her warehouse a little visit last night." Kalli tried not to sound smug.

Zoe looked at her with more interest, her blue eyes sparkling. "That was you? I should have known when I saw the aftermath of what happened. Those guys didn't look very pleased with what went down. I had been thinking of trying to track down whoever was behind it and warning them that Eris might come after them, but now I guess I don't have to." Zoe paused, looking at Kalli with interest. "So, I know what he does for a living, but what have you been up to? Are you a cop too? Is that why you're following Eris?"

Kalli shook her head, suddenly feeling unworthy. She'd always believed in her work, in the importance of it. However, compared to her former friend, who was an international police officer, what she did seemed a whole lot less impressive. "I run a shelter for domestic abuse victims."

A knowing look entered Zoe's eyes, her expression softening. Her hand reached across the table and rested on Kalli's arm, squeezing gently. "I can't think of a more fitting profession."

Kalli searched for any hint of irony or disdain, but she didn't find one. Zoe seemed perfectly sincere in her belief. Warmth flooded into her, and she let out a breath she hadn't known she'd been holding. She hadn't realized until that moment exactly how much she'd been worried about the other Amazon's reaction. "Thanks."

"So if you run a shelter and you're a college professor, what on earth are you doing chasing after Eris?" Zoe asked with a frown.

Sam gave Kalli a look, cocking his eyebrows upward in an unspoken question. She could tell he was going to leave it up to her whether she wanted to share their reasons with Zoe. After a split second of hesitation, she decided to bring Zoe into the fold. After all, she'd been one of her closest confidants when they were in Themyscira, and she was a cop. If she couldn't trust Zoe, she probably couldn't trust anyone. What was twenty-five hundred years apart in the grand scheme of things?

"We think that Eris is trying to return to Themyscira," she said.

Zoe's eyes widened. "How on earth could she do that with the veil still in place? None of us know how to find it. That's why we're out here in the first place." She leaned closer, the volume of her voice dropping slightly.

Sam raised his hand sheepishly, his mouth quirking up at the end. "I'm afraid that's my fault. I've been studying the Amazons my entire life. My research led to the general area where the city was likely located, though I wasn't able to determine the specific spot." He ran his hand through his hair, giving it an adorably rumpled look.

Zoe whistled quietly. "So you think evil minion number one might be trying to make her way back to her evil overlord."

"That about sums it up," Kalli said. She took one last bite of her pasta, then shoved the plate away.

"And here I was thinking it was just about selling guns to terrorists," Zoe said, then sipped her wine.

"The guns shouldn't be an issue anymore," Kalli said without elaborating. She hoped that Larson had gotten her photos and had already closed in on the warehouse, maybe with the ATF in tow.

Zoe shrugged. "Who knows what other stockpiles she may have, or if she has something worse than guns floating around. What if she plans to bring them back to Themyscira?" She shook her head. "I'm going to have to figure out what to tell my bosses."

Kalli picked up the tab for dinner before Sam could even open his wallet, earning her yet another glare. She just smiled in return.

They made their way to the departure gate. After speaking to the airline staff at the desk, Zoe was able to switch her seat to sit next to

Kalli and Sam in first class. They boarded their flight, surrounded by businesspeople and tourists heading out on vacation.

Since their flight went overnight, Zoe took immediate advantage of the goodies from first class, pulling on her free eye mask and shoving in earplugs. As soon as they took off, she reclined her seat flat into a bed, rolled over, and went to sleep.

Kalli didn't know what to do with herself. She wasn't tired, even though she knew she was going to be incredibly jet-lagged if she didn't get some rest. Most of the passengers around her were starting to do the same thing Zoe had. The sky outside the windows was pitch black, a few stars twinkling just bright enough for her to see.

She glanced in Sam's direction, but he'd already pulled out a book and was reading. Turning her gaze to the back of the seat in front of her, she did her best not to think about him. She had no idea why he was suddenly occupying such a large part of her brain, considering she'd just met him the day before.

She'd spent most of her time as queen of the Amazons holding off swarms of invaders, all led by men convinced that they could rule Themyscira better than any woman. She'd proved them wrong then, just as she'd been proving men wrong for millennia. She didn't need a man in her life. She was just fine on her own.

With a huff, she mashed her finger on the button to transform her own seat into a bed and rolled onto her right side, her back to the man in question. For the first time in four thousand years, she was starting to wonder if she was missing out on something.

Chapter Ten

I T FELT LIKE HE'D only just managed to fall asleep when the overhead lights on the plane came on and the flight attendants started walking around with breakfast sandwiches and warm towels. It took a Herculean effort to pry his eyes open and focus on what was going on around him. They were about to land in Athens.

Sam blinked rapidly and sat up, glancing around to get his bearings. Zoe was still conked out next to him, apparently able to sleep through anything. Kalli, on the other hand, was already sitting up, looking like she was wide awake and ready to go. The extremely jet-lagged part of his brain hated her for it. She caught his eye before quickly looking away again.

She'd been acting funny since they'd arrived at the airport in DC. He couldn't put his finger on the problem, but they seemed to have lost a bit of their easy rapport, and he was starting to miss it. She kept looking at him sideways, as if she was worried about something, but he had no clue what.

In contrast, Zoe seemed to be an open book. She was far more outgoing and friendly than her former queen, and an incurable flirt. If he'd passed her on the street, he might have guessed she was a sales rep or maybe a fitness instructor. Nothing about her screamed cop or, for that matter, Amazon.

She and Kalli obviously had a history, but he couldn't quite pin down what it was. When Kalli had first realized who she was, it had been almost like she'd been seeing a ghost. It was only since Zoe had noticed him that Kalli had been acting oddly.

In fact, she was almost acting jealous.

Which was ridiculous and probably all in his head. Zoe appeared to flirt with everyone, and it wasn't like he and Kalli were dating. He had to rein in his hopeful thoughts before Kalli noticed something was up.

The flight attendant handed him a towel, which he used to wipe his face, clearing some of the fog from his brain. It wasn't the same as getting a full night's sleep, but it would have to do. He accepted the tray of food, digging into the bacon, egg, and cheese croissant.

There had been no direct flights from Washington, DC, to the island of Lemnos, so they had a layover in Athens before they were supposed to take a puddle-jumper flight to the island. Thankfully, the stop was short, and they were on the island well before lunchtime.

Sam was tempted to suggest they head to a hotel to catch up on a few hours of sleep before they went anywhere, but his two lovely traveling companions didn't look tired at all. He, on the other hand, felt like he'd been flattened by a steamroller. Maybe Amazons needed less sleep than humans.

They stepped out of the terminal into the sunshine. The landscape was just as exotic as he was expecting, full of rocks and scrubby trees. The houses and buildings were classic Greece, with shining white walls and bright terra-cotta roofs set off wonderfully against the bright-blue water.

He inhaled deeply, breathing in the salty air. He'd always loved traveling. It was one of his favorite parts of his job. He'd been to several places in Greece during his research project, but it never got old. There was just something so different from the stark gray stone and brick that made up Washington, DC, and he couldn't help but enjoy the change.

He wasn't the only one who noticed it. Zoe glanced around quickly and didn't seem overly impressed, but Kalli was a different story. He watched her eyes close slowly as she spread her arms and enjoyed the sunshine. It was only in the mid-sixties, but looking at her, he would have thought she was bathing in the tropical heat. Her eyes opened, and she glanced around.

She looked . . . right. Like she belonged here. Lemnos wasn't the location of Themyscira, but the exotic scent and feel of the island suited her much better than the cramped buildings and constant hustle of the big city. She was a woman who deserved to live in a place of beauty and wonder, and DC wasn't it.

Zoe had used her contacts with Interpol to get them a suite at a hotel in the capital city of Myrina, the largest port on the island, which made it the logical place for Eris to base her smuggling operations. Zoe grabbed them a taxi for the short but winding drive to the city.

When they arrived at the hotel, the bellman took one look at Zoe and Kalli and practically tripped over himself to grab their luggage. He awkwardly gestured for them to precede him into the hotel's lobby, taking the opportunity to ogle them from behind. Anger rose in the back of Sam's throat, and he tapped the man on the shoulder. The bellman glanced around like he hadn't even noticed Sam standing there.

"That's not the way to treat a lady. I'd suggest you tuck your eyes back into your head before they notice. Trust me, you don't want to make those women mad." Even though he wasn't normally a violent man, he wanted to punch this sleaze in the nuts.

Kalli had reached the tiled floors of the lobby. She glanced around and realized he wasn't with them, giving him a questioning look. He held up a finger. "Are we clear?" he asked, glaring at the shorter man, unabashedly using his extra height to his advantage.

The bellman glanced between Kalli and Sam, then nodded. "We're clear. Sorry, sir." He bobbed his head a few times in Sam's direction.

Sam nodded once in acknowledgment, then turned and entered the hotel.

"What was that about?" Kalli asked.

"Nothing, really. Just taking care of something." He shrugged. She didn't need to know about the jerk checking out her ass.

She gave him another puzzled look but let it drop. They walked over and waited behind Zoe, who was checking in at the front desk.

The hotel lobby was ultramodern, with lots of shiny silver accents and simple leather furniture. The lime-green couches looked particularly uncomfortable. The hotel had also been liberally decorated with potted plants, the leafy greens matching nicely with their futuristic-looking furniture.

Thankfully their suite was much better. The main living room was complete with a couch, a plush chair, and a big-screen TV. There was a kitchenette and dining area near the door, and off to either end of the living room were doors leading to the two bedrooms.

Zoe took a quick walk around the expensive-looking room and declared, "It'll do." She dragged her excessively large suitcase to the door on the left and claimed one of the bedrooms.

Kalli and Sam stood awkwardly in the living room. "You can take the other bedroom," he said, waving his arm in the general area of the far room. He had to forcibly stop his mind from picturing her there.

Kalli stared at him and shifted her weight from one foot to the other. "No, you should take it. I've slept in worse." She licked her lips, drawing his attention to their lush fullness. Not wanting to repeat the bellman's rude behavior, he yanked his gaze back up to her eyes.

He managed a smile. "So you've said. I promise you, I'll be fine on the couch. I've slept in tents in the desert, so this is definitely a step up."

Kalli opened her mouth to protest again but was cut off by Zoe, who had reentered the living room. "Guys," she said, rolling her eyes at them. "The couch pulls out into a bed."

"Oh," Kalli said, her cheeks flushing adorably. Without saying another word, she spun around and headed into the other bedroom.

"Wow, you'd think after four thousand years she'd have figured out how to handle a hot guy," Zoe said. She walked into the kitchen and grabbed an apricot out of the fruit bowl on the counter.

Sam glanced at her, uncertain how to respond. He didn't want to insult Kalli, nor did he want to argue about his own level of attractiveness. In the end, he said nothing and dragged his suitcase into the corner of the living room.

"I'd say you guys are cute, but you haven't seemed to figure this whole relationship thing out yet," Zoe said, hoisting herself up to sit on the counter and biting into her fruit.

Sam's eyes narrowed. "We're not in a relationship." His stomach squirmed uncomfortably. This was probably something he should be discussing with Kalli, not Zoe.

Zoe laughed. "I know, I can tell. What I don't know is why not. It's obvious you guys have the hots for one another." Her blue eyes sparkled as she grinned at him.

Sam crossed his arms in front of himself defensively. "We just met two days ago."

Zoe's eyebrows winged upward. "Really? That I wouldn't have guessed. Have you slept together yet?" She took another bite.

He retreated a step backward. "Of course not." Though, thinking back to that night at her house, he was more than up for it.

Zoe looked him up and down, the same way the bellman had been checking her out downstairs. "It's a shame, really."

He sputtered, but before he could come up with a coherent response, Kalli walked back into the room. "What's a shame?"

Sam didn't have the capacity to come up with a quick lie, but thankfully Zoe was fast on her feet. "I was just saying that it was a shame that he's never been to Lemnos before. It's a nice little island."

Sam shuffled his feet on the carpet and tried to look like this wasn't news to him.

"Unfortunately, we probably won't have much time to sightsee while we're here. We have our work cut out for us," Kalli said, all business as usual.

"Right, we need to find Eris," Sam chimed in, trying to cover up his awkwardness. He ignored Zoe's knowing glance and focused on Kalli.

Kalli nodded. "We definitely need to do that before she moves on. But there's something else I think we should do while we're here."

Zoe finished munching on her apricot and jumped off the counter to throw the pit in the trash. "What's that?" She came around the end of the kitchen counter and joined them in the living room.

"There's something I think we should try to find while we're here. I'm not sure if it's still around, or if we could ever find it again. The island has changed so much since the last time I was here." Kalli almost seemed like she was talking to herself.

Zoe made a circular motion with her hands. "Spit it out."

Kalli rolled her shoulders back, straightening her spine. "Do you remember what we did before we left the island and went our separate ways?"

Zoe's eyes went wide, her mouth opening silently.

"What am I missing here?" Sam glanced from one woman to the other, feeling totally out of the loop.

It was Zoe that answered. "When we decided to leave the island, we knew we needed to keep a low profile. We didn't want to draw too much attention to ourselves for being Amazons. The veil had already come down on Themyscira, and the deal was that people outside of that boundary weren't supposed to remember about the city or the Amazons. We were supposed to be hidden from the rest of the world."

Kalli picked up the story. "We didn't want to be seen wandering the world as heavily armed warriors, as we would have stood out among the traditionally male-dominated cultures of the time. We agreed to keep the minimum weaponry we needed to protect ourselves, and we hid the rest."

"Why didn't they take your weapons when they kidnapped you?"

Zoe answered. "They did. Nyx gave them to the Greeks as payment for kidnapping us. When we escaped, we took them back."

Sam shifted, tucking his hands into the pockets of his jeans. "So you're telling me that there's a hidden cache of Amazon weapons somewhere on Lemnos?" His researcher's heart gave a little lurch at the thought of all those artifacts.

"It's possible." Kalli shrugged. "At least, as long as it hasn't been found already."

He felt a deep vee form between his eyebrows as he squinted at the two women. As excited as he was at the idea of that many archaeological artifacts, realism settled on his shoulders like a lead blanket.

"It's been several thousand years. There's no way the weapons would have survived and still be usable." He looked directly at Kalli. "You saw the exhibit. The swords we found were way too far gone for them to be of any use today."

Kalli dropped her gaze toward the carpet, rubbing her fingernails back and forth across the leg of her pants. "In theory, you're right," she finally said.

He rolled his eyes, crossing his arms in front of his chest. "Okay, so this is me missing some piece of the puzzle again." He was a professor with two PhDs. He wasn't used to feeling ignorant.

Zoe shrugged and pursed her lips. "What do you know about the Greek god Hephaestus?"

"I have a doctorate in Greek mythology, so plenty. I have a feeling that's not where you're going with this, though." When she cringed slightly, he continued: "I think I'm going to need a drink for this." He skirted around the couch and the kitchen counter and headed to the fridge. Just as he was hoping, he found several bottles of complimentary beverages inside. He grabbed a beer, turning to offer one to each of his companions. Zoe nodded, so he grabbed one for her, too, but Kalli shook her head. Her loss.

After cracking open the bottles, he handed one to Zoe, then went back into the living room and settled down on the couch. He finally answered her question. "Hephaestus was the god of forges and metalwork. What's that got to do with anything?"

"Lemnos is, or at least was, sacred to Hephaestus. It was believed that one of his forges was located on the island." Zoe joined him, sitting on the opposite end of the couch. Kalli perched on the very edge of the chair, her body rigid.

Sam took a swig from the bottle. It was sweeter than he normally went for, but it wasn't bad. "Let me guess. You made another deal with a Greek god?"

Kalli tilted her hand back and forth. "Sort of. We didn't make a deal with him so much as prayed to him and offered him a sacrifice if he would grant his protection to our weapons. We figured it was possible we might need them again."

"A sacrifice?" he asked, a hint of skepticism slipping out.

Zoe made a sound of disgust. "Not a human sacrifice, if that's what you're asking. It was a goat."

Realistically, he'd known that the Amazons would never have sacrificed humans. Their entire culture was based around protecting people. He cleared his throat to cover the awkward silence. "So basically, if it hasn't already been found—and if a Greek god held up his end of the deal—there may be an armory full of Amazonian weapons somewhere on the island."

Kalli and Zoe both nodded at him.

"Where is it?"

"That's the tricky part," Kalli said, finally slumping backward into her cushy armchair. "I have no idea."

He turned to the blonde woman. "Zoe?" he asked hopefully.

She shook her head. "I couldn't tell you. I'd totally forgotten about it until Kalli mentioned it."

"Well, I guess we have our work cut out for us." He slouched against the couch, nursing his beer.

Zoe knocked back the last of her drink. "We should probably split up. One person can go scout around for Eris while the others try to find the weapons."

Kalli shifted in her seat. "I'm not sure splitting up is a great idea."

Zoe went to the kitchen to dispose of her beer bottle. "Sure it is. We'll cover more ground this way. I'll go find Eris's warehouse, and you can take Dr. Hunky over here to look for the weapons cache." She plowed on before Sam had a chance to object to being called Dr. Hunky. "I can take care of myself, if you remember," she added.

Kalli launched herself to her feet and started pacing. "Of course you can. I didn't mean to imply that you couldn't."

Sam could see the war going on behind Kalli's eyes. Her protective instincts had kicked in. He hadn't known her very long, yet he felt like he could read her like a book. He understood her, maybe even better than she understood herself. She'd just gotten Zoe back into her life, and she wasn't ready to risk losing her again. She wanted to make sure they would both be safe.

"So it's settled then. I'll catch you guys on the flip side." The door closed behind Zoe with a small click.

Kalli sighed. She'd clearly let Zoe go despite her own reservations, counting on the other warrior to do what was necessary. In spite of the doubts he knew she had about herself, Sam was certain she'd been an amazing queen. It was obvious in how she behaved around Zoe.

"I guess that leaves the two of us," he finally said.

Kalli glanced at him, clearly pouting. It was totally inappropriate to be thinking about how much he wanted to nibble on those lips.

"I guess it does. We're going to need a car."

He yanked his mind back on track.

The front desk was able to point them to the nearest car-rental facility, where they got the biggest SUV they could find. Kalli had no idea how much weaponry they'd hidden, so they didn't take any chances. What they were going to do with the weapons once they found them, he had no idea. A giant stash of swords and shields wasn't likely to go unnoticed. That was a problem for the future, however. First, they had to locate it.

Lemnos wasn't a huge island, but it was big enough that they couldn't cover the whole thing in a day. Kalli had no idea where to start, so the plan—if you could call it that—was to drive around the island and hope to spot a familiar landmark. The task was going to be next to impossible given how much had changed in the twenty-five hundred years since she'd last set foot there.

Sam decided it was best if he drove so she could look around freely. He tried to stick as close to the coast as possible, hoping that Kalli would recognize where they might have landed when their boat beached. They drove in and out of towns and along stretches of deserted roads. They didn't talk much as he drove, and she stared despondently out the window.

He could feel her frustration radiating off her. He couldn't imagine what it must be like to have been alive for as long as she had and to try to dig out a memory from that far back. He could barely remember his parents taking him to Disney World when he was seven, and he was only in his thirties. She had so much history to sort through that his brain couldn't even grasp the extent of it.

His hand flexed on the gearshift, but he kept it where it was. He wanted to reach out and take her hand, but he wasn't sure it would be welcome. What he'd told Zoe was true. Despite everything that had gone on—and the fact that they'd flown halfway around the world together—they'd only known each other for two days.

Despite that, the longer he was around her, the more he was impressed with her. He'd started out fascinated with her simply because she was a stunningly beautiful Amazon warrior, a member of an immortal ancient race. When he'd first figured out what she was, he'd secretly been hoping he could finally prove to his peers that he'd been right all along, that the Amazons really had existed.

But things had changed. He still thought what she was and what she could do was amazing, but he was also starting to realize that she herself was just as incredible. She kept him slightly off balance, and he was always hoping she would reveal another fascinating tidbit about herself. She was obviously strong, both physically and mentally, but she was also caring. Why else would she run a women's shelter or worry about what Zoe was up to when she was out looking for Eris?

He trusted her and had no reason to doubt anything she'd told him so far. He had to admit, though, his brain did get squirmy when she started talking about making deals with deities. He'd never been particularly religious—most academics weren't—but she talked matter-of-factly about Greek gods as if their existence wasn't something to be questioned, just understood and accepted.

He had no idea what to do with that. He couldn't quite believe that some legendary god had granted Kalli a favor and hid her weapons for her. Or, even more improbable, that one had cloaked an entire city for her. It was true that no one had been able to find Themyscira, but it seemed more likely that it was lost to the sands of time than protected by a mythical deflector shield.

The more he was around her, however, the more he wanted to believe.

After several hours of driving around in circles, they headed back to the hotel in Myrina. Sam's stomach was growling, so they stopped at a restaurant and grabbed some takeout, bringing it back to eat in the suite. They ordered extra, not knowing whether Zoe would be back to join them.

When they got to the room, Zoe was already there. She turned to them as they closed the door. "Ooh, food. My fave." She bounced off the couch and joined them in the kitchen.

Sam grabbed plates and silverware out of the cupboards and took them to the small table off the end of the kitchen island. Kalli opened the bags and started pulling out cartons. They'd gone a bit overboard, ordering anything that sounded good. She opened containers of hummus and pita, tabbouleh, spanakopita, authentic Greek salad, and baklava, which looked so delicious he wanted to eat the entire tray of it himself.

"Any luck?" Zoe asked as she dug into the food, heaping large piles of everything onto her plate.

Kalli shook her head. "No, nothing. You?" Kalli finished opening the food cartons and sat down to make up her own plate.

Zoe nodded. "Some. I think I found the warehouse, but there wasn't much activity going on that I could see. I'm not sure why it showed up on both our radars as currently being used. I didn't see a soul."

Sam couldn't hide his disappointment. He hadn't thought it was going to be as easy as just showing up and having everything fall right into their laps, but neither of them finding anything was frustrating.

"Maybe tomorrow we shouldn't split up. If we all go together, the three of us might spot something that one person alone may have missed," he suggested.

Zoe nodded slowly. "Maybe you're right. So where do we go?"

"The warehouse," Kalli said. "As useful as it would be to find the weaponry, the real reason we're here is because of Eris. She needs to be our priority."

"Agreed," Sam said. "I'll try digging into my notes again. Maybe there's some reference I missed the first time around that will help us out."

"Sounds like a plan," Zoe said.

They went their separate ways after dinner, with Zoe heading to her room, Kalli to the kitchen to clean up, and Sam digging out his journals. There had to be something that could help them. He just needed to find it.

Chapter Eleven

KALLI WATCHED SAM AS he rifled through his enormous luggage in the living room. Her vantage point from the sink had her perfectly placed to discreetly ogle everything he did, and she wasn't going to complain. The term *Dr. Hunky* didn't do him justice.

Zoe had retreated to her bedroom, which left her and Sam alone in the main room of the suite. He was deeply engrossed in whatever it was he'd scribbled in the dozens of notebooks he'd brought from his apartment. She watched as his glasses slid down his nose slightly, then saw him absently push them back into place. Something tilted in the general region of her heart.

She had no idea what was so adorable about Sam, but she couldn't deny what she was feeling. He was so delightfully geeky, and he wasn't a complete slouch in the muscles department either. He was the perfect blend of smart and sexy. And, not to be discounted, he didn't seem to mind letting her take the lead.

The rhythmic nature of washing their dinner dishes allowed her brain to wander freely. She could almost see what it would be like to be with Sam long-term. Despite barely knowing each other, they seemed to have a way of fitting together that felt natural. He was obviously more into brainy stuff, and she was more into brawn, but they could each hold their own in the other's department.

She could picture them together back in DC, exploring the city or simply hanging out on her couch, watching TV. As much as she enjoyed her work, it would be nice to have someone to come home to, someone who could help her relax and unwind. Sam seemed like he needed someone in his life who would be willing to push him to have a bit more fun, to get out of his stuffy professor role and into some excitement.

She reached out to grab another dish but came up empty. She'd finished them all while daydreaming about a life that could never happen. She was an Amazon, and she was immortal. He was human and had a limited expiration date. Did she really want to get even more emotionally attached to someone she was bound to lose eventually anyway? Besides, she'd spent her extremely long life making sure she didn't have to change for a man, and she wasn't about to start now.

But Sam wasn't like that. She knew that in her heart. He would never ask her to change or give up who she was. If she was forced to admit it, he probably respected her and her power more than any man she'd ever met. Of course, he was also the only one who truly knew what she was, and he didn't seem to mind. In fact, he seemed to love it.

Maybe she should just sleep with him and get him out of her system. That was probably all this was, pent-up desire that had gone too long unfulfilled. There was no reason not to take matters into her own hands. They were both consenting adults, and she was pretty sure she wouldn't have to work hard to convince him.

She focused on his gorgeous profile. She opened her mouth to invite him into her bedroom, then chickened out. For some reason she couldn't bring herself to proposition him when she knew full well that she was just trying to scratch an itch. He deserved more than that.

Making up her mind, she left the kitchen and almost sprinted to her bedroom. She wanted to shut the door between them, but it felt rude. She hovered near her bedroom door, unsure what to do. Her strange behavior must have caught his attention because he glanced in her direction. Now she really had to say something.

"I think I'm going to turn in." It sounded weak even to her own ears. "Jet lag." It was a handy excuse.

Sam smiled in her direction, his brown eyes like molten chocolate. Obviously unaware of the inner battle she was fighting, he said, "Sleep well."

Kalli fled, closing the door. She could no longer see his face, but she was certain it was going to haunt her all night. What was wrong with her?

She woke up ridiculously early the next morning, which wasn't surprising since she'd gone to bed at seven p.m. She stayed in bed as long as possible, but she couldn't seem to hold herself still. It had been several days since she'd last gotten in a good workout, and she was tempted to head to the hotel gym. Burning off pent-up energy might help get her mind back under control.

She changed into capri workout pants and an exercise shirt, then tugged on her sneakers. She was also craving a shot of caffeine, so she was hoping there was coffee in the kitchen.

As quietly as possible, she opened her bedroom door, not wanting to wake Sam. She tried to tiptoe to the kitchen, then almost jumped out of her skin when she heard a voice from the direction of the table.

"Good morning," Sam said.

Kalli closed her eyes and took a deep breath, willing her pulse to settle back down. She glanced at the messy sofa bed, then to the kitchen table, where she found Sam sitting in nothing more than a pair of boxers.

Her mouth started to water, and it wasn't because he was drinking a steaming hot cup of coffee. Her eyes traced his body, starting at his neck and moving down his exquisitely muscled chest. She spotted rock-hard abs above his navy boxers and well-muscled thighs. Guilt rocked through her, and her eyes jumped back up to his face.

He'd noticed her perusal of his body, but his only reaction was one raised eyebrow. He made no move to put on clothes. Apparently he was totally comfortable in his state of undress. Kalli definitely wasn't a prude, but when she was doing her best to not think about jumping his bones, it wasn't helpful if he spent his time without his clothes on.

"Coffee's hot," he said, sipping from his own mug.

Mutely, she nodded. She walked to the counter and poured a cup. Maybe the caffeine would help her form a coherent thought. After a few sips, she found her voice. "I was going to go down to the gym."

He nodded. "Mind if I join you?"

Watching him get all sweaty in the gym was not what she had in mind, but she didn't have a polite way of saying no. "Sure," she said, trying not to let the strain show in her voice.

She finished her coffee slowly, hoping he would change his mind. He didn't. Instead, he threw on a pair of loose basketball shorts and a T-shirt and waited patiently for her to finish. Resigned to not being able to get him out of her head, she followed him down to the gym.

She normally preferred boxing or lifting weights, but today she felt like she could use something that would get her heart rate going and allow her to work out some of her jitters. She jumped on a treadmill and started pounding away, watching the distance slowly increase on the attached screen.

It was immediately obvious how Sam was so well muscled for having a mostly sedentary job. He walked over to the rack of weights and started doing curls, his biceps and pecs slowly bulging and releasing for her captive gaze. She stumbled slightly on the treadmill as she watched but caught herself before she did any serious damage to her ankle or the machine. Cursing herself for getting distracted, she wrenched her gaze away from where he'd switched to doing shoulder presses and back to her own machine.

For the rest of the workout, she studiously avoided looking in his direction. It wasn't a great time to get seriously injured, and she had no intention of making a giant fool of herself. After five miles, she slapped the stop button and climbed off, crossing to the opposite side of the room from where Sam was doing squats. She pulled out a yoga mat and did a few stretches, her muscles feeling the warm burn of being well used.

With silent agreement, they headed back up to the room, Kalli concentrating on not ogling the slightly sweaty sheen on his tanned arms. Kalli unlocked the door, then hung back in order to avoid accidentally brushing up against his warmth as he entered the room. She attempted to smile at Sam and got a half smile in return.

"For God's sake, you two, just get a room already. It'll be less awkward for us all." Zoe's voice startled Kalli out of her concentrated effort to ignore Sam. She blushed furiously, but her embarrassment quickly changed to annoyance. She needed to get ahold of herself. Kalli glanced quickly at Sam, who appeared less taken aback than she was, before fleeing to her room to shower.

When she came back into the room, she found Zoe and Sam huddled over the table, staring at a map of the island. "What are you up to?" she asked.

Zoe looked up. "Trying to figure out a plan of attack for today. I figure we can go drive around for a while during the day, looking for the weapons cache, then head out to the warehouse tonight, when things might be more active."

Kalli nodded, coming to stand between them. "Makes sense."

They ate a quick breakfast, then climbed back into the car, Sam once again behind the wheel. He tried a different route than he'd taken the previous day, driving in the opposite direction in hopes that it might look different enough to jog a memory. They saw plenty of picturesque villages and views of the sea, but nothing that looked promising to either Kalli or Zoe. Reluctantly, they returned to the city for dinner and killed a few hours in the hotel room before heading out again.

Kalli dressed in all black, just as she had for their warehouse infiltration. Zoe and Sam both followed suit. This time Kalli drove the short distance, then parked a few blocks from their final destination. They got out of the vehicle and left it behind, not wanting anyone to hear them approach.

Zoe led them to the building she'd scouted the day before. This building was considerably smaller than the one Eris had used in Washington, DC, and from what Kalli could see, there didn't appear to be any movement at all. She and Zoe did a quick perimeter sweep, leaving Sam safely behind a neighboring building, but nothing seemed out of place.

The building next to Eris's appeared to be abandoned and in terrible condition, which made it an ideal place for them to set up shop. Kalli once again pulled her cat burglar routine and had them inside the building in less than three minutes. They found a spot on the second floor that overlooked the main entrance to Eris's warehouse, and they made camp.

Hours passed and nothing happened. Not a single person went in or out of the building they were surveilling. They took turns playing lookout and rotated who got to sit on the only box in the entire building, an uncomfortable wooden thing only slightly warmer than the concrete floor.

Kalli was torn. Part of her wanted to stay and watch the building, hoping that they would see some activity. A second part of her brain wanted to break into the warehouse and be done with it. The last, and most logical, part of her brain told her to call it quits for the night.

Well after midnight, she stood, drawing the attention of her two companions. "We should head out for the night. There's nothing going on here."

Sam popped right up, stretching and shaking the feeling back into his limbs, clearly more than willing to take off. Zoe looked more reluctant. "Why don't you two go back to the hotel. There's no point in all of us sticking around here."

"You don't want to come?" Kalli asked, surprised. The chilly warehouse wasn't the most hospitable place in the world, and it wasn't like they'd seen anything that had hinted at Eris's presence.

Zoe shook her head. "I might tap some of my Interpol sources and see if maybe we got our data wrong about this place. You guys don't need to hang around for that."

Kalli looked at Sam, who shrugged. "You sure?" she asked one last time.

"Positive." Zoe pulled out her smartphone and began digging through it, as if to prove her point. "I'll find my own way back."

With more than a little reluctance, Kalli led Sam from the warehouse and back onto the streets. It was chillier than she'd anticipated, and she shivered as they walked back to the car.

"Are you cold?" Sam asked, immediately stripping off his coat and draping it around her shoulders. Kalli stared at him in shock, lightly grasping his coat's collar. She'd never had a man give her his coat. It was such a small thing, but at the same time, it felt huge. She'd always thought of chivalry as a sexist concept—it probably still was—but to her surprise, it felt nice to be on the receiving end. He hadn't taken even a moment to think about himself before he'd given his jacket to her.

"What?" he asked.

She smiled and kept walking toward the car. "Nothing. You're just a really good man."

He gave her a puzzled smile, his now-bare arm brushing up against hers as they walked. "You say that like it's a bad thing."

She shook her head. "No, not a bad thing at all. Just unusual, I suppose." In her experience, good men were rarer than Halley's comet.

"Unusual? You've been alive for four thousand years, and you're telling me that you haven't met other nice men?" he asked skeptically.

They reached the car and climbed in, Kalli behind the wheel. She started the car and cranked the heat but didn't put it into drive. She turned to face him. "Yes, that's exactly what I'm telling you." It seemed like it was time for confessions. "I'm a warrior. I'm accustomed to soldiers and men that wanted to conquer, both our land and our people. I've watched the systemic suppression of women for countless generations. I run a domestic abuse shelter precisely because I know what sort of monsters men can be."

"We're not all like that," he said quietly, pain in his eyes. His hand lifted like he was going to reach out and touch her face, but he let it drop before it got there.

She nodded. "I'm beginning to understand that."

"Kalli, I would never hurt you. Not if I could help it." His brown eyes stared directly into her own, not glancing away or blinking until she nodded slightly.

She felt a shift in the area around her heart. "I think I believe you." It was a lot for her to admit.

"I'll keep trying to convince you," he said.

Her eyes swept over his face. She hadn't wanted to get seriously involved with anyone, but she wasn't sure she could help it anymore. Sam was working his way into her heart and her life, and even though she wasn't entirely comfortable with it, she wasn't sure there was much she could do about it.

Well, there was one thing she could do about it.

Before she could change her mind, she leaned across the center console and captured his mouth in a warm kiss. Sam let out a surprised murmur, but his hand immediately went to the back of her neck, drawing her even closer.

She let herself sink into the warmth of the kiss, enjoying the firm press of his lips against hers. She could feel the heat radiating off his body, despite the distance that still separated them. She wanted to cling to him, but the awkwardness of the car prevented it.

His tongue ran along the seam of her lips, and she parted them, allowing him to dive inside and claim her mouth. Her tongue danced and played with his in a mating ritual as old as time. She reached up, running her hands through his thick blond hair, and pressed their mouths together more firmly.

His hands went to the coat he'd just draped over her shoulders and tugged it off. Unfortunately, she was wearing her own coat beneath that, and it was zipped all the way to the top. Sam muttered a curse under his breath as he tried to tug at the zipper.

Some sense of reality came back. "We shouldn't be doing this," Kalli said, pulling away.

Sam immediately retreated to his side of the car, a shutter coming down over his face. "You're probably right," he said, rubbing his hand over his lips. "It probably isn't smart to get involved right now."

Kalli wasn't sure how serious he was being but hoped not very. "I just meant we shouldn't be doing this in the car in the middle of the street."

Relief flooded his face. "Oh, thank God." He leaned over and dropped a quick kiss on her mouth. "I was really hoping you weren't changing your mind."

She smiled and put the car in gear. "You're not getting away that easily."

Chapter Twelve

THE DRIVE BACK TO the hotel seemed to take forever, even though logically Sam knew it was only a few minutes. As far as he was concerned, they couldn't get there fast enough.

The stakeout had been extremely boring and nothing at all like their first trip to Eris's warehouse. It made him glad he wasn't a cop for a living. He'd passed the time staring at Kalli and trying to remember anything he could from his notes about the location of Themyscira.

He wasn't sure exactly what it was about her that he found so irresistible. Zoe was equally muscular and attractive, yet he didn't turn into a fountain of testosterone when she was around.

Kalli's brown hair brushed her shoulders, drawing his eyes to her pulse, which he could see beating erratically in her neck. At least she was as worked up as he was.

She glanced at him, bringing his attention to her face. Her blue eyes were both intelligent and piercing. Her gaze went straight through him, making him feel like he was heating up from the inside out.

Her outfit was sexy as hell too. The way her black leather pants clung to her legs and rear end made him thankful to be a man. Many times during their hours-long stakeout he'd had fantasies of running his hands up those pants and cupping the warm flesh underneath. He shifted uncomfortably in his seat.

Nothing had made him happier than when she'd leaned across the car and kissed him. He'd been thinking about kissing her all night or, if he was honest with himself, since the moment he'd met her. He hadn't been disappointed. Her soft lips had felt divine under his own, and he'd had to remind himself to take things slowly. After hearing her confession about not knowing any nice men, her behavior made a lot more sense. He was damned if he was going to scare her off and prove her right. He needed to do this the right way; she was worth a little patience.

The car slammed to a stop. Gazing around him in a slight daze, he realized that they'd arrived back at the hotel. Grinning wolfishly, he glanced at her. "Race you upstairs," he said, shoving open his door and running toward the hotel.

Kalli made a slight squeak, but he heard the rapid cadence of her footsteps coming up behind him. They reached the door at the same time, her hand coming out to grab his elbow. "Slow down. We look ridiculous," she said.

Not wanting to embarrass her, he complied, his hand covering hers. He attempted to saunter nonchalantly across the lobby, but when they got to the elevator, he mashed the button furiously until the car arrived.

They made it to their floor and, with a bit of fumbling, managed to extract a room key and push open the door. The door clicked shut behind them, and Sam tugged Kalli to a stop. She looked at him questioningly.

"Are you sure about this?" he asked, searching her face for any uncertainty or discomfort.

He found none. Instead, she smiled and took his other hand. "Never been more sure of anything." With that, she pulled him closer, pressing seductively against him. She was almost as tall as he was, and the alignment of their bodies felt just about perfect, her core pressing intimately against his own.

He reached up and slid his hand under her hair and around the back of her neck, drawing her lips to his for a heated kiss. Her hands plunged into his hair, and she pressed herself firmly against him. He sank deeply into the kiss, his tongue tasting her silky lips.

He explored the length of her body and traced her curves. He dropped his hands to her legs, acting on his earlier fantasy of running them up the leather pants to cup her butt.

Kalli took it as an invitation and wrapped her legs around his waist, boosting herself up so she was twined around him. She used her own strength to cling to him, torso to torso, mouth to mouth.

He felt like he was drowning in her. He wanted to go on kissing her forever but also couldn't wait for more. He pulled away from her kiss and glanced around, trying to navigate toward her bedroom. She took the opportunity to prey on his neck, licking it up and down, giving him love bites, then soothing them away.

With some difficulty he managed to open the door to her room without dropping her. He made it to the bed before tipping them both onto it, using his weight to pin her in place.

He swooped down, claiming her mouth once more, pushing his tongue inside and making her his. He leaned back far enough to get his hands between them and remove her coat, tossing it to the floor without a second thought. He yanked up the hem of her shirt and tugged until he had it over her head. Her beautiful body was revealed, and he drank in the sight of her lean torso and her breasts, lovingly hugged by black lace. His hands traced their way up her skin, skimming her rib cage before cupping her lace-covered breasts.

The sensation drove him wild. He wanted skin.

He needed skin.

With a low growl, he dropped his hands to the button on her leather pants, then yanked down the zipper. He tried to tug the pants off, but his body was trapping them in place. He quickly rolled off her and stood next to the bed, watching her shimmy out of the pants, which clung to her like a second skin.

With a saucy grin she rose to her knees and dropped the pants over the edge of the bed. Kneeling there, wearing nothing more than black lace panties and a bra, she was the sexiest sight he'd ever seen. She crawled toward him on the bed, crooking a finger to make him come closer.

"Now it's your turn," she said as she grabbed his black T-shirt and tugged it over his head. As soon as it was gone, her mouth latched on to his neck, shifting slightly as she kissed and licked her way down his torso. Her hands skimmed his stomach, the muscles quivering beneath her touch.

His whole body clenched as her fingers found his fly. She inched the zipper down so slowly he was worried he might embarrass himself. Finally, after several torturous moments, she pushed, dropping his black jeans and boxers to the ground in one shove.

His breath hissed out as her warm hands found his shaft, which immediately responded to her touch. His eyes drifted closed as he let his head fall back, enjoying her gentle stroking. She cupped his balls, and his eyes shot open again, his head dropping to ravage her mouth with his own.

He edged his way onto the bed, forcing her to back up to make room for him. "My turn." He caressed her torso, reaching around her back until he could release the clasp of her bra. He tugged it off and flung it across the room. He pushed gently until she fell back to the mattress. He grabbed her panties and sent them flying too.

He let himself sink slowly on top of her, relishing the feeling as every inch of his harder body came in contact with her softer one. They fit together so perfectly he never wanted to let her go.

He lifted himself slightly to the side and let his hands roam over her silky skin, cupping her breast and flicking her nipple back and forth with his thumb. She gasped and he smiled. She was an incredibly powerful woman, and knowing he could make her come apart was heady stuff.

Almost of its own accord, his hand slid down her torso, taking the time to skim her ribs and the softness of her belly before locating the curls beneath. His finger plunged into her folds, the moist heat enveloping him. He found her clit and began to rub gently, not wanting to rush, just trying to awaken her, to give her some heat and pleasure.

She groaned, "Sam."

He didn't stop what he was doing. "What?"

Her eyes were halfway closed, and her hand came up to cup his jaw. "The way you're making me feel." Her hips bucked slightly and pushed into his hand.

He smiled and rubbed a bit harder, a bit faster. "You like that?"

She didn't speak, simply nodded. Her hand worked its way out from where he'd had it pinned and grabbed his cock. She ran her fingers over it lightly, teasing it. She suddenly wrapped her whole hand around him and pumped, making him groan.

As much as he'd wanted to tease her and seduce her, he hadn't counted on her dishing it right back. The movements of her hand as she pumped and twisted were driving him to the edge.

"Enough," he said, his voice hoarse and rough. He rolled on top of her, pushing her into the plush, white comforter. Without any warning, he plunged himself inside her, her sheath closing around him in an iron grip. He groaned and dropped his forehead to meet hers. "Kalli," he whispered.

She tried to wiggle underneath him, but he reached down and placed his hands on her hips, stopping her. "No, not yet." He crossed the last inch and placed his mouth gently on hers, taking it in a deep and drugging kiss.

When his anticipation receded just enough that he knew he wasn't going to embarrass himself, he finally opened his eyes, meeting her intoxicating blue gaze. He pulled out and drove home, holding her attention and loving the bliss he saw on her face.

Her hands ran through his hair, massaging his scalp. Her gorgeously toned legs wrapped around his waist, her ankles locking near his lower back. The move drove her pelvis upward, allowing him even deeper access into her body.

It sent him over the edge. His pace went wild as he pounded into her. He reached out with one hand, grabbing her breast and flicking the nipple back and forth. His hand slid lower, squeezing between their slapping bodies to flick at her center. Her eyes squeezed shut as she came, her head flung back, her brown hair spilling across the bed.

Watching her come undid him and sent him crashing over the edge after her. With a final pant, he collapsed on top of her, crushing her into the mattress.

Slowly, reluctantly, she unwound her legs from around his body, dropping them to the bed. Her hand traced lazy circles around his back. "I'll move. Just give me a second," he said, somewhere in the neighborhood of her ear.

He could practically hear the smile in her voice. "Don't rush on my account."

With far more effort than it should have taken, Sam heaved himself sideways. He felt the loss immediately, both of her heat and her closeness. Before he could move far, she grabbed his waist, pulling him against her side. Her head tipped sideways, coming to rest on his shoulder, the crown of her hair tickling his nose.

At a loss for words, Sam contented himself with holding her close, smelling the vaguely fruity scent of her hair, and feeling the softness of her skin where his hand was cupping her arm. "Well, that was…"

"Amazing." She sighed and snuggled closer.

He smiled contentedly. He should probably get up, at least to close the door to her bedroom, but he couldn't make himself move. Giving up, he snuggled closer to his Amazon queen.

Sam stifled a yawn. He glanced at the clock: almost three in the morning. Kalli was probably as exhausted as he was, and they had another long day coming. They were in Greece for a reason, and sadly it wasn't for vacation.

Unfortunately, they were lying on top of the fluffy white comforter rather than underneath. Kalli seemed perfectly content in her nakedness, but the fact that her nipples were still as hard as eraser tips meant she was probably cold.

Sam started to roll over, hoping to pull down the blankets and crawl underneath.

"Where do you think you're going?" Kalli said, rising up onto one elbow to look down at him.

"I was just going to…" The fire in her eyes had him trailing off once more.

"Uh-uh. You're not going anywhere yet. I haven't finished with you." She pushed herself up to her hands and knees, then shoved his shoulders back against the mattress. She flung her leg over his hips and straddled him, her core coming to rest intimately against his.

Sam never would have thought he'd be ready to go again so quickly, but his body was already going hard beneath her damp heat. She shimmied her hips in an exotic lap dance, reaching up to cup her own breasts in the process. She seductively licked her lips, which made him think about other places she could be using that mouth.

He shifted his hips and found himself perfectly positioned to slip inside her. With one smooth upward thrust, he buried himself, causing Kalli to arch her back in response.

He tried to move again, but she pinned him in place. "My turn."

Her hips stayed exactly where they were, not moving or rotating, but her hands were all over him. They started at his shoulders, slipped over his chest, and flicked his nipples the same way he'd flicked hers. They made their way down to his rock-hard stomach and came to a stop, just barely touching the place where he was inside of her.

He bucked his hips again, but she used her superior strength to stop him. Instead, she reached down and cupped his balls, toying with them gently, rubbing them and rolling them in her hand.

Impossibly, he got even harder. Just when he was ready to start begging, she finally moved. She slid her hips slowly up and down, up and down. She was driving him wild with her slow but constant movement.

His hands went to her hips, trying to encourage her to go faster, but she changed it up on him again. Her hips started circling slowly, making figure-eight motions that left him gasping for air. It was the most pleasurable torture he'd ever experienced.

He tried to let her set the pace, but his hips began thrusting almost involuntarily. For once she didn't stop him, setting up a driving rhythm that made her entire body tense and her breasts jiggle up and down.

He couldn't tear his eyes away.

She leaned forward, her breasts bobbing and swaying in front of his face. He tried to rear up and grab one of them with his mouth, but her relentless motion had them moving so much he couldn't latch on.

With almost no warning, his heels dug into the bed, and his back arched as he came harder than he'd ever come before, his body pouring itself into hers for what felt like ages. He reached between them and used one finger to find her clit, flicking it. It didn't take much. Within seconds she was right there with him, her whole body stiffening before she collapsed on top of him.

Sam could have lain there forever, not moving an inch, But the sound of the door to the suite opening and closing sent panic alarms through his brain. Well aware that the bedroom door wasn't quite closed, he grabbed the comforter, yanking hard so that he could fling it over the two of them as they lay, still connected, on the far side of the bed.

His eyes went wide, tension creeping into his throat. It wasn't that he was embarrassed about sleeping with Kalli, but he didn't particularly like broadcasting it quite so blatantly. He glanced at Kalli's face and was surprised by her catlike smile. She didn't seem bothered at all by the fact that they were about to get caught in the act.

"Finally," Zoe's overly dramatic voice sounded from just outside the door before it was pulled shut, closing the two of them in the warm silence left behind as Zoe retreated.

"Well, that didn't go quite as planned," he said, rolling his head back against the pillows, embarrassment heating his cheeks.

Kalli just smiled, licking her lips. "Oh, no? Should we try again?"

He stared at her, mouth hanging open in shock. "That's not what I meant."

She sat up, moving her hips so that he slid out of her body. She patted his cheek and winked. "I know. I was just teasing you."

She shifted slightly so that she was lying next to him, her arm draped over his waist, her head snuggled on his shoulder.

He felt awkward. Not just because Zoe had clearly seen exactly what they were up to, but because he wasn't sure how to act with Kalli. He gave in to the temptation to let his arm circle her body and hold her close to him but wondered if that was what she really wanted. She'd always been so standoffish that he couldn't help wondering if she would have preferred if he left and went back to his bed in the living room.

"Don't you dare," she said.

"What?" He hadn't said anything out loud, had he?

She lifted her head, propping her chin on his chest and looking him in the eye. "Don't run away, even if it's only to the living room."

How had she known what he was thinking?

"I know I've been reluctant to get involved with you, but don't take that the wrong way. It had nothing to do with you. You're an amazing, sexy man."

He ran his hand absently down her hair, stopping on the silky skin of her naked back. "Then what was it?"

She sighed, her warm breath passing over his neck. "You were right back in my kitchen in DC. I don't like getting involved with people long-term. It's too painful, seeing them die or watching them leave me. When I'm with a man, I make sure it's casual."

He didn't like the sound of that. There was nothing casual about his feelings for Kalli, even though deep down he knew she was probably right. They could never be together long-term. It wouldn't work. He would always continue to age, and she wouldn't. What eternally sexy woman would want to be with a man who would eventually wrinkle and wither right before her eyes?

"I see," he said, though he still didn't. He hated the thought of missing out on whatever time they had together, however, so he didn't want to ruin the moment.

Kalli lifted her head even farther, her searing blue eyes pinning his. "You see what?" she asked.

He glanced away from her face, focusing on her naked shoulder instead. "I see why you don't want to get involved. It makes sense." He rolled away from her and stood, making his way around to the other side of the bed, where his pants were heaped on the beige carpet.

Before he could reach down and grab them, she rolled herself across the bed and stopped him, her movements nothing but a blur. At times he forgot that she was a preternatural being. Glancing down at the hand she was currently using to prevent him from moving was a stark reminder.

"I think you may have misunderstood me. I was trying to say that I originally didn't want to get involved with you because I know where it leads. It leads to years of pleasure followed by centuries of pain."

Sam didn't move, pinned in place by the force of her stare and her grip on his wrist. He skimmed her face, trying to read her expression. "I get it. That's why I'm trying to let you go. I would never want to cause you centuries of pain. Not when I can prevent that."

She shook her head, relaxing her iron grip. "That's exactly my point. It's far too late for that. I'm already involved." She leaned in and kissed him, her lips soft and encouraging. All plans of retreat fled his mind, and he tugged her against him. He would take whatever she was willing to give him and be grateful. When it was time for her to move on, he would have to accept that.

"Now get back over here." She cocked her head toward the bed, and he followed her gladly.

Chapter Thirteen

KALLI WOKE UP FEELING warm and comforted. She couldn't remember the last time she'd actually let a man spend the night with her. She'd gotten more and more careful about it over the years.

Without opening her eyes, she arched her back slightly, pressing into the warmth of the strong male chest behind her. Her arm was nestled next to Sam's, and she moved so she could press his arm closer into her stomach, hugging him to her. Eventually there would be pain, but not now.

Her slight movements must have jostled him awake, because his voice was rough in her ear as he said, "Good morning, beautiful."

She smiled, still not opening her eyes. She could stay like this for ages and not get tired of it. Her body felt gently used in a way that no workout would ever come close to matching. "Hey there, yourself," she responded.

"You know what I think we should do today?" he asked, his head still buried in her hair.

Lots of ideas of ways they could spend the day went shooting through her head. There was a hot tub with jets in the bathroom, for instance, or the chair near the window that they hadn't tested out yet. "What's that?" she purred.

"Climb a mountain."

Kalli's eyes flew open. That was not on her list of possibilities for the day. "Oh?" she asked, trying not to sound too disappointed.

"Yeah. When I was going through my notes yesterday, I realized that there may be a reason why you and Zoe haven't been able to figure out where you stashed your weapons all those years ago."

His fingers began tracing small patterns on her stomach, and she did her best to ignore the sensation so she could focus on what he was saying. Kalli rolled onto her back, forcing Sam to scoot away a few inches so she could fit. Of course he was talking about the weapons and their mission. It wasn't like they were in some hotel on an exotic Greek island just for fun. They were there for work. "Why do you think that is?" she prompted him, forcing ideas of spending all day naked in bed to the back of her mind.

"Well, back when the Amazons were around, during the Greek empire, this whole area was a hotbed of volcanic activity. Now, not so much. However, Lemnos is supposed to be sacred to the god Hephaestus, right? What better place for Hephaestus to make a forge than in a volcano?"

She nodded. "I'm following."

A smile flew across his face as he was talking, the corners of his eyes wrinkling. "But if the volcanoes no longer exist . . ."

"They would just be mountains," she finished his thought. She sat up, holding the sheet to her chest. Her mind was whirling. Everything he was saying made sense. In fact, now that he'd brought it up, she vaguely recalled the volcanoes he was talking about. If they'd erupted at some point, they would look totally different than they had when she'd been there thousands of years ago.

Of course, that brought up a totally different problem. If the weapons had been buried in a volcano that erupted centuries ago, would they even still be there? Volcanoes were one of the most destructive forces in nature, so it was extremely likely that it could have obliterated their cache. There was only one way to find out.

"You are brilliant," she said, leaning back to plant a huge kiss on his lips. "Who knew an academic could be so sexy?" She waggled her eyebrows at him, making him smile.

He tried to pull her down on top of him, but she resisted. Even though she'd just been thinking about spending all day in bed with him, now that he'd told her his theory, she couldn't let it go. Of course they would have buried their weapons trove at the base of a volcano that was the forge of Hephaestus. That was where his power would have been the strongest, so it would have been easiest for him to guard them there.

She shook her head, trying to clear it. You'd think she would have remembered an important detail like the volcano, but unfortunately her immortality didn't come with a photographic memory. Well, there was nothing to be done about it now. They had an idea of where to search, and she was eager to get started.

She rolled over, gracefully flipped off the bed, and landed on her feet. She moved so rapidly that Sam was still looking where she used to be, and it took him a second to catch up. He looked startled, though he masked it quickly.

Damn. She was usually better about hiding what she was. Her preternatural strength and grace didn't usually pass for human, and she had to tone it down slightly when she was around people who didn't know what she was capable of. Which was basically everyone. She'd gotten so comfortable around Sam that she'd forgotten to rein it in.

"Made you look?" she tried to joke. It was definitely her experience that men didn't like to be around women who upstaged them or were more capable than they were physically. She bit her tongue and stared at him.

He smiled, scooting toward the edge of the bed and sitting up. He met her gaze head-on. "Never feel like you have to hide who you are around me. Remember, I knew exactly who and what you were before I got you naked. I can handle it."

Warmth spread around her insides as a knot of tension loosened in her stomach. Tentatively, she smiled back. She wasn't used to being this uncertain around a man, and it was unsettling. In past relationships with men, however long they'd lasted, she'd always made sure to keep the upper hand. She was an Amazon and a former queen at that. Being in charge was second nature. This new thing she had going with Sam was different, and she had to feel her way slowly.

Every other man she'd been involved with had taken issue with her strength and her need for control. That was one of the main reasons her interactions with the opposite sex had always been short. Most men had thought she would change her ways once she was with them, to tone herself down and be more womanly, whatever they thought that meant. They were always disappointed when it didn't happen. More often than not, things never went further than one night.

Sam was totally different. As she stared into his warm brown eyes, taking in his cheeky grin, she could almost believe him when he said he didn't want her to hide who she was.

Unfortunately, he hadn't seen the real her yet, so as far as she was concerned, the jury was still out. That thought sobered her, and her smile faded.

"We should get dressed and get a move on, go check out this volcano of yours," she said. His face crinkled in confusion, and he opened his mouth to speak, but he obviously thought better of it. Good. It was probably better that way.

"Yes, ma'am," he said, obviously trying to lighten the suddenly somber mood.

He sauntered across the carpet and headed into her attached bathroom. He didn't quite shut the door behind him. She stepped just a bit to the right and could clearly see his gorgeous body in the mirror as he grabbed a towel off the rack and turned on the shower.

He stepped inside, pulling the door shut behind him, blocking her view.

With a sigh, she turned around and perched on the edge of the bed, her back to the bathroom. What was she doing? She knew better than to get involved with people. It was hard enough to have friends and colleagues, but having lovers was something else entirely. Sam was sneaking his way into her heart in a way she wasn't prepared for and didn't entirely welcome. If she opened herself up to him, it would mean more pain down the road.

It was probably already too late. She didn't want to admit it to herself, but there wasn't much she could do about her feelings for Sam. It seemed unbelievable that they'd only just met. She felt so close to him, closer than she'd been to another person in a long time. Maybe even since she'd been forced out of Themyscira.

Since it appeared her heart was already involved, she might as well make the best of it. With a small nod, she stood and followed in his footsteps, nudging the bathroom door open.

"Got room for one more?" she asked.

Sam spun around and faced her through the foggy shower door. A slow smile spread across his lips, and he bit his bottom lip. "Only if it's you."

Her heart racing, she joined him in the shower and made it worth his while.

Twenty minutes later, they finally made their way out of the bedroom, fully clothed, and headed to the kitchenette to scrounge up some breakfast. She'd just opened the door to the refrigerator when someone spoke behind her, startling her. "Finally coming up for air?" Zoe asked from the small table in the dining area.

Kalli's eyes drifted closed as she took a deep breath, trying to slow her heart rate. She must have walked right by Zoe on her way to the kitchen and hadn't noticed her. Her senses must be muddled. Finally, she opened her eyes and saw her friend's knowing smirk. "Good morning, Zoe," she said, not answering the other woman's question.

Sam didn't even hesitate. "Even Amazons must need food occasionally," he said, winking in Kalli's direction.

Kalli had to fight down a blush. She wasn't normally a shy person, so her sudden awkwardness felt foreign. Ignoring them both, she reached in the fridge and got out some orange juice, then grabbed a glass from the cupboard. Sam found a blueberry muffin that looked tasty enough that she thought about stealing it.

"So what's on the agenda for today, more sexual Olympics? We are in Greece, after all." Zoe looked perfectly innocent, sipping away at her mostly empty cup of coffee.

Kalli rolled her eyes. "Nope, we actually have a plan." She filled her in about Sam's theory regarding the mountain.

Zoe let out a low whistle. "Makes a lot of sense. It would also explain why we weren't seeing anything we recognized."

Kalli nodded. "Yep. My thoughts exactly."

"What are we waiting for?" Zoe said, pushing to her feet. "Let's do this."

They climbed into the car and set off. Sam was driving, with Kalli and Zoe keeping watch. They figured that the best place to start was a mountain previously called Mosychlos, which used to be a volcano. It took them about forty-five minutes to drive there, but as soon as they arrived, Kalli sat up a bit straighter in her seat.

"I'll be damned," she said, her heart thudding.

"Bingo," Zoe agreed, leaning forward from the back seat until she was between Kalli and Sam.

Sam pulled into an available parking space, and they decided to get out and walk. The mountain was now a tourist spot, so there were people all over the place. Kalli's heart sank at the sight. Even if this was the spot where they'd buried their weapons all those centuries ago, it didn't seem possible that they'd remained undiscovered. The sheer volume of visitor traffic made it all the more unlikely they would find what they were looking for.

With a sigh, Kalli followed the others out of the car. Sam still seemed excited about the idea that this could be it, and Zoe was right there with him. Clearly they hadn't come to the same conclusion she had.

They set off around the base of the mountain, hoping to spot something that would look familiar. Kalli could just barely remember marking the burial site, but it seemed far-fetched that a marker would still be here after all this time.

It took them about an hour to hike around the base of the mountain. It wasn't until they were almost back to the parking lot that Zoe finally spoke.

"Wait," she said, stopping in her tracks.

Kalli paused, though she wasn't sure what Zoe was expecting to find. The weapons were clearly gone. "What?" she asked, trying to keep her exasperation to a minimum.

"It was here," Zoe continued, looking at the mountain next to her.

Kalli rolled her eyes, hoping Zoe couldn't see her. She turned to face the big pile of dirt that they'd been walking around, expecting to see the same nothing she'd been seeing all day. Instead, something caught her eye, something that didn't belong.

Sam was the first one to move. He approached the side of the hill and rubbed his finger over the rock they'd been staring at. Kalli could just see a faint etching in the stone, a bow crossed with an arrow, a spear, and a sword. The symbol of the Amazons.

"It's not possible," Kalli said. How could this have been here for thousands of years and yet no one had noticed it? Someone should have found it before now.

"It may be impossible, but here it is," Sam said with a smile. He began brushing away the loose gravel and dirt near the stone. Zoe jumped in eagerly, clearing debris as fast as her hands could manage.

Kalli wasn't sure why she wasn't more excited. This was what they were here for. This was why they'd come. It had been her idea to find the weapons cache, if it still existed, so why was she suddenly doubting that this was a good idea?

She scanned the area, but she could no longer see any tourists wandering around. It was as if they'd disappeared or as if they were suddenly hidden from sight. Which didn't make any sense. When they'd buried the weapons all those years ago, she'd prayed to Hephaestus to protect them, but she hadn't asked for any sort of shield for them, not in the same way she'd asked for Themyscira to be cloaked.

The emptiness was eerie. Something was wrong, but Kalli couldn't put her finger on what. She wanted to tell the others but didn't know what she should even say.

Shaking off the feeling, she joined Zoe and Sam at the side of the mountain. They were both scrabbling frantically at the dirt, their excitement obvious. Kalli had another idea. She reached out and brushed her hand slowly across the stone with the Amazon symbol.

At first nothing happened. Then a slow rumble seemed to come from the depths of the mountain. Kalli jumped back, suddenly terrified that she'd done something wrong. It occurred to her that they were digging into a dormant volcano. Logically, she knew that nothing she'd done could have woken up a volcano, but the shaking ground and falling dirt seemed to want to make a liar out of her.

With a quick shout, Sam jumped away just as a large stone came tumbling down the hill and landed exactly where he'd been standing. Kalli grabbed Zoe by the shirt collar, yanking her away from the falling debris.

"What did you do?" Zoe asked, panting.

Kalli shrugged, not entirely sure. "All I did was touch the stone."

"Of course," Sam said. "That's probably why this is still undisturbed. You asked for the protection. It makes sense that you'd have to be the one that breaks it."

With a loud boom, a large pile of dirt collapsed, revealing the opening to a cave. The rumbling stopped and the dust began to settle. This had to be it.

Kalli forgot all about her feeling of unease. This was what they had come for. This was theirs, the Amazons'. With a wicked grin, which was returned by Zoe, Kalli shoved her way inside the cave.

There was no light, so she pulled out her newly replaced cell phone and turned on the flashlight feature. The opening of the cave led to a short tunnel, but she couldn't see where it ended. Ten feet in, the tunnel took a hard right, ending in a wide cave.

There was no doubt they were in the right place. She lifted her arm, allowing the light from her phone to land on the contents of the room.

"I'll be damned," Sam said reverently.

Laid out in front of them was a neat row of beautifully crafted armor. The tiny amount of light coming from her phone reflected off shiny shields, spear tips, and sharpened swords.

"Bingo," Zoe said, coming up behind them.

There had been only eight of them captured by the Greeks, but Amazons rarely went anywhere without weapons and armor. There was so much it might not even fit in the car.

Sam pulled out his own phone and turned on the light. He took several tentative steps forward, his hand stretched toward the nearest shield, his face a mask of rapturous bliss. The bronze embossing depicted an Amazon in battle, charging down an opposing warrior while on horseback. The Amazon was wielding a spear, and her opponent was cowering in terror.

Kalli watched as he ran his fingers reverently over the metal. Against all scientific fact, the weapons were perfectly intact, not tarnished or damaged in the least. He bent down to examine a sword, thankfully not attempting to touch the blade.

"This is sharp, almost razor sharp," Sam said, glancing in her direction. "This shouldn't be possible. You saw the one we found at the museum. It was almost unrecognizable."

"Hephaestus obviously listened to our prayers," Zoe said, walking over to pick up a sword. There was an immediate change in her demeanor. Zoe was always intimidating, but as soon as she picked up that Amazon weapon, something shifted. It was almost like a cloak of power settled around her shoulders. "This feels good."

Kalli slowly walked down the row, her heart breaking just a bit. The weapons and shields were perfectly preserved, but she knew what she wasn't going to find among them. The queen of the Amazons was presented with a new set of armor when she rose to the throne. Her royal armor should have been there among all the rest. It wasn't.

When Nyx had staged the coup, she'd made sure to tell Kalli exactly how unworthy she was to be the queen of the Amazons. Nyx had taken her throne, but she'd also taken her crown and armor. A final humiliation for the deposed queen.

At the far end of the row was a plain shield with no engraving. This was what Nyx had given the Greeks in place of her royal armor. This was what she had carried after they'd overthrown the soldiers and reclaimed their weapons. Kalli slowly reached out and picked it up. It felt strange, after living for centuries in the modern world, to once again be hoisting a shield on her forearm. As soon as it settled into place, however, a sense of rightness washed over her.

Kalli reached for the sword resting directly behind her shield. It fit her hand like it was made for her, despite the fact that it wasn't her original sword. It didn't matter. Swords were second nature to her. She gave the sword a quick twirl, sending the blade singing through the air so fast that Sam glanced up to see what she was doing.

"Feels good, doesn't it?" Zoe said as she slung a bow and a quiver of arrows over her shoulder.

Kalli didn't have the words to answer her. She'd been avoiding thinking of herself as an Amazon for so long that it was hard to make the mental switch back. She'd been deposed. She was holding generic armor and weapons from the armory. She didn't feel very heroic, but Sam and Zoe were looking at her expectantly. She needed to do this for them.

"Absolutely," she responded.

"So how do we go about lugging all of this out of here?" Sam asked.

"I don't think you'll have to worry about that."

Kalli spun around, pointing her sword at the new voice. Eris, standing in a pool of lantern light, was blocking the entrance to the cave, and she wasn't alone. Four big men stood behind her, muscles bulging out of the sleeves of their shirts. Their cropped haircuts and tactical gear screamed ex-military.

"Eris," Zoe said as she rolled her shoulders and spread her feet into a fighting stance.

Eris smiled in her direction, but it didn't reach her eyes. "Zoe. I'd say I've missed you, but we both know that isn't true."

"Eris, what are you playing at?" Kalli tried to reason with her. "What do you hope to gain by going back to Themyscira? What scheme do you have, and how does it involve our people?"

Eris turned her sneer in Kalli's direction. "Our people? We were betrayed. You were forcibly removed from power. How on earth can you still think of them as 'our people'?" Eris spun to look at Zoe, who cocked her eyebrow in response. "You, I might expect this from. You were truly caught in the cross fire. It was only your friendship with our queen here"—she practically snarled the honorific—"that led to your banishment."

"And what led to yours?" Kalli asked, taking a slight step forward and purposefully drawing Eris's gaze. Maybe if she could keep Eris talking, she would think of a way to get them out of this alive. Zoe was highly trained and well armed, but Sam was a professor. Because of her, he was about to get caught in the middle of a fight.

Again.

Eris lunged in her direction but pulled up before she got too close. "I wasn't banished. It was a mistake."

Kalli lowered the tip of her sword toward the ground. "A mistake? Is that what you've been telling yourself? That you were cast out by accident? Nyx doesn't make mistakes, or don't you remember that?"

Eris shook her head and took a half step back. She glanced rapidly from Zoe to Sam before landing back on Kalli. "My exile was a mistake. I was caught in the wrong place at the wrong time."

"Whatever you have to tell yourself in order to sleep at night," Zoe said, her hands clenched around her sword.

Eris sneered. "It doesn't matter anyway. That mistake is about to be corrected, once and for all."

Kalli glanced in Sam's direction, hoping he was smart enough to stay out of this. She wanted to scream and throw herself in front of him to protect him from what was about to happen. Everyone else in this room was a trained fighter. Sam wasn't. He used his brains for a living, not his brawn. She would never be able to live with herself if anything happened to him while she was supposed to be looking out for him. She squeezed the handle of the sword to stop her fingers from trembling.

She couldn't fail, not at this.

"So, what, you take the weapons and go back and storm Themyscira? You prove once and for all that you belong with them? Or do you plan to stage another coup, kicking Nyx to the curb?" Kalli kept the attention on herself as she stalked slightly closer.

Eris threw her head back and laughed. "That's what you think this is all about?" She had to hold her sides because she was laughing so hard. "You think I want a handful of rusty metal trinkets so I can go rejoin the ranks of those who betrayed me?"

Kalli's heart dropped. That was exactly what she'd thought, what they'd all thought. They'd come chasing across the globe to stop Eris from returning to the side of her dark queen. If that wasn't her plan, Kalli didn't know what was. She carefully schooled her features into a blank mask.

"If you aren't here for the weapons, why are you following us at all?" Zoe demanded.

Eris chuckled again. "For him, obviously." She pointed in Sam's direction. Before Kalli could blink, Eris had flung herself across the cave and grabbed Sam by the arms. He tried to struggle, but Eris was too fast for him. She wrenched his left wrist behind him and yanked it up toward the center of his back. She wrapped her other arm around his shoulders and started retreating toward the exit. Sam tried to kick backward at her legs, but she yanked his arm even harder.

Sam cringed in pain, his mouth opening on a silent shout.

"What are you waiting for?" Eris screamed, gesturing to her bodyguards.

The four goons leaped into action. They were big and strong, but they weren't Amazons. One of them charged Kalli, a smirk spreading across his face. She grabbed his wrist and tugged, using his momentum against him and sending him shooting past her into the stone wall behind her. The second man lunged at her, and she attempted to crack him over the head with the hilt of her sword, but his beefy arm got in the way knocking the sword out of her hand. She retaliated by smashing the heels of her hands into his sternum and forcing him into the wall with his buddy.

She heard Zoe engage the other two, but Kalli's eyes frantically sought Sam's. Eris was dragging him down the tunnel and out into the daylight. He was doing his best to resist, but with the grip she had on him, his struggles were futile.

"Sam!" she shouted, taking a half step toward the cave entrance.

"Not today, lady." One of the soldiers had recovered from his headfirst encounter with the wall. He lashed out and grabbed her wrist, keeping her from following Eris and Sam.

Kalli used his grip on her arm to bend his wrist backward as she spun around him. She reached down to grab her sword off the floor, but before she could the second man managed to grab her from behind. His arms clamped around her waist and pinned her arms to her side.

Desperate to escape, Kalli lifted both knees to her chest, forcing the man holding her to support her full body weight. She used her slight advantage to slam both her feet into her attacker's knees, hearing the satisfying crunch of broken bones.

He dropped like a stone. Unfortunately, he didn't release her, so she fell with him, his weight pinning her to the ground. The air left her lungs in a giant whoosh.

Light-headed, she tried to look around. Zoe was across the room, moving like lightning, spinning and twirling, a sword in each hand. The men she was fighting were trying to get closer to her, attempting to fend off her swings with shields, but she was holding her own. They were the ones bleeding, not her.

A steel band wrapping tighter around Kalli's ribs brought her attention back to the man behind her. He was down but not out. He wasn't going to be walking anywhere anytime soon, but unfortunately his arms still worked.

Feeling only slightly guilty, she slammed her fists into his broken knees. He screamed in agony, finally letting her go. She rolled away just as her first attacker came back for more. He aimed a vicious kick at her head, but thankfully her enhanced reflexes had her ducking out of the way just in time.

Her fist came up, slamming into his groin. The man collapsed to his knees, bringing his face closer to where she was crouched. She slammed her hand like a knife into his windpipe, crushing it. He keeled over, gasping hoarsely and clutching his throat as he struggled to breathe.

The clanging of metal on metal brought her attention back across the room to Zoe. Kalli grabbed her own sword and shield, preparing to help her friend.

A blur of motion flew across the room, grabbing one of the two men attacking Zoe and slamming him backward into the ground. The newcomer slammed a hand into the downed man's chest, cracking several of his ribs and making him go limp.

Once her second attacker was down, Zoe used one of her swords to knock the shield out of the remaining soldier's hands, sending it clanging across the dirt floor. She brought up her two blades so they were making an X around his neck, backing him none too gently into the wall and pinning him there.

The sudden stillness was eerie. Kalli glanced around, verifying that all their attackers were incapacitated. They were. That left only her, Zoe, and . . .

"Selene?" Zoe said incredulously as she glanced at the new arrival.

The third Amazon rose slowly to her feet with a smile, tucking her mass of light-red curls back over her shoulder. "In the flesh."

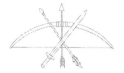

Chapter Fourteen

K ALLI DIDN'T HAVE TIME to be amazed at finding Selene alive after all this time. Her brain could make room for only one thought.

"Sam!" Kalli screamed, running from the cave and back into the blinding light. She heard footsteps behind her but didn't turn to see who had followed. She needed to get to Sam.

She glanced around frantically, hoping to see some sign of him or the direction Eris might have taken him. There was nothing, the parking lot empty except for their rental car. The fight had lasted only a few minutes, but it was obviously long enough for Eris to kidnap Sam.

"Sam," she said again, tears threatening to choke her.

"Who's Sam?" Selene asked, coming to stand next to her.

Kalli swallowed down her emotions. "He's an anthropologist who studies Amazons," she answered quietly.

"He's her boyfriend," Zoe chimed in, coming up on Kalli's other side.

Kalli rolled her eyes. The term was so juvenile. She was over four thousand years old. There should be a better term for it than *boyfriend*. Besides, despite what the ache in her heart was telling her, they'd never gotten that far in their relationship. What was between them was so new she had no idea what to call it.

Selene let out a low hum, drawing Kalli's eyes to meet her friend's curious green ones. "Boyfriend, huh?" She smiled to take the sting out of her teasing. "What do you think Eris wants with him?"

"The location of Themyscira," Zoe answered. "He's spent years studying our culture. Apparently his museum exhibit had a map that gave the general location of our homeland."

Selene rocked back on her heels, letting out a low whistle. "Eris is trying to go back? Why?"

"That's a good question," Kalli said. "But we shouldn't talk about this here. We need to find a way to haul all this weaponry back to the hotel. I don't want tourists stumbling on this place and getting hurt."

By the time they made it back inside the cave Eris's men had vanished, but Kalli could barely bring herself to care. Somehow she managed to oversee the recovery of the weapons cache even though her brain was acting on autopilot. Sam was gone. What could a pile of weapons mean in the face of that?

She helped Zoe and Selene move everything out of the cave and into their vehicles. Between their car and Selene's, they had plenty of room for everything, even the spears. Thankfully the tourists had disappeared, allowing them to haul their cargo out without being noticed.

Kalli did most of it instinctively, her mind spinning with questions. Where was Sam? What was Eris planning on doing to him? Where would she take him? Was he hurt? She couldn't even process that she'd let him get kidnapped right out from under her nose.

She'd failed. Again. Sam was gone, and it was all her fault.

She didn't protest when Zoe took the car keys out of her hand. She vaguely overheard Zoe telling Selene something about a hotel, but before she could process it, she was being led to the car and pushed into the passenger seat.

Zoe was silent for most of the ride back to the city, for which Kalli was grateful. She couldn't handle any of Zoe's anger or disappointment. She had plenty of that on her own.

They pulled into the parking lot at the hotel, but before Kalli could get out of the car, Zoe reached out and grabbed her arm. "We're going to get him back."

Kalli met her eyes, noticing for the first time the concern on her friend's face. "Sure," she said. Anything to make Zoe stop looking at her like that.

Zoe's hand gripped her even tighter.

Kalli barely registered the quick pain.

"We will get him back. I promise you that," Zoe vowed.

After another quick squeeze Zoe let go, and Kalli followed her out of the car. Selene was already waiting in the lobby, and the trio headed upstairs to their suite.

"Nice digs," Selene said, taking in the pristine white carpets and the large windows overlooking the city.

"We've been using it as our base of operations," Zoe said.

"What operation is that exactly?" Selene asked, pacing the living room and nosily looking at all of Sam's luggage.

The one to make Eris pay for what she'd taken. "We're tracking Eris," Kalli said instead. "I ran into her in Washington, DC, at Sam's museum exhibit. Sam and I have been tracking her ever since, trying to stop her from rejoining Nyx."

"I ran into them at the airport," Zoe chimed in helpfully from the kitchen. "What are you doing here? Not that we're not happy to see you after all these years." A grin split Zoe's face.

"It seems that tracking Eris is the thing to do around here. I've been after her too. I heard a rumor she was up to something in Greece, so here I am."

Selene plopped onto the couch, shoving one of Sam's bags out of the way. Zoe joined her, sitting cross-legged and wiggling to get comfortable. Kalli reluctantly perched on the edge of the chair.

"So Eris is trying to rejoin Nyx? Why would she do that?" Selene asked, picking up a notebook and flipping through it.

"Well, that's what I thought her plan was, and that would have been bad enough, but now I don't think that's what she's after," Kalli said, shifting uncomfortably in her seat as she watched Selene touching Sam's possessions. She fought down the urge to smack the notebook out of Selene's hands.

"Yeah, today she made it sound like that wasn't the end goal," Zoe said, fiddling with the seam on her jeans.

"Then what is her plan, and why does she need an anthropologist?" Selene asked, dropping the notebook onto the coffee table with a dull thud and glancing at Kalli.

Kalli had been puzzling over the exact same thing since they'd left the cave. Only one thing made sense to her. If Eris wasn't going back to attempt to regain her place at Nyx's side, she was going for something even bigger.

The Amazons didn't have much worth stealing. They were a tribe of warriors who valued their weapons above anything else. But then what had Eris's threat meant when she'd said that something would happen to them? Was it possible the Amazons were protecting something she wanted?

There was only one possible explanation. "She's after Harmonia's gift."

Zoe's head popped up, her fingers stilling on her jeans. Selene glanced from Kalli to Zoe and back. "Harmonia's gift?" Zoe almost whispered.

Kalli nodded. "It's the only thing that makes sense. She's after the source of the Amazons' powers. The gift our mother gave us when she and Ares first created us."

Selene jumped up from the couch and began pacing back and forth across the white carpet. "Of course. Eris is an arms smuggler, right? She could get her hands on the most destructive weapons known to humankind. She's looking for something more. Something she can't get on the black market."

"If the gift is the source of the Amazons' powers, would Eris be able to siphon them into herself?" Zoe asked, eyes wide.

"The legend says that she who possesses Harmonia's gift gets the power. There's a reason that it's kept hidden. If no one knows its location, then no one can try to take it for themselves," Kalli explained.

It felt right. Eris had sided with Nyx during the coup but probably only because she'd believed she was going to be at Nyx's side, her second, her trusted adviser. All of that had been taken away from her, but it didn't mean her desire for power had disappeared along with it.

"We need to stop her. Not that we didn't already intend on doing that, but this is unreal. Doesn't she realize what will happen if she takes it? The Amazons will be powerless, mortal." Zoe's agitation was feeding Kalli's. A headache began a slow throb behind her temples.

"She doesn't know what it looks like." Selene stopped pacing but started rapping her knuckles against one another as she talked. "No one knows what Harmonia's gift looks like, right?"

Kalli felt the weight of both Zoe's and Selene's gazes as they pierced her. They were looking to her for guidance, and she wasn't sure what to say. They wanted their former queen, and she was just a woman who ran a women's shelter. "Harmonia never showed any Amazon an object of power," she said carefully.

"But it exists, right? I mean the gift is real." Selene stopped fidgeting and plopped back onto the couch, once again pushing her mass of red hair out of the way. "We've heard about it for thousands of years. It must be real."

Kalli knew she had to tread lightly. There were truths that had been entrusted to her when she'd been crowned, and she had sworn to protect them with her life. "I believe it is, yes."

"We need to get there first. We can't allow Eris to locate the gift. Can you imagine what she would do with that much power?" Zoe asked, impatiently pushing blonde hair behind her ear.

"I bet Eris has imagined it. I bet she's spent the last twenty-five hundred years thinking about it," Selene said, slouching down in the couch and staring at the ceiling.

"How do you suggest we find Themyscira before her? She took Sam, remember?" Kalli said, panic rising in her throat. She didn't like feeling so helpless. At her shelter, she always knew what to do. She was in charge, and she followed her instincts. When it came to anything that had to do with the Amazons, she was afraid her instincts had vanished a long time ago.

"We have these," Selene said, popping off the couch and grabbing all the notebooks she could find from the end table. "You said these were Sam's notes, right? So maybe there's something in here that will tell us where to look."

For the first time since they'd been ambushed in the cave, Kalli felt a sliver of hope. The notebooks wouldn't be as good as the man himself, but she would use everything at her disposal to get him back. "Selene, you're brilliant."

Selene shrugged. "Eh, nothing special."

"What are we waiting for? Let's do this." Zoe grabbed the stack of notebooks out of Selene's hands. Zoe sorted the books into piles by dates. "I figure that you two can get started on these, and I'll go call Interpol. I'll let them know she's on the move again and that she may have a hostage." Selene's eyes narrowed in Zoe's direction before her expression went blank. Kalli wondered what that was about but couldn't spare the time to worry about Selene. Sam was more important.

Zoe stacked the books into three piles, then headed into her room and shut the door. Kalli nodded resolutely. This could work.

It had to work.

Hours later, Kalli threw the notebook she was holding across the room, snarling slightly when it hit the bare wall with a satisfying thud before sliding down to land open faced on the floor.

Selene looked up, raising one eyebrow as she glanced at the book. "Problem?"

"We're no further than we were when we started. We still have no clue where Themyscira is or where Eris is taking Sam." Kalli's breath felt shallow, her fingernails biting into her palms. There wasn't time to freak out, not if she wanted to get Sam back, but her brain refused to listen.

Selene stuck a bookmark into her notebook and closed it, resting it lightly on the coffee table. "We've barely started, Queen Kalliope. We'll find it."

Kalli jumped to her feet and crossed the room to look out the window at the town below. "Don't call me that. I'm not your queen. Not anymore." Queens didn't get innocent civilians kidnapped while trying to clean up their own messes.

Selene came up behind her, her footsteps muffled on the plush carpet. Kalli didn't turn around. She couldn't face the disappointment she would see in her friend's eyes.

"Hey," Selene said, resting a hand on Kalli's shoulder. "This isn't your fault."

Kalli rolled her eyes, still unable to look at her. "Of course it is. Who else is to blame? I'm the one who dragged Sam halfway across the globe. I'm the reason he's here in the first place."

Selene let out a loud, scoffing laugh. "That's a bit conceited, isn't it?"

Kalli whipped around, her anger zeroing in on her target. "Conceited? What are you talking about?"

Selene rocked back on her heels, crossed her arms over her chest, and stared her down. "I realize that you're used to being in charge, that you've always been the one held responsible. But think about this for a minute. You're telling me that an intelligent man—with a PhD, no less—had no say whatsoever in his own actions, and is only here in Greece because you dragged him?"

Kalli opened her mouth to respond, but Selene cut her off again, a head full of steam. "And another thing. You are not the one who kidnapped Sam and took him Hades knows where. That was Eris. You can't claim that one either." Selene took a step closer, shoving her finger at Kalli's chest.

"What's going on?" Zoe asked cautiously as she walked back into the room.

"I'm teaching our queen here a lesson about guilt and blame," Selene said, not even bothering to glance around. "She thinks she's responsible for what happened to Sam."

"That's total crap," Zoe said.

"I know that, but apparently she doesn't." Selene slowly lowered her finger, but her stare burned into Kalli, leaving a ball of fire somewhere in her navel.

"It's just that . . ." Kalli tried to explain herself, but she was cut off again.

"Lighten up, Kalli," Zoe said quietly. "You'd think that all the sex you had last night would have relaxed you a bit more." She cocked her head to the side and smirked.

Talk about hitting the nail on the head. "That's just it!" she yelled as she shoved away from her friends and stalked across the room to get as far away from them as possible. The large room was suffocating her as surely as a pillow over her mouth. "Nothing good ever happens when I relax. Every time I lighten up, there are consequences. That was true when I actually was your queen, and it's especially true now with Sam."

She wanted to throw something. Stalking back over to the couch, she grabbed the nearest throw pillow and launched it as hard as she could. It hit her bedroom door with a soft thump. "When you're in charge and you don't cross every *t* and dot every *i*, people get hurt. Good people. They die, they get injured, they get kidnapped. And that's on you, because you were the one that led them there."

The pillow hadn't been satisfying enough. Crossing to the kitchen, Kalli grabbed a plate. She raised her arm, intending to smash the dish as hard as possible onto the kitchen tile. Before she could manage it, Zoe darted across the room and grabbed her wrist.

"People die. People get hurt. People even get kidnapped. It happens all the time, every day. And you know whose fault it is?" Selene came up beside Kalli and gently pulled the plate out of her hands. "The person who attacked them."

Kalli looked from a pair of compassionate green eyes to a pair of understanding blue ones. She'd been braced for blame or disgust but saw no signs of it. These women were standing by her, believing in her. They didn't fault her for what was going on. Taking a shuddering breath, she felt her heartbeat slow, and an icy knot in her gut start to thaw.

Zoe released her grip, and Kalli slowly lowered her arm. "You're not alone in this. We'll be here, standing by your side. We'll face this threat together, the way Amazons always do," Zoe said quietly.

"All for one, one for all, right?" Selene chimed in, making Kalli bark out a reluctant chuckle.

"I think the Three Musketeers were a bit after our time," Kalli said, but the point was made. For whatever reason, these two were sticking with her.

⟶⟫⟫⟩ ⟨⟨⟨⟨⟵

Selene exited the swanky hotel and headed to the parking lot. Her trunk was still packed with weaponry, so she'd have to be extra careful not to draw any attention to herself. Not that that was very likely. Being sneaky was her business.

She dug her phone out of her pocket and hit redial. She called Ambrose enough that she didn't even need to go digging for him in her contact list. The other end rang once before a crisp British accent answered. "Have you arrived then?"

The car clicked softly as she unlocked the doors and slid behind the wheel. "Of course."

"No trouble?"

The fight at the cave flashed before her eyes. It was probably good that she'd arrived when she had. Not that Kalli and Zoe couldn't take care of themselves, but at the rate Kalli was starting to freak out, there was no telling what she might have done. "Nothing I couldn't handle."

She could hear Ambrose smiling through the phone. "Whatever would you do if you didn't get in at least one good scuffle before dinner?"

She chuckled. He knew her too well. "How are things at Blackburn?" she asked, changing the subject.

"You mean since you left less than eight hours ago? Everything is going swimmingly. Not one of our current ventures will be mishandled, I promise you. Legitimate or not."

She took a deep breath and rolled her shoulders, then started the car. Logically, she knew that she had nothing to worry about. Ambrose was more than capable of running the business in her absence. He'd done it many times before. She was just feeling more unsettled than she'd expected by seeing her friends again.

Thousands of years ago, she, Kalli, and Zoe had been extremely close, sharing everything and relying on one another in times of trouble. But now, after having been separated for so long, there was a distance between them. One that she didn't dare change.

They could never know what she really did for a living.

There was a reason Ambrose was her only friend, and even he didn't know everything about her. He would freak out if she ever tried to explain her life as an Amazon.

No, it made more sense to keep her two lives separate. Ambrose knew about her current life, and Kalli and Zoe knew about her past. Best to leave it at that.

Bringing herself back to the present, she sighed. "Thanks, Ambrose. Sorry for bothering you."

"Nothing you could do would bother me."

"I don't buy it, but thanks anyway. I'll check in soon." She hung up the phone and tucked it into her pocket.

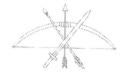

Chapter Fifteen

WHEN SAM WOKE UP, it was so dark he could barely tell he'd opened his eyes. The uneven bumping and the sound of crunching gravel told him he was in the back of a moving vehicle, but he couldn't tell what kind. It smelled of new upholstery and gunpowder.

Eris.

He had no idea how much time had passed since he'd been taken. Eris had dragged him out of the cave, shoved him into the back of an SUV, and shot him up with something that obviously made him black out. It could have been hours or days since he'd been admiring the weaponry with Kalli and Zoe in that cavern.

Kalli was probably panicking. She already felt responsible for the weight of the world. She didn't need his kidnapping on her conscious.

Cautiously, he glanced around, trying not to draw any attention to himself. He didn't need to have bothered. He was alone in what appeared to be the back of a large van. They must have swapped vehicles at some point while he was passed out.

He tried to move but quickly discovered he was bound and gagged. Mentally cursing, he tugged on his bindings, the plastic zip ties cutting into the skin of his wrists.

He struggled to sit up, which was challenging without the use of his arms or legs. A few awkward worm motions later and he managed to maneuver so he was touching the metal wall of the van. With a heave, he pushed himself upright, catching himself just before he overbalanced and tipped in the opposite direction.

The damp rag in his mouth didn't make it easy to breathe. He rubbed the cloth against his shoulder, trying to dislodge it, but it wouldn't budge. Giving up, he looked around and took stock.

He'd been hoping there would be something in the back of the van with him, something sharp enough to cut through his bindings, but Eris was too smart for that.

He was going to have to try something else. Before he'd started traipsing around the globe from field site to field site, he'd made a promise to his family that he would learn how to defend himself in case it ever became necessary. He'd done his best to keep up his fighting skills, but some of the other lessons hadn't been used in a long time. Even so, the mechanics of escaping zip ties probably hadn't changed much.

Since his attackers had been smart enough to secure his wrists behind his back, escaping wouldn't be quite as easy as if they'd been in front. He maneuvered his way onto his knees, inching away from the walls of the van to give his arms room to move. With a slight cringe, he raised his arms as high as they would go away from his back.

He really hoped this worked.

He braced himself for impact as he slammed his hands down toward his butt as hard as he could. His elbows splayed wide, and his bound wrists crashed painfully into his ass. He had to repeat the motion a few times, but to his surprise the tiny plastic handcuffs snapped off. He took a second to rub the raw skin on his wrists before he yanked the damp gag out of his mouth and threw it across the van. He licked his lips, trying to get the disgusting taste out of his mouth.

His feet were harder to free, since he didn't have the same momentum he had with his arms. After a few minutes of twisting and tugging, he managed to break his legs free too.

His body tingled as blood flowed freely back into his extremities. There was no time to nurse his injuries.

He had to escape—now.

As quietly as possible, he crawled to the back of the van, the coarse carpet scratchy against his palms. There were no windows, so he couldn't see outside. He had no idea where he was, but he didn't want to be around when they finally came to a stop.

He took a steadying breath, then ran his hand up the seam between the two doors, locating the handle. Just as he was about to open the door, the van came to a screeching halt, knocking him off balance and away from the exit.

He scrambled back to the door, but it opened before he got there. Eris stood in the opening, the moonlight outlining her features as she inspected him like a piece of meat.

"Free, hmm? You're more clever than I gave you credit for. I'll have to keep a closer eye on you." She winked, then gestured for the muscle-bound man behind her to grab him.

The moon was barely giving off enough light to walk without tripping, but Sam tried his best to scan the area as he was dragged out of the van. They had arrived in front of a low, one-story house, but, as far as he could tell, there was nothing else around for miles. No neighbors, no streetlights, nothing that might indicate there was civilization nearby.

Even if he managed to escape from Eris and her men, there wasn't anywhere he could run. He had no idea where he was and no idea which way to head to find someone who could help him. Panic threatened to climb up his throat, but he swallowed it back down. He couldn't afford to lose his head while he was being held hostage.

Kalli would come. He just had to hang on to that.

The black-clad soldier dragged him by the upper arm into the house, shoving open a door off the long central hallway. Inside was nothing more than a mattress on the floor and a thin-looking gray blanket. With a rough push from the soldier, Sam found himself falling onto the mattress, his knee taking the brunt of his weight as it sank straight through the thin bed.

"She'll come for you when she wants you," the man said, slamming the door behind him as he left.

Sam heard the metal snap of several locks being thrown. Glancing around, he realized that he'd been moved from one small windowless box to another. There was just enough light leaking under the door that he could gauge the size of the room, and it wasn't much bigger than the mattress he was lying on.

The mattress was almost paper thin, but at least it was better than sleeping on the hard floor. He muffled a groan as he rolled onto his back, his knee throbbing when he moved. Even if he'd had a way to escape, the golf ball forming on his leg meant he wasn't running anytime soon.

He took stock. He wasn't hurt, apart from his knee. Eris wanted something from him, which meant he was safe for now. She wouldn't kill him if there was still some way he could be of use to her.

She wanted Themyscira.

She was trying to find it but must have been having trouble. For all her money and connections, she still couldn't locate it. She needed him, which gave him the power.

The sound of approaching footsteps sent his heart racing. It was too soon. He needed to stretch this out as long as possible so Kalli had time to find him. The footsteps paused outside his door, but to his relief, whoever it was kept walking. He let out a long, slow breath, his shoulders loosening.

All night he lay in bed, straining for the sound of someone approaching. Every time he heard the heavy tromping of boots outside his door, he was sure that this was it. Each time he had to calm himself as they passed.

He must have fallen asleep at some point, because the next thing he knew, the door was thrown open and light was pouring inside, far brighter than the hazy incandescent bulbs from the hallway would have been capable of producing.

Still blinking away the glare, Sam felt an iron grip lock on to his upper arm and yank him to his feet. He came eye to chin with a man who looked like a clone of The Rock. The man's muscles bulged menacingly as he grabbed Sam's shoulders and roughly spun him around, shoving him into a walk.

"Let's go."

Sam had to swallow down his fear. He tried to remember whether he'd ever been in a situation quite like this before, but despite a few close calls with some likely crooked police on one of his earliest digs, he had nothing to compare it to. His palms were slick with sweat, and he surreptitiously wiped them on his pants as he walked.

The house was bigger than it had seemed the night before. His guard yanked him down a long hallway leading away from the door. At the far end of the plain white hall was a door painted jet black. The guard yanked Sam to a stop before using his beefy fist to pound a staccato rhythm on the door.

"Enter," a voice commanded from within.

The man opened the door and shoved Sam inside. He stumbled slightly, wincing as he used the back of a chair to catch himself before his bad leg caused him to fall. He glanced up just in time to see Eris's catlike grin.

"Welcome. Why don't you have a seat?" She gestured graciously to the chair he was still using to brace himself. He didn't know what her end game was, but Sam didn't trust her sudden niceness. It likely didn't bode well for him.

Glancing around at the starkly furnished room, he gingerly sat on the edge of the chair. There wasn't much more in the room apart from the chair he'd taken, the chair she was sitting in, and a small empty desk that she was using as a footrest. It made him wonder what she used the barely functional office for.

"You can leave us." Eris flicked her fingers dismissively toward the guard who had followed him into the room. With a quick head bob, he left, closing the door behind him with a snap.

He and Eris were alone. Sam racked his brain for what he knew about her. She was a black-market dealer who specialized in weapons. She was ruthless, according to the information that Zoe had dug up on her from Interpol. She didn't let other people's incompetence get in her way and was violent when dealing with people she thought had crossed her. Oh yeah, and she was an Amazon.

Perhaps he'd had a romantic vision of Amazons. He'd always pictured them as good and kind, as warriors who helped those less fortunate than themselves. He'd seen them as selfless and charitable, using their gifts to right wrongs.

Eris had shattered those beliefs. She was hard, cold, and ruthless. She ran guns and led mercenaries. She was nothing like Kalli and Zoe. Kalli had been everything he'd ever imagined an Amazon to be. Eris was her antithesis.

Her red hair was pulled up in a tight ponytail and tied in place with a leather strap. She was no longer wearing her signature black leather. Instead, she was sporting olive-green cargo pants and a tight black tank top that showed off her ample curves. She had a gun strapped to her right hip and a knife sheath wrapped around her left thigh. She looked every bit as if she would kill him for looking at her the wrong way.

Her gray eyes stared at him much the same way he was staring at her. The shrewdness was obvious, but so was the cruelty. She leaned back and cocked her head.

"You intrigue me, Dr. Treadwell."

He wasn't sure how to respond to that.

"All the information my people found about you tells me that you are nothing more than an academic, a college professor." She got up slowly, her movements both sultry and lethal. She started to slowly circle his chair.

Sam wanted to follow her with his eyes—to keep her where he could see her—but he also wanted to stand his ground. She was an Amazon, and he was unarmed. If she wanted to hurt him, she would, and there wouldn't be anything he could do about it. Stubbornly, he kept his eyes facing front, not getting drawn into her mind games. "I am. I'm an anthropologist."

He jumped slightly when her hand settled on his shoulder, then cursed himself for reacting. He could hear the smile in her voice as she responded. "So what is a scholar doing in the middle of the desert?" He braced himself as she ran her black-tipped fingernails down his arm as she sauntered back to her seat.

"I'm pretty sure I'm in a desert because you brought me here. Last I knew, I was on an island in Greece." The snark probably wasn't a wise move, but at least he wasn't lying.

Her lips narrowed, and her fake smile vanished. "Dr. Treadwell, may I call you Sam?" She kept talking as if she hadn't just asked him a question. "Sam, it isn't a wise idea to cross me. I can make your life a living hell if I want to."

Knowing he was pushing his luck, Sam leaned back in his chair and crossed his arms insolently. "I'm sure you could. But you need me or else I wouldn't be here." He stared her down. He hoped he wasn't overplaying his hand and that his analysis from the night before was solid. She had to want information from him. Otherwise, why keep him alive?

"Where is Themyscira?" she demanded, slamming her hands flat on her desk and leaning toward him.

Sam tried not to smile. He had her, at least for the moment. "Now why would I give you that information?"

Her smile was back, but it was tinged with cruelty. Her hand twitched toward the knife on her thigh, but she didn't reach for it. "Because you'll wish you'd never heard of the Amazons if you don't."

He nodded, trying not to betray his clenching stomach. He felt sweat popping out on his upper lip and hoped she didn't notice. "That's undoubtedly true. So I'm supposed to believe that once I tell you what you want to know, you'll let me skip along my merry way?"

"You have my word." Her fingers clenched around the arms of her chair, her talon-like fingernails making long scratches in the wood.

"You'll have to forgive me if I don't believe you."

His only play right now was to stall for as long as possible. He had to figure out a way to escape. Kalli was probably already looking for him, so he had to give her time to find him.

She would come for him.

Eris lunged out of her chair. Her hand slapped him harshly across the face, sending a loud crack ricocheting across the room. His head hit the back of the wooden chair. He could have sworn he saw cartoon birds circling his head as he tried to blink his vision clear.

Eris snarled at him, no longer the attractive seductress and every inch the stone-cold killer. "You'll regret your choice soon enough."

She backhanded him across the other cheek, sending fire across his face and making his eye feel like it was going to explode.

"Anton!" Eris yelled. The door opened, and the same guard reappeared. "Please escort our guest back to his quarters. It appears he's going to be staying with us for a while."

Sam found himself being yanked to his feet. Apparently his meeting with Eris was over. At least he'd bought himself some more time. Every hour counted. He had no intention of allowing himself to be a part of whatever scheme Eris was concocting.

Anton practically dragged him down the hall to his room. He pulled open the door and unceremoniously dumped Sam on the same hard mattress from the night before. The guard slammed the door shut and slid the bolt home.

Sam was once again locked in the dark.

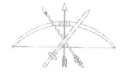

Chapter Sixteen

KALLI STARED OUT THE hotel room window at the distant Mediterranean Sea. The aqua-colored water was so peaceful. She wished she and Sam were in Greece together on a relaxing vacation, or even a boring one with lots of visits to museums and ruins. Anything but this.

She missed him more than she'd thought possible, considering how short of a time they'd been together. He'd inched his way into her heart, taking up residence in a place she hadn't known existed.

She'd been an Amazon for more than fifteen hundred years before she'd been forced out of her home. Unfortunately, the rest of the world hadn't seen women as powerful in their own right. For countless generations women had been subjugated, only allowed to do what the men in their lives allowed them to do.

It was part of the reason the Amazons had been created. To show women—and the world—that they were strong, that they didn't need a man in their life to support them or take care of them. The

AMAZON IN EXILE   181

Amazons had taken up the cause and run with it, fully embracing the idea. It had gotten to the point where wanting a man had been seen as a weakness. Something to be pitied and shunned.

Yet here she was calling that very basic premise into question. She knew, without a doubt, that she could take care of herself. She did not need a man in her life to protect her or provide for her. But maybe she needed one to feel complete.

She'd never wanted to think about it before, but there had always been a part of her, deep inside, that had felt like something was missing. That there was something she didn't understand in the world but that she didn't know how to grasp. Because she hadn't understood it, she'd always just shoved it down into a tiny corner of her mind, ignoring it in favor of the life she did understand—leading and protecting others.

Sam had made a crack in that tightly protected box, and its contents were starting to spill out. She found she could no longer ignore the feelings inside her.

Yes, she could live her life all by herself, but did she have to?

"They're in Türkiye." Zoe's words snapped Kalli out of her reverie.

"Really?" Her heart thudded. It was the first solid lead they'd had in the two days since Sam had been captured.

Zoe nodded. "Interpol thinks their intel is solid. It seems she has a building east of Ankara."

It made sense. From everything they'd pieced together from Sam's journals, the coast of Türkiye on the Black Sea was the most likely location of Themyscira.

The door to the hotel room opened, and Selene swept inside, her red curls bouncing with energy. "Türkiye," she said excitedly. She came striding over to the couch and stopped in front of them, her face falling as she noticed their gazes. "Why are you guys staring at me?"

"How do you know they're in Türkiye?" Kalli asked, her left eyebrow going up. She hadn't asked Selene what she did, apart from hunting Eris, and Selene hadn't exactly been forthcoming.

"I have sources. They're very reliable." Selene sounded a bit defensive but didn't volunteer any further information.

"Well, it just so happens that your mysterious sources corroborate what my official ones believe," Zoe said.

"So we go to Türkiye," Kalli said. "I guess we need to pack."

"We need to be smart about this," Zoe said. "We won't just be able to walk up to her base of operations and knock on the door. We'll need a strategy." She began collecting Sam's notebooks and stacking them in neat piles.

"And we'll need to be sneaky," Selene chimed in. "I'm good at sneaky."

Kalli drew in a deep, calming breath. They had a lead now. It didn't matter that it had been two days since she'd last seen Sam's face. He was smart. He would have found a way to survive.

He had to be alive.

She tuned out the good-natured bickering between Zoe and Selene, who were arguing about the best way to approach Eris's hideout. The choices seemed to be deception or frontal assault.

The sudden silence caught her attention again. She turned to find both Zoe and Selene watching her.

"What?" she said, suddenly self-conscious.

"We've got a plan," Zoe responded.

"But you're not going to like it," Selene added with a wry smile.

The women explained what they'd hashed out, and they were right—Kalli didn't like it at all. Unfortunately, she didn't have an alternative, which was how she found herself standing on a desolate runway in the middle of the night, waiting for their ride.

"Are you sure this is legal?" Zoe asked as she readjusted one of the cartons of weapons they'd recovered from the cave.

Selene shrugged. "For the most part."

Zoe rolled her eyes. "I'm going to pretend I didn't hear that."

The whirring of a rotary engine cut through the night, making the three of them glance toward the sky. A small twin-propeller plane was just cresting the distant line of trees, only visible because of the lights on the front and wings.

"Here we go," Selene said, reaching down to pick up a battered army-issued duffel bag.

The pilot landed on the dirt runway and cut the engines. Seconds later, someone popped open the side door to the plane, dropping a small set of stairs. They made quick work of loading their surprising amount of luggage into the tail of the plane before strapping themselves in. The whole process took less than ten minutes start to finish. Without a word, the pilot ran through his safety checks, and they were airborne.

Kalli was tempted to push Selene about how she'd managed to get them a pilot and a plane on such short notice, but every time the conversation veered toward Selene's life, the other woman changed the subject. With a mental shrug, Kalli let it go. If Selene didn't want to discuss it, there was probably a good reason for it.

After a short flight, they landed on an equally deserted runway, but this one had a dark cargo van waiting for them. They unloaded all their luggage and trunks full of weapons into the van, filling the back almost to capacity. With a simple nod, Selene grabbed the car keys from the man who was waiting for them and hopped in the driver's seat. Kalli and Zoe climbed in and Selene took off, leaving the man standing in their cloud of dust.

"He'll be fine," Selene said, forcing Kalli's gaze away from the sight of the man standing forlornly behind them. "He does this all the time."

"Something else I'm going to pretend I didn't hear," Zoe chimed in. "An Interpol agent probably shouldn't be skating this many legal gray areas."

Selene just scoffed. "This is Eris. If she's planning what we think she is, bending the law is a small price to pay for stopping her before she figures out how to exploit the Amazons and gain their power."

Privately, Kalli agreed with Selene. As much as she preferred to operate within the confines of the laws and rules, she'd learned during her time on the throne that sometimes those laws and rules hindered more than they helped. She couldn't let Eris hurt people. Not on her watch.

Selene drove for what felt like hours but was likely far less. Kalli had to stop herself from falling asleep in the passenger's seat. Luckily for her, they were traveling on some of the bumpiest dirt roads she'd ever been on, which kept jouncing her awake every time she dozed.

Just as the sun started to rise, Selene pulled up in front of a low stone house and cut the engine. There wasn't much to see. The house was the same shade of tan as the hill that sat behind it. The only interesting feature, if you could call it that, was a small bush that someone had attempted to plant by the front door. By the withered looks of it, whoever it was shouldn't have bothered.

For the third time that night, they hauled all their boxes around, unloading them from the car and stowing them in what was probably supposed to be the living room. The room was conveniently right by the front door and devoid of all furniture.

Even with her strength and level of fitness, lugging around all their cargo made Kalli's shoulders hurt in a way they hadn't for a long time. As soon as they were done unloading, she picked the closest box and dropped onto it in exhaustion.

"There are beds in the other rooms," Selene said. "We should probably try to get some rest. We should move on Eris's house tonight."

Kalli trudged down the hallway and picked one of the rooms at random. She lay down on the bare mattress and tried to sleep, aware that she wasn't going to be much good to Sam if she was too tired to play her role in the rescue operation. Even knowing that, her eyes wouldn't close, her body unwilling to give in to sleep. Instead, she watched the shadows made by the sunlight filtering through the dirty window as they slowly marched across the ceiling.

Time passed slowly. She wished they could just get it over with, but that wasn't the plan, and she had to trust the plan. She didn't have much choice, and Sam probably didn't have much time left.

It was going to work.

A short eternity later, a soft knock startled her out of her reverie. The bedroom door creaked open, showing Selene backlit by the hallway light.

"It's time."

Her stomach sank. Even though she'd been waiting for this all day, or really since Eris had kidnapped Sam in the first place, she suddenly wasn't sure she was ready for this. What if something went wrong? What if their plan didn't work and Sam died?

She sat up, doing her best to ignore the churning in her gut. She could do this. She had to.

Kalli took the piece of paper Selene was holding. It was a map to Eris's base of operations. Somehow, through her unknown network of connections, Selene had managed to get them a house that was only a few miles from where Eris was keeping Sam. Kalli memorized the map, then handed it back. In her other hand, Selene held out a set of keys.

"Off you go," Selene said.

The night was dark as pitch. There wasn't much in the way of civilization nearby, so the main source of ambient light was the moon. The headlights on the beat up pickup truck she was driving did little to alleviate the unrelenting darkness, and Kalli was barely able to differentiate between the road and the barren landscape.

At last she saw a point of light in the distance. She drove straight for it, knowing exactly what she would find. Moments later, she pulled up in front of a low-slung house that looked like it had seen better days. There were no cars to be seen, but they had to be hidden nearby. She'd arrived at Eris's base.

Just for effect, she waited for a few minutes, sitting in the driver's seat, her headlights shining straight through the house's front windows. She knew she was drawing attention to herself, but that was the point.

Sam was inside that house. She was going to get him back.

She reached inside herself for the steellike reserve that had always suited her so well when she was queen. She'd been in far worse situations than this. With a mental shake, she stiffened her spine.

Time was up.

She climbed out of the truck, leaving the headlights on, and slammed the door as loudly as possible. She stood there in the yard, in full view of anyone looking out the windows, and stretched, lifting her arms to the sky and bending sideways like she felt nothing more than a bit sore from being in the car for too long.

She took a moment to limber up, knowing full well that her tight leather pants and tank top showed off her body to its best advantage. It wouldn't hurt if whatever guys Eris had with her were a bit distracted.

At long last, the front door of the house opened, and a man walked out. Any doubt she might have had about this being the wrong house fled as soon as she saw the jacked-up man standing on the porch. There was no way a man would have that many muscles—or weapons—and just happen to be an innocent bystander.

"I believe you have the wrong place," he said, not taking more than a step away from the doorway.

Kalli smiled, cocking her left hip out and propping her hand against it. "No, I don't believe I do."

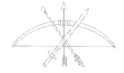

Chapter Seventeen

S AM ACHED FROM HEAD to toe. The hard wooden chair was pressing into his bruised legs and shoulders, sending shards of agony shooting through his body. He was sure his whole body was sickly shades of purple and green, and every time he licked his lip, he could feel a giant swollen knot and a split that bled sporadically.

"Let's try this again, shall we?" Eris practically purred as she circled his chair, tracing a finger down one of his arms and up the other before jabbing it harshly into a pressure point at the base of his neck.

Sam squeezed his eyes tightly shut, trying not to react. He couldn't help it, though. A tiny whimper slipped past his lips, his breath escaping as harsh pants.

"Aww, baby," she leaned down and whispered in his ear. "You want me to stop? All you have to do is tell me where Themyscira is."

He was tempted to tell her something, anything. His time since he'd been kidnapped had passed in a blur of constant pain punctuated by tiny reprieves of unconsciousness. He had no idea how much time had passed; it could have been hours or weeks for all he could tell.

He opened his mouth and tried to talk, but nothing came out. Eris crossed in front of him and smiled, a cruel look making her eyes narrow and her mouth turn up at the ends. She lifted her finger ever so slightly, the pain in his shoulder slowing to a dull throb.

"You were saying?" she purred.

He licked his lips and spat blood on the floor at her feet. "I'm pretty sure it's in Timbuktu."

She backhanded him sharply across the cheek, making his already black eye throb in pain. It wasn't smart to keep pissing her off, but he couldn't let her win. "Or maybe"—he turned to look her straight in the eye—"it's at the bottom of the Mediterranean like Atlantis."

She let out a snarl. She pulled back her arm, and he braced for the blow, cringing away as far as he could get while trapped in his chair.

Someone rapped sharply on the door. Eris's hand halted midswing, her eyes racing from him to the door and back. He could tell that she wanted to follow through, but since she'd warned her men not to interrupt unless it was important, he could see her weigh her options. Finally, her hand dropped to her side.

"Enter."

Anton opened the door. "She's here."

A feral smile spread across Eris's face as she sauntered over to her minion. She patted his cheek in a thoroughly condescending manner. "Good boy." She blew the mercenary a kiss, but her gaze zeroed in on Sam. "I guess I won't need you after all."

Sam's heart started to race. There was only one woman whose arrival could make Eris that happy.

Kalli was here.

With an almost seductive finger wave in Sam's direction, Eris crossed to the door. She looked at Anton. "You know what to do."

Anton's face split in a terrifying smile, his eyes focusing in on each and every one of Sam's injuries. He stalked closer to the chair and rolled his neck, a loud crack splitting the tense silence.

Sam swallowed painfully. Kalli might have found him, but it looked like his time was up.

⤜⟩⟩⟩⟩ ⟨⟨⟨⟨⤛

"Ma'am, you need to leave."

Kalli had to stifle a laugh. The guy on the porch was doing his best to look intimidating, but he had no idea whom he was dealing with. She was an Amazon, and she was royally pissed off. This guy didn't have a chance in hell.

She smiled. "Why don't you go get Eris for me? It's okay. You can take your time. I'll wait." She winked and waved him off dismissively. To add insult to injury, she suddenly became fascinated with the state of her cuticles.

Out of the corner of her eye she saw his fists clench at his sides. Finally, he turned around and stuck his head back inside the house. He muttered something under his breath before turning back around and closing the door. This time, rather than attempt to engage her in conversation, he just stood there, arms crossed over his chest, making his considerable muscles bulge to the breaking point.

As she waited, Kalli kept her face impassive. Deep inside, however, her stomach felt like lead, and her mind was spinning a thousand miles an hour. She hoped they were doing the right thing. She wouldn't be able to survive it if she was putting Sam in more danger by being there.

A manicured hand tapped the solid wall of muscle blocking Kalli's view of the doorway. The man shifted two paces to the right, allowing the door to swing freely as Eris emerged into the night. A satisfied smile spread across her lips as her arms crossed in a mirror image of her mercenary.

"Kalliope. To what do I owe the pleasure?" Her eyes skimmed Kalli from head to toe before she sneered dismissively.

"I came to make a deal." Kalli shifted her weight to the balls of her feet, the slight movement making Muscles reach into his waistband, where she assumed he was carrying a gun.

"A deal? What on earth do you think you have that would be of value to me?" Eris chuckled slightly, and her eyebrows rose to her hairline.

Kalli swallowed. Here went nothing. If they were wrong, this whole plan was about to blow up in their faces. "Harmonia's gift."

⟫⟫⟫ ⟪⟪⟪

Selene could barely make out the footprint of the building. The pressing darkness both worked in their favor to mask their approach and hindered their ability to make progress. The house Eris was using as a base of operations was nestled not far from a series of small hills, which they were using as cover. Unfortunately, there was a wide-open expanse between the edge of the hills and the entrance to the building.

A slight tug on the back of her jacket brought Selene's attention to Zoe, who nodded in the direction of their target. Two men dressed in all black, and with more guns than anyone could possibly need in the middle of nowhere, had just come around the side of the house. Each man scanned the area with a small flashlight.

With a muffled curse, Selene jumped behind a mound of dirt just before the beam landed on the spot where she'd been crouching. They needed to take care of these guys—and fast. There wasn't a lot of room for error. If they didn't hold up their end of the deal, Kalli would be hung out to dry.

That wasn't an option.

Selene pointed from Zoe to the man on the right, then pointed to herself and the man on the left. Zoe acknowledged her with a quick nod before crawling away.

Selene didn't hesitate. She dashed up the hill she was hiding behind and used it to launch herself at the soldier. The man let out a surprised grunt as she plowed into him. Both of her fists landed in his gut, and her momentum carried them to the ground. She went with the forward motion, tucking into a ball and rolling, then propelled herself to her feet.

Her target was still on the ground trying, and failing, to suck in a deep breath. He reached for one of his many guns, but she beat him to the punch, ripping it out of his hand and smacking him upside the temple with it. He sprawled on the ground, out cold. She crouched next to him, putting her fingers on his neck. He was still alive. She pulled out several zip ties and used them to secure his hands and feet.

She glanced up, noticing that Zoe was kneeling on the back of the second soldier, neatly securing her own target. They still made a fantastic team, even after thousands of years apart. The thought brought a smile. She'd missed these women. She quickly vowed that no matter what happened with Eris, she would make sure she never lost track of her friends again.

Warrior senses on high alert, Selene nodded at her partner, and they stood simultaneously, making their way across the ground to the back of the building. There was a door exactly where her intel had said it would be. Unfortunately, though unsurprisingly, it was locked. She fished her lock-picking kit out of her back pocket and went to work as Zoe stood guard behind her. Within seconds, the lock clicked. Selene gently tugged the door open, standing slightly to the side in case guards were waiting on the other side.

When no alarm went off, she tugged the door wider with a smile. It was nice when the bad guys made it easy on you. She stepped inside, moving far enough in for Zoe to join her. The hallway had doors on both sides. They had no idea which one held Sam.

Just when she thought they were going to have to check every single one, the door to her left opened. She got a glimpse of a small office that had little more than a desk and two chairs, one of which appeared to be holding a very bloody Sam. Standing between her and Sam, however, was one of the largest men she'd ever seen. He was easily close to seven feet tall, as she found herself eye level with his collarbone. His muscles looked like they were on the verge of ripping his shirt open every time he breathed.

Crap.

She could take this guy, but close-quarters fighting wasn't what she'd had in mind. Not to mention, they'd been hoping to get in and out without drawing attention to themselves. Looked like that plan was shot to hell.

The man's eyes narrowed. She was pretty sure it was only his surprise that had kept him from attacking so far, but he was over that. With a roar, he launched one beefy fist straight at her face.

Chapter Eighteen

E RIS'S ARMS DROPPED TO her side as the smile fled her face. Her eyes narrowed as she took a step toward the edge of the porch. Kalli heaved a mental sigh of relief. They'd been right. Eris was after the gift.

"Why would you come here and offer me such a powerful treasure?" Eris asked, not quite able to keep the eagerness out of her voice.

"You know why. You have Sam." Kalli met her gaze without flinching.

"Sam?" She tsked her tongue several times. "My, how you've changed. You used to be the queen of a society that scorned men."

"And you used to be one of its warriors for good. We're not all what we used to be."

Eris flinched slightly, then sneered. "Warriors for good? Is that what you think we were? Well look where that got us." She gestured vaguely to their desolate surroundings. "We could rule this world, but we chose not to. We chose to be good."

"Do you accept my deal, or not?" Kalli asked. As interesting as it was to dissect Eris's particular brand of chaos, Kalli had one thing on her mind: Sam.

Eris took several steps forward, stepping off the porch and onto the dirt. "You don't have Harmonia's gift."

Score one for Kalli. Eris was definitely interested in what she had to offer.

Kalli shook her head. "No, I don't. But I can tell you how to get it. I used to be queen, remember?" She shrugged like it was no big deal.

Kalli could see Eris considering her words. "And what about your sidekick Zoe? She's okay with you just coming here and offering me such power? How do I know she's not hiding in your vehicle right now?" Eris clearly wasn't aware of Selene, but Kalli wasn't about to point it out to her.

Kalli held her hands out, her fingers splayed widely. "Search it if you'd like. There's no one here with me. Zoe doesn't even know I came."

Eris nodded quickly to Muscles, who pulled his gun and slowly approached the truck. Kalli took several steps sideways, giving him a wide clearance. He peered through the windshield and side windows into the cab, then went around the rear and searched the bed.

"It's clean, boss."

With a nod, Eris acknowledged him and turned back to Kalli. "So it would seem we may be able to deal after all. How do I find it?"

Kalli couldn't believe she was about to say this. "It's in the Royal Hall of Themyscira. It's hanging on the wall."

Eris's mouth opened slightly. "Hiding in plain sight."

"The power belongs to all Amazons. It isn't something that should be hidden away and never appreciated."

"Well, I do appreciate the information." Eris saluted Kalli and turned to head back into the house.

"Wait," Kalli called after her. She couldn't let Eris go before she got Sam back. "Now it's your turn to hold up your end of the deal. Give me Sam."

Eris spun back around, openly laughing. "Why would I do that? I've already gotten what I need from you. I might as well kill him."

"What about the location of Themyscira?" she yelled desperately.

Eris just laughed harder. "I've got that part covered. Your man was nothing more than a pretty plaything. And you know how I love to play with my food before I eat it."

All reason fled. With a guttural roar, Kalli charged. She saw a moment of panic in Eris's eyes before Kalli's fist cracked her across the left temple. Eris spun around but went with the movement, pivoting until she came full circle and slammed her left fist into Kalli's gut.

Kalli's breath went out with an oomph. Panic rose as she struggled for breath, but she used the feeling to direct her energy back into the fight. She sent a sharp uppercut at Eris's jaw, following up with a roundhouse to the ribs, her foot feeling the give as Eris's bones snapped beneath the pressure.

The torso blow didn't even slow her. Eris's hands swooped down in a chopping motion, catching Kalli on both sides of the neck.

Their movements became a blur of speed. Kalli stopped thinking and operated on pure instinct. She was a fierce fighter. You didn't get chosen to be the queen of a warrior civilization without being able to fight.

Kalli ducked under a blow from Eris's arm but got caught across the thigh by a follow-on kick. She returned the favor by stomping on the back of Eris's knee, sending her into a kneeling position. With as much energy as she could muster, she punched her opponent across the cheek, hoping to lay her out. Unfortunately Eris saw the move coming and dodged sideways, aiming for a groin shot.

Kalli launched herself, flipping midair and landing behind Eris, out of the reach of the other woman's punch. The smart watch on her wrist vibrated. It was the signal she'd been waiting for, but she was trapped. There was no easy way out now.

From the corner of her eye, Kalli could see a growing crowd of thugs pouring out of the house. They were frozen in place, clearly trying to decide whether they should engage. Eris must have noticed them, too, because she shouted, "She's mine!"

Eris sprang to her feet with a snarl, launching herself toward Kalli, who sidestepped easily. "Is that all you've got?" Kalli taunted. "You couldn't take me when we were training together. What makes you think you can do it now?"

"Kill the hostage," Eris snarled as she aimed both fists at Kalli's stomach. Kalli tried to dive sideways, but she didn't move fast enough. The sharp, burning pain told her one of her ribs was broken.

As she was forced backward by the blow, Kalli watched as several men went back into the house to carry out their boss's orders. She flew into a blind rage. Ignoring the pain in her body, she let her fists and feet fly, catching Eris across the leg, upper arm, and the side of her head. Blood came pouring out of Eris's nose, making her look like a grisly sort of clown.

Eris stumbled and fell to her knees. Satisfaction rose up in Kalli as she went in for the final blow. This was it. She was going to put an end to this.

"Ticktock, Kalli!" A large black cargo van came out of nowhere, Zoe hanging out of the driver's-side door.

Kalli hesitated. She was so close. Everything would be over soon. Eris was down, and Kalli could make sure she stayed that way.

"Gotta go now!" Zoe yelled again.

Zoe was right, and Kalli knew it. She dropped her fist, watching Eris fall to the ground. She turned and sprinted as fast as she could toward the truck. Kalli launched herself into the driver's seat, slammed the door, and threw the car in gear.

She followed the van as closely as she could but kept glancing at the house as it grew smaller in the rearview mirror. The dark had practically swallowed the house when a giant fireball ripped through the night, the sound deafening even from this distance. A moment later the shock wave hit her, making her glad she was already seated. The explosion was massive, lighting up the night for several miles.

The fight was over, but everything was starting to catch up to her. As the tension in her body slowly ebbed, the pain started to sink in, creeping into her muscles and blossoming from where her ribs were likely broken. She glanced down at her hands, which were covered with Eris's blood.

She'd had her. If only she'd had a few more moments, she could have ended her. The Amazons were not truly safe until Eris was eliminated from the equation. She'd had the chance tonight, but she'd failed. Once again, she hadn't been strong enough.

The van pulled to a stop, and Kalli pulled the truck up next to it. They were back at the house where she'd failed to take a nap earlier in the day. She opened the driver's door and climbed out of the vehicle.

"We can't stay here. You only have a moment," Zoe said, nodding in the direction of the back of the van.

Kalli turned, her heart suddenly pounding in her throat. She took a few tentative steps forward, then forcibly yanked the door open.

"Kalli." The voice was weak, but it was music to her ears.

"Sam!" She climbed into the back of the van, her arms out to hug him to her, but she stopped just short of touching him. He was covered in bruises and had two black eyes. He was squinting at her, his beautiful brown eyes glazed with pain. "What did they do to you?" she rasped.

"Nothing that my beautiful Amazon queen couldn't rescue me from," he said, wincing as he attempted to smile. "I knew you would find me somehow."

His Amazon.

Of course, because that was how he saw her. No matter what she'd told him about herself, he still had her pegged as some all-powerful warrior. That was what he expected from her.

She wanted to weep. This whole situation was her fault. Sam had been taken because he'd been helping her, and now he was injured. She would never forgive herself. She wasn't good enough, not at being an Amazon queen and not at being a lover. Most guys didn't have to worry about winding up black and blue because their girlfriend was a magnet for evil.

Kalli leaned away from him, ignoring the shock in his gaze. He tentatively reached out with one hand, but she backed up even farther, her shoulder hitting the rear door of the van. She had to do the smart thing here. She had to be strong.

"As soon as we make it someplace a bit safer, I'll see that Zoe gets you to a hospital." Her voice sounded stilted, even to her own ears. "Once you get the medical attention you need, we'll arrange for a flight back to DC."

Sam's outstretched hand slowly lowered down back to his side, the other one holding his abdomen. "You're sending me away?" he asked, disbelief evident even though he could barely talk without gasping. "After everything we've been through together?"

Exactly. He'd been attacked more than once while they'd been together. Given the state of his injuries, he couldn't afford to get in another fight.

She steeled her nerves, bile rising in her throat. She'd finally opened herself up to a man, and look where it got her. She was an immortal warrior, and short of outright death on the battlefield, she could heal from almost anything. He was a fragile human who had only a handful of decades on this planet. Even those few years could be cut short by being involved with her. She couldn't do it to him.

"Thank you for your assistance, Dr. Treadwell, but I believe your services are no longer required." She nodded once in his direction. "I'll send Zoe in to make you comfortable for the journey."

She turned her back on him and climbed out of the van, leaving him behind.

⇢⇉⇉ ⇇⇇⇇

"You're an idiot," Selene said cheerfully as she helped Kalli load the rest of their supplies into the cargo area.

Kalli did her best to hide her emotions as she did what needed to be done. "Why, because I'm loading heavy crates while injured?" she asked as she fished out an ACE bandage from one of their medical kits. She knew exactly what Selene meant, but she wasn't going to make it any easier on her.

Selene just rolled her eyes. "Not exactly, princess." The redhead nodded at Sam, who was sitting on a bench seat in the back of the van, leaning against the wall for support. The ride was going to hurt like hell, but there was no other way to get him to a doctor.

Looking away from Sam, Kalli tugged up the hem of her shirt. She wrapped her chest tightly with the bandage, trying to immobilize her broken ribs as much as possible. With a frustrated huff, Selene stomped over and did it for her, yanking harder on the bandage than was strictly necessary.

"I don't know what you're talking about," Kalli said, trying to ignore the pointed glances of her longtime friend.

Selene took a step back and looked at her, crossing her arms across her chest. "You know what? I actually believe you. I don't think you have a clue what you're doing."

The back door of the vehicle slammed closed, and Zoe came to stand next to them. "What doesn't Kalli know?"

Kalli's eyes narrowed at Zoe, but Selene answered her question anyway. "Kalli has no idea what she's doing wrong." Selene waved her hand vaguely in the direction of Sam.

Comprehension dawned in Zoe's eyes. "Oh, that." She nodded. "Yeah, big mistake there. No offense."

Kalli straightened her spine, swallowing a hiss as pain shot through her ribs. "I know exactly what I'm doing."

Selene rolled her eyes again. "Yeah, you're being all noble and self-sacrificing. You're throwing away the best thing to ever happen to you all because you're afraid of what might happen next."

Kalli could think of worse options. She wouldn't be able to deal with it if Sam was killed while under her protection. She was saving them both. "I'm doing what needs to be done. Just like I've always done."

Zoe nodded. "Queen Kalliope had to do what needed to be done every minute of every day. She was who we looked to for leadership and protection. Kalli James, on the other hand, can have her cake and eat it too. Enjoy your life. Live a little." She shoved Kalli's shoulder lightly.

She appreciated what her friends were trying to do, but they were wrong. Enough was enough. "The decision has been made. Now let's move out before we get caught."

Kalli yanked open the passenger door of the van. She climbed into the middle jump seat and did her best to ignore her friends.

She was right. She had to be.

⇝⇝⇝ ⇜⇜⇜

Sam could hear the low murmur of voices through the thin wall separating the front seats from the cargo hold but couldn't make out what the women were saying. It didn't matter either way, as it wasn't like he was going to be part of the mission anymore anyway.

He tried to get some sleep, but his body felt like it was being stabbed every time they hit a bump on the winding dirt road. That left him alone in the dark with nothing but his thoughts.

Had Kalli really ended things?

Thoughts of Kalli were all that had gotten him through the torture Eris and her men had thrown at him. He'd gone into himself, ignored the present, and focused on her beautiful face. He'd pictured her smiling sweetly as she punched and kicked her way through Eris's thugs, taking them down a peg or ten.

After Zoe and Selene had rescued him, Selene had filled him in on the plan, but it hadn't helped. The sound of the explosion had rocked him to his core. He'd been certain that Kalli had been caught up in the blaze.

It was only after he'd heard the crunch of the truck's tires when she'd pulled up next to the van that he'd started to have hope again. He'd heard her footsteps, and then, miraculously, there she'd been, staring at him.

She'd taken one look at him, and a mask had slipped into place. A cold, hard, unreadable mask. She was not the same Kalli he'd made love to in Lemnos.

This Kalli was cold and unfeeling, not the type of woman who would dedicate her time and money to a domestic abuse shelter.

Was she right? Maybe he was out of his league. He was just a professor with a possibly unhealthy obsession with Amazons. That didn't make him one of them.

As much as he didn't want to admit it, maybe she had a point. The pain shooting through his body every time the van jounced made it obvious that going to the doctor probably wasn't a bad idea. But then what? He would get sent back to DC like a good little boy?

He couldn't picture going back to his old life, not after having met Kalli. He'd spent his entire life studying Amazons, only to come face-to-face with them. Of course, he couldn't very well explain that to his colleagues, at least not without the risk of exposing Kalli, Zoe, and Selene. Where did that leave his career?

And where did that leave his heart? In the short time since he'd met Kalli, he'd already begun to think of her as a permanent presence in his life. She was such an amazing person, and she didn't seem to recognize that about herself. He couldn't picture the rest of his life without her.

Of course, he was also mortal. He would age and die one day, all while she stayed young and beautiful forever. He would leave her, even if he didn't want to. She would then have to carry the weight of that around with her for the rest of her existence. Could he inflict that pain on her long-term for their short-term happiness?

She was probably right to send him away. Their lives were too different for it to make sense. He was an academic who relied on his brains, and she was a warrior who relied on muscle. He was human, and she would live forever. He was middle class, and she was filthy rich. They didn't belong together.

He drifted off to sleep, trying to make himself believe the lie.

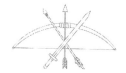

Chapter Nineteen

KALLI JOLTED AWAKE AS the van came to a sudden stop. Her ribs still ached like a bitch. The ACE bandage had helped, but even with the accelerated healing powers that came with being an Amazon, she couldn't mend broken ribs in less than six hours.

Glancing out the windows, she saw that they were once again in the middle of nowhere. Everywhere she looked was green vegetation, but not a whole lot of civilization. Off in the distance, she could see large hills that may have been called mountains if someone wanted to be generous. They were parked in front of yet another abandoned-looking stone house.

There wasn't a hospital in sight.

She glanced left and right between Selene and Zoe. "I told you to take us to a hospital. Dr. Treadwell should be assessed by a medical professional after his ordeal."

"Oh, so now it's Dr. Treadwell, is it?" Selene's voice rose sarcastically as she yanked the keys out of the ignition, flung the door open, and climbed out. "I see you still haven't pulled your head out of your ass."

There were few times she missed being queen, but right about now it would have come in handy. "He shouldn't be here," she repeated through gritted teeth.

Zoe laid a hand on Kalli's forearm, drawing her attention. "We couldn't exactly show up with a van full of weapons and explosives, now could we? It might have raised a few questions."

Zoe had a point. Kalli hated to admit it, but she hadn't thought her plan through all the way.

"Fine. Let's at least get inside then." She forced her way out of the vehicle, looking dismally at their new hideout. "Looks lovely."

"Beggars can't be choosers," Selene said. "It'll have to do for now."

Kalli flinched when she heard a groan coming from the rear of the van. The back door opened slowly, and Sam inched his way out, trying to mask how much pain he was in and failing miserably. Zoe crossed to his side and helped him stand.

"I thought we were going to a hospital?" he asked, his voice marginally stronger than the night before.

"Yeah, well, these two disobeyed orders. We'll find you one shortly," Kalli said. A knife of pain twisted in her gut. His bruises looked even more painful in the light of day than they'd looked the night before.

"Always happy to disobey orders," Selene said with a smile, looking Sam up and down. "I'm Selene, by the way."

"Sam." He reached out and tried to shake her hand.

She waved him off. "No offense, but you look like I could knock you over with a twig right about now." Her green eyes flashed. "You're kinda cute, though, under all that purple and green."

Kalli's eyes narrowed as she watched Selene watching Sam. "So where exactly are we?"

"Straight to business I see. Well, suit yourself." Selene spun on her heel and headed into the house.

The living room wasn't totally empty like the one they'd stayed in the night before. However, the most it could boast for itself was a scratched wooden table and one chair that looked like it might break if someone actually tried to sit on it. Selene crossed to the table and pulled out a roll of paper, carefully spreading out a large map of Türkiye. She jabbed her finger to a small town along the coast of the Black Sea.

"We're currently fifteen miles outside of Terme. This is as close as we could get to pinning down the location of Themyscira based on your notes." Selene looked at Sam.

"We're still looking for Themyscira?" Sam asked as he cast a sideways glance at Kalli. She wanted to force him to take it easy but figured she could pick that fight again later.

Selene nodded, her face grim. "We can't assume we stopped Eris or even slowed her down by much. The fact that we stopped and warned Kalli to leave means we also warned Eris something was going on."

Guilt hit Kalli like one of Eris's punches. She'd gotten so wrapped up in her fight with Eris she hadn't stuck to the plan. She was only supposed to have distracted Eris while Selene and Zoe did the rest, but she'd missed her cue to leave and had needed to be rescued. If she'd reacted with her head instead of her heart, Eris might have walked right back into that house, never knowing what was coming. Instead, her impulsive decision had cost them an edge.

"Eris already knows where to find Themyscira," Kalli said.

Selene stopped studying the map and looked at her. "How do you know?"

"She mentioned it before we fought."

"Well, crap," Zoe said, plopping down on the wooden chair. The wood started to crack under her weight, and she promptly jumped back up.

"How did she figure out where it was?" Selene asked. Her eyes slid toward Sam.

Sam stared her down as much as he could through his puffy black eyes. "Not from me."

"If you didn't tell her, then she must have already known. And if she already knew, why did she go to the trouble of kidnapping you?" Zoe asked.

Kalli's stomach turned sour. "Because of me." Three sets of eyes looked at her like she was imagining things, but this was exactly why she wanted Sam to leave. He was in danger as long as he was with her. "I'm serious. She told me that he was nothing more than a plaything. It was a trap. She kidnapped him to lure me there."

"Why would she do that?" Zoe, at least, didn't sound immediately dubious.

"Harmonia's gift. Everything comes back to that. She lured me there deliberately, hoping I would trade information for Sam's life."

Kalli took a few steps away, bracing her hand on the wall as everything fell into place. "She knew how to get to the city, but not how to find the gift. It was a setup."

"Look, I don't know what this gift thing is supposed to be, but you didn't actually tell her where it was, did you?" Sam asked, taking a half step in her direction.

Kalli shook her head. "No, I didn't." Not the truth of it anyway. She could feel the room let out a collective sigh of relief.

Selene nodded. "Then we still have an advantage. She may know where the city is, but she doesn't know what she's looking for or where it is."

"So how do we find the city, preferably before she does?" Sam asked, his eyes catching hers defiantly.

Kalli glanced around the room. They were all looking at her, hoping she would lead them. They wanted answers, and she wasn't sure if she had any to give. "I don't know."

She felt their disappointment like a sliver of ice to the heart. She'd let them down, again.

"Maybe we should all just try to get some rest. We all had a pretty big night last night, and you two look like hell," Zoe said.

Selene looked like she was ready to protest, but Kalli jumped in before she could. "Yeah, that sounds like a good idea." Spinning on her heel, she turned toward one of the doors off the main room, hoping to find a bedroom. She lucked out on her first try and stepped inside, closing the door quietly behind her. She could hear low murmuring but didn't even try to make out what they were saying. With a deep sigh, she crossed to the bed, toed off her shoes, and crawled onto the mattress.

The rigid set of Kalli's shoulders as she'd walked away should have been enough to scare him off. Kalli had done plenty to push him away, but he sensed this went deeper than she'd let on. This wasn't about him no longer being of use. There was something much bigger at play.

He glanced at the other two Amazons. Selene just shrugged, but Zoe spoke up.

"She's been in a mood ever since you were taken. She feels responsible for what happened."

Sam nodded. It made sense. Kalli held herself to impossible standards. "She feels like everything rests on her." His heart went out to her as their conversation from the previous night came back to him. He suddenly saw everything from a different light.

"Maybe I should go talk to her?" Zoe asked, taking a hesitant step toward the closed door.

Sam shook his head. "I'll do it." He forced his aching body to hobble across the wooden floor and opened her door without bothering to knock.

Kalli was lying on the bed, curled up on her side and facing away from him. He eased his body onto the mattress slowly, scooting until he was spooned up behind her. He gently put his hand on her hip, careful not to brush her injured rib.

He thought she was going to pretend to be asleep, but eventually she sighed. "Why are you here?"

The words sliced into him, making him pull back and lift his hand off her hip. "Do you not want me to be here?"

She rolled over so she was facing him, nose to nose. She winced as she looked at his black eyes, then dropped her gaze to his neck, one of the only nonbruised places on his body.

Her hand tentatively reached out to rest against his heart. "Of course I want you to be here. What I'm asking is why you want to be."

The tension in his gut eased slightly but didn't go away. "I'm here because I like being around you. You're an amazing woman."

"But I'm not! I know you have this thing for Amazons, but clearly I'm not all that we're supposed to be. Look what they did to you!" The words were harsh, but underneath the anger he could hear pain.

He grabbed her by the chin, forcing her to look him in the eye. "Let's clear one thing up right now. I'm not with you because you're an Amazon. I'm with you because you're an amazing person. You care, more than you want to at times. Your heart would encompass the entire planet if you could find a way." Warmth blossomed in his chest, a truth he hadn't wanted to admit. "I love you, but I love you for being you, not because you're an Amazon."

Kalli's mouth dropped open comically. "You love me?" The words came out as a whisper. Her hands went to her neck, pulling a chain out from under her shirt so her hands could worry it.

Sam tried not to laugh, but he did crack a smile. "I know you're new to this whole relationship thing, despite being a few millennia old, but yes, this is what it looks like to be in love. To want to be with someone through the good and the bad."

"Well, the bad just keeps on coming. Sam, I have no idea what I'm doing. Those women are expecting me to lead them, and I have no clue what to do next. We have no way to find Themyscira, and if we can't find it, we have no way to stop Eris."

She kept sliding the chain through her fingers, absentmindedly rolling it around.

"We'll figure it out together." He brushed a quick kiss against her lips. A flash of something shiny caught his eye.

He glanced at her necklace and noticed the ring hanging off it. The wiry design and shimmering blue stone triggered his memory. "Is that the ring from the bookcase in your bedroom?"

Kalli glanced down, obviously unaware that she'd been playing with it. "Yes. It's actually part of a matched set, a ring and a circlet. They're only supposed to be worn by the reigning queen of the Amazons."

"It didn't get taken from you?"

She shook her head. "When the Greeks kidnapped us, they took the crown but didn't know to take the ring. Presumably Nyx is wearing the circlet, unless she's been overthrown since I left."

An idea was slowly forming in the back of his mind. "So only the current ruler is supposed to wear them?"

She nodded.

"What would happen if you put it on?"

She blinked at him several times before she answered. "I honestly have no idea. I haven't felt worthy of it for a long time. I took it off twenty-five hundred years ago and haven't tried it on since."

He smiled, some of the tension in his stomach releasing. "I think right about now would be a great time to give that a try."

"Sam, I don't know about this."

He grabbed her hands between his and gently squeezed. He wished she could see herself through his eyes. "Kalli, you can do this. You were chosen for a reason. Maybe this was it. Maybe the entire reason you were deposed was so you could come riding to the rescue and save the Amazons from a terrible fate. Who are you to question the gods?"

The last part may have been a bit overdramatic, but it seemed to work. With a sigh, Kalli pulled the chain over her head and removed the ring. She hesitated, then resolutely shoved it on her right index finger.

A shock wave of power started from where the ring met her body and radiated outward, forcing him back. Before he even had a chance to ask what had happened, Zoe and Selene burst through the door, knocking it off the hinges so it hung drunkenly on an angle.

"What was that?" Selene said, her voice awed.

Sam shifted to a seated position as fast as his battered body would allow. Kalli followed much more slowly. She glanced from Selene to Sam and then down to the ring on her finger. Her mouth opened, but no sound came out. Sam saved her the trouble. "That was your queen reclaiming her throne."

Zoe took a step into the room, noticing what Kalli was staring at. "It's the queen's ring. I had no idea you still had it."

Kalli finally looked away from the glinting sapphire and met her friend's eyes. "I've always had it. I just didn't think I deserved to wear it anymore."

Selene crossed to the bed and sat down on the corner of the mattress, her hand reaching out to rest on Kalli's foot. "You are the rightful queen of the Amazons. That's always been the case, no matter what happened."

Zoe came and sat on the other corner of the bed, making Sam glad he'd moved his feet out of the way. "Do you think they felt that in Themyscira?" she asked, tucking her blonde hair behind her ear and glancing in Kalli's direction.

Kalli looked just as baffled as the rest of them. "I have no idea. I didn't even know it did that." She laughed. "I've had that thing for thousands of years, and I apparently know next to nothing about it."

"What do you think this means?" Selene asked. "Only the reigning monarch is supposed to be able to wear the ring. Yet somehow you can wear it even though Nyx staged a coup."

Sam smiled. "I think what it means is that she never actually stopped being the queen. Nyx may have taken her throne, but she was never the rightful ruler. That's still Kalli." As he said it, something shifted slightly near his heart. He'd just gotten through confessing that he loved her, and now it turned out that she was still the reigning monarch of a society of women who hated men. As happy as he was for her, that she would be able to reclaim her rightful place, it could mean the end of whatever was just starting to build between them. Either way, he was going to support her. He loved her, and he wanted what was best for her.

"Do you think the ring can somehow help us find Themyscira again?" Zoe asked, her blue eyes flashing.

Kalli's nose wrinkled, and she squinted. "No, but I think I might know something that can."

Selene's eyes took on a wolfish gleam as she opened her mouth to say something, but Kalli held up her hand to wave her off. "I appreciate your enthusiasm, but this is something I think I might need to work on by myself. I promise I'll let you know as soon as I have something more concrete to go on."

Zoe stood up from the bed and tugged on Selene's arm. "We'll leave you to it."

When they reached the doorway, Zoe turned around and dropped into a gesture halfway between a bow and a curtsy, a huge smile on her face. "Your majesty." Selene mirrored the gesture, then set the door back in its frame as much as she could.

Sam watched them go and then turned back to Kalli, leaning in to brush a soft kiss across her lips, making her smile. "Your majesty," he said, bowing slightly.

She shook her head. "I may be the queen of the Amazons, but I'm not your queen. Please, for the love of the gods, keep calling me Kalli." She crossed the scant few inches between them and drew him into a kiss, much deeper than the one he'd given her. She tried to shift closer to him, then hastily pulled away, letting out a gasping breath of pain. "Stupid accelerated healing, why aren't you done yet?" she whispered.

With a chuckle, he planted another feather-light kiss on her lips. "You may have accelerated healing, but not all of us are that lucky."

With a reluctant sigh, she pulled away. "I know. I'm sorry. It's really not a good time, for many reasons."

Understanding, he slid off the bed. "You have some stuff to work through. I'll let you get to it."

She crawled across the mattress to pull him into one last kiss. "I'll find you when I'm done."

He smiled, but it was bittersweet. "You better."

Sam left the room, then made his way out the front door of the house, putting more than just physical distance between himself and Kalli. He had no idea what her idea was for finding Themyscira, but he wondered if it even mattered. Kalli was now once again the queen of the Amazons. She was going to have lots of responsibilities and obligations, and they weren't something he would easily be able to help with or relate to.

He came to a stop next to the van, leaning his aching body against it. Every single movement was agony, a reminder of what he'd been through at the hands of Eris and her men. The thought of being back together with Kalli had been the only thing keeping him sane through the days of torture and pain. Her face had stayed with him, a constant reminder to be strong.

And now he might lose her.

Kalli was the reigning monarch of an entire culture who despised men. He was a college professor who lived halfway around the world. What could he offer someone like her? More importantly, would his mere presence and the relationship they were building make her people lose faith in her ability to rule? He could never do that to her. He wouldn't be the thing that stopped her from reclaiming her destiny.

After the battle was over, he would have to be strong. He would need to do what had to be done and walk away. She could do what she was born to do, and he would go back to his boring existence.

Pain that had nothing to do with his physical injuries shot through him. He had no idea how she'd managed to squeeze her way into his heart as quickly as she had, but there she was. Leaving her would be the hardest thing he'd ever had to do.

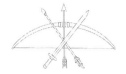

Chapter Twenty

K ALLI NEEDED TO BE outside. Despite having no idea where she was, the giant map on the table notwithstanding, she needed to be around nature. She needed to connect to the land in the way she used to.

Technology, electricity, and indoor plumbing were all marvelous inventions, but they distanced people from the land that helped sustain their lives. Her homeland had been wonderful for its time, but it had been rustic. She could still, after all these years, perfectly picture the stone houses in their village and the Royal Hall where they'd feasted and celebrated.

Harmonia, the mother of all Amazons, was a wood nymph who originated from an ash tree. Being in nature and living off the land was a part of who the Amazons were deep inside. Being part of it helped make them stronger, helped turn them into the powerful warriors they came to be.

Kalli needed to feel that strength. She still didn't know what it meant that she was able to wear the queen's ring, or what to make of the rush of power that had happened when she'd put it on. Hopefully it meant that she was supposed to be the one wearing the ring.

In fact, she was counting on it.

The fields behind the house were the bright green of spring, with small flowers and weeds popping out of the ground in splashes of color. She headed for a nearby stand of trees, drinking in the sun and the breeze, letting the feelings seep into her body and help her heal. The trees, whether through coincidence or fate, were ash.

Feeling a bit foolish, Kalli knelt at the base of the largest tree, her head bowing and her eyes drifting closed. For a moment all she did was breathe in and out, soothing her mind and her soul. A slight vibration passed across her skin, almost as if the tree were trying to reach out and share its energy. She could almost feel her mother's presence in the wood.

"Harmonia, mother of all Amazons and sacred nymph," she finally spoke. "I need your guidance. I've lost my way, and I've been adrift for too long. The Amazons are facing a grave peril, possibly more so than ever before. One of our own is going to betray us. She intends to kill anyone who stands in the way of her gaining the power that resides in each of us. I'm trying to stop her, but I'm stuck. I need to find Themyscira and return before Eris carries out her plan, or this could be the end of your daughters. The end of the Amazons."

A touch as light as the breeze lifting her hair made Kalli open her eyes. Standing in front of her was a woman, or at least the image of one. She wasn't quite solid, and she hovered several inches above the grass, which didn't shift or rustle as the woman moved. She was beautiful beyond anything Kalli had seen, with flowing brown hair that went past her waist and a sumptuous green dress that looked like it was made of velvet and mist. She appeared no older than Kalli, despite being ancient.

The resemblance between them was like a kick to the gut. Kalli couldn't compete in the overall awe factor, but they had the same small nose, the same rosy lips, the same blue eyes. It was startling to see how much they had in common, especially since Kalli had believed herself unworthy of being an Amazon for so long. To look at her mother, the immortal nymph, and see so much of herself staring back at her was bewildering.

Harmonia beamed with pride. Her fingers reached out and almost touched Kalli's face, her wispy fingers feeling like nothing more substantial than down feathers.

"My beautiful daughter. I've missed you."

Kalli wanted to say that they'd never actually met, but it felt rude to point that out when she was asking for help.

Harmonia smiled. "Just because we've never met doesn't mean I haven't been watching you, guiding you when I can."

Apparently her mother could read her mind. Note to self.

Kalli wanted to be strong, wanted to simply ask what she needed to and leave, but her mouth had other ideas. "If you were watching, why didn't you help me? Why did you let me stay lost for so long?"

A bittersweet look crossed her face. "It wasn't time. Now it is. I can't always interfere as much as I'd like."

"But you wanted to?" Kalli sat back on her heels and searched out her mother's gaze.

Harmonia's head dropped sideways, her stance softening. "Of course I did. I hated to see my favorite child suffering."

"Favorite child?" Kalli forgot all about her plan to stay kneeling and jumped to her feet, her height coming within an inch of her mother's. Her voice rose as she spoke. "How can you say I'm your favorite child? Besides the fact that we've never spoken before today, I was deposed and kidnapped. I've spent the last twenty-five hundred years on my own, not even living among my people."

"And yet you wear the ring." Harmonia's voice remained level, both eyebrows going up.

The fire went out of Kalli, stopping her before she responded. She glanced down at her right hand, watching as the sun glinted almost painfully off the brilliant sapphire she wore there. "Was that you? The burst of power, was that yours?"

"No, my child. That was yours. It was power you've always had in you. You just forgot how to use it."

"I had to be reminded," Kalli said.

Her mother smiled and tucked her hands behind her back. "Yes, your young man. He's lovely. Not bad on the eyes either."

Kalli's mouth dropped open with unflattering disbelief. Not only was it strange to hear your mother tell you that your boyfriend was attractive, but this was quite literally the mother of the Amazons, the biggest man-haters on the planet.

Harmonia rolled her eyes and shook her head. "Just remember that in order to be someone's mother, I had to first be someone's lover."

When she put it that way, it seemed kind of silly. "So you're not opposed to him? I mean to us?" Kalli asked, tentatively.

"Do you care for him?"

Kalli nodded, afraid to speak.

"Do you love him?" Harmonia pressed.

Kalli turned away from her mother, unable to look her in the eye anymore. She'd asked a valid question, but Kalli wasn't sure she had an answer to it. Was what she had with Sam merely chemistry?

If it was nothing but physical attraction, the last few days would have gone differently. She still would have found a way to rescue Sam from Eris's clutches, but she wouldn't have nearly lost her mind in the process. When she thought back on how she'd reacted and how she'd treated Zoe and Selene, guilt settled into her stomach. She'd been a basket case, and there was only one logical explanation.

"Yes. I love him." Instead of feeling nervous, a sense of calm flowed into her. She loved Sam, and suddenly it was the most natural thing in the world. Yes, she was the queen of a society that detested men, but that was a problem for a future time. Right now she wanted to find him and scream her love from the rooftops.

"How does that help me?" Kalli asked, turning once again to face her mother's wispy form.

"Oh, it doesn't. I was merely curious." Harmonia giggled.

Kalli rolled her eyes, then sobered. "Eris is trying to return to Themyscira. She wants to take the power that you imbued us with for herself."

Harmonia's eyebrows went up. "You know that the object she's after won't do what she wants it to do."

"I know that, but she doesn't." To save Sam, Kalli had told Eris what she'd wanted to hear. Thankfully Eris didn't fully understand what she was looking for. "She's willing to kill everyone to get the power she's after. I need to stop her, but I can't figure out how. I don't know how to go back." Kalli tempered the frustration she felt so it wouldn't seep out in her tone.

"Kalliope, why is it impossible for you to find Themyscira?" her mother asked like she was lecturing a small child.

Kalli huffed out an irritated breath. "Because it's cloaked. I asked Hermes to hide it from the world back when I was the queen."

Harmonia didn't say anything, just watched her with a small smile.

Finally, it clicked. "Mother, you're a genius." Kalli wanted to jump up and down, but that didn't seem like a particularly dignified thing to do the first time you met your mother.

"Be safe, my daughter." With one last nod, Harmonia vanished.

Kalli stood next to the ash tree that was the embodiment of her mother, and for the first time since Sam had been kidnapped, she felt good. Yes, it was strange that she'd finally spoken to her mother after being alive for as long as she'd been. She'd always been a bit resentful that Harmonia hadn't been around, that she hadn't had a more traditional upbringing, but that wasn't what she'd needed. She was an Amazon, and more than that, a queen. If she'd had the typical loving mother and gentle upbringing, she probably wouldn't have been able to do what she'd done in her life. She may not have been able to make some of the impossible decisions she'd had to make, like who would live and who would die in battle.

She was who she'd been raised to be. A warrior queen, and this queen needed to save her people.

"Hermes," she said, looking up toward the cloudless sky. "Messenger of the gods, I beseech you. Appear."

Nothing happened. Kalli stood in the middle of the grassy field, the small crop of ash trees her only companions. She glanced around, hoping against hope that another wispy figure would appear. None did.

"Damn it." Her mother must have been wrong. She may be wearing the ring, but she didn't seem to have the power she once had.

No. This wasn't allowed to fail. Her people were in danger, and she was the only one who could save them. "Hermes, I swear, if you don't get down here immediately, I'll kick your ass."

"I think I'd like to see that," a voice said from behind her.

Kalli practically jumped out of her skin, spinning around to face the man now standing less than five feet from her. He was dressed in a full three-piece suit, despite the warmth of the spring day. His short blond hair was fashionably cut, and his face contained just the right amount of scruff to be attractive. His green eyes screamed intelligence and a bit of amusement.

Kalli rapidly looked around. There was nothing in sight. No cars, no hovering helicopter. This man had appeared out of thin air, which meant only one thing. "You're Hermes?" she asked, trying desperately to keep the disbelief out of her voice. She should probably apologize for threatening him.

"Don't you recognize me?" he asked, spreading his arms and spinning around in a circle, like he was showing off. She was remembering long, braided hair tucked under a winged helmet and winged shoes. He looked nothing like what she'd expected.

Still uncertain, Kalli reached out and poked his arm, hitting solid muscle, not wispy mist. "But you're here. Like, really here."

Hermes shrugged. "I'm the messenger of the gods. I go where I must." He pulled an iPad out of thin air and began rapidly searching through it. "Speaking of that, I really don't have a lot of time. My schedule is filling up as we stand here making small talk."

Pulling her tattered confidence around herself like a cloak, Kalli straightened her shoulders. "Hermes, I need to ask you a favor."

His eyes barely skimmed hers before focusing again on his iPad. "Haven't I done plenty of favors for you before? I cloaked your entire city in a veil for you. No one can find it anymore."

Kalli shook her hands to release tension. "That's exactly what I wanted to talk to you about. I need you to bend the rules for a bit. I need to find Themyscira."

His fingers flew over the tablet, the light from the screen sending flashing colors across his perfectly tanned face. Finally, he opened his hand and the iPad simply vanished. "That wasn't the agreement."

"I know, but this is important. One of the Amazons that was banished with me is planning to return. She wants to steal the source of the Amazons' powers, and she has the guns and firepower she needs to kill them all." Kalli refused to beg, trying instead to infuse her words with a sense of urgency.

"And how does she know how to find it?" Hermes asked, his voice almost bored.

It was a valid question, and yet again Kalli didn't have an answer. She just knew that Eris had found a way, and she needed to stop her. "I don't know. But it's up to me, to us, to stop her." Kalli glanced at the house in the distance. Hopefully none of the others could see what she was doing.

"And you want me to help you."

It wasn't really a question, but she answered it anyway. "Yes, I can't do this without your help." It couldn't hurt to flatter his ego with the truth.

The way his shoulders shifted and his head came up a bit straighter told her she'd hit the mark. "That's true." His gaze narrowed, and she met his eyes, his green ones boring into her blue ones like drills. "You look like your mother."

The change of topic threw her for a loop. "Yes, I guess I do."

Hermes sighed. "Very well. I'll do this for you, but only because I happen to like your mother. Your father's a bit of an ass."

Kalli had to stifle a laugh. "You would know better than me, since I've never met him, but I suppose Ares might get that way sometimes. He *is* the god of war."

"Trust me, you're better off." With that, he lifted his foot and grabbed a loafer that probably cost more than her entire wardrobe. He plucked at the side of it, and for just a moment the smooth Italian leather faded away to show a leather sandal with wings on either side of the ankle. Hermes removed his hand from the shoe, and the image vanished, returning back to something that could probably be seen in boardrooms across the globe. In his hand, however, was a snow-white feather. "Take this. It will allow the bearer to see through my veil. Don't lose it unless you want your enemies to use it against you." He dropped the feather into her outstretched hands.

Before she had a chance to thank him, Hermes was gone.

Kalli stared at the sky. In the span of just under fifteen minutes, she'd met both a wood nymph and a god. When she'd ruled all those years before, she'd prayed to the gods, but she'd never actually met one of them. She was humbled they'd thought her worthy enough to meet in person. She must be doing something right. Hermes wouldn't have come to her if she wasn't the rightful queen.

She glanced down at the feather in her hand, her fingers brushing over it softly. Such a fragile thing, something so easily lost. One strong wind, and everything they'd worked for would be gone forever. She doubted Hermes would give her such a gift twice. Kalli carefully tucked the feather into her pocket, gently patting the fabric covering. The last thing she wanted was to damage it.

She turned and faced the house. Inside were three people counting on her to get this right. She wasn't about to let them down. Resolutely, she walked toward the house, her long strides eating up the ground. She squared her shoulders and pushed open the back door. Whatever Eris had planned, Kalli was ready for it.

When she walked into the living room, she found Sam sitting on the floor in the corner, poring over a stack of his journals, carefully turning page after page. Zoe was leaning over the table, staring at the map, tracing her finger along the coast of the Black Sea, a look of deep concentration on her face. Selene was nowhere to be found.

"You're done," Zoe said, her head swiveling in Kalli's direction. "Selene's just gone to make some calls for more supplies. I swear, I have no idea where she's getting all this stuff. Interpol does not work as fast as whatever network she has going for her."

"I'm back," Selene said as she walked into the room from the opposite direction. "As to where the supplies come from, you're probably better off not knowing."

Sam's head came up at that. He looked like he was going to ask a question but glanced at Zoe's face and clearly thought better of it. Instead, he looked at Kalli. "Did you get what you needed?"

She smiled for the first time in what felt like forever. From her pocket, she drew the small white feather. "We're going to build ourselves some wings and fly there?" Zoe asked with a grin.

Kalli shook her head. "It's from Hermes. It will guide the bearer through the veil and into Themyscira."

"You spoke to Hermes?" Sam asked, rising to his feet and brushing the dust off the back of his pants. "Like the god?"

Kalli nodded. "I also spoke to our mother," she said, glancing at Zoe and Selene. Both women took a step closer to her, twin looks of awe on their faces. "She was the one who guided me to Hermes."

"Did she say anything else?" Zoe asked hopefully.

Embarrassment flooded into Kalli, making her cheeks warm. She glanced at Sam but couldn't look him in the eye. "She may have a bit of a crush on my man."

Blood rushed into Sam's cheeks, mirroring what she was sure her own looked like.

Selene snorted loudly, not bothering to hide her laughter. "Well, at least our mom has some taste. I always wondered what she saw in Ares."

Zoe cleared her throat loudly. "So what are you supposed to do with the feather?"

Kalli appreciated the change in topic and accepted it gratefully. She shrugged, walking over to the table. "No idea, but here goes nothing." She placed the feather flat on her palm and closed her eyes. At first she felt nothing, but then her hand began to tingle. She glanced down at the map. Clear as day, right in the middle of the area Zoe had been searching, was a large dot labeled *Themyscira*. "Someone get me a pen, fast."

Sam grabbed the one he had tucked behind his ear and handed it to her, watching closely as she leaned over the map and inked in the details only she could see.

"I'll be damned," he said, walking back to his pile of journals and rifling through it. He finally grabbed a tattered one with a black leather cover and brought it back to the table. He flipped it open to a page somewhere in the middle, showing a map that had clearly been hand drawn. It depicted the area immediately around Themyscira, but it didn't have any context to show where it might fit on a larger map of the area. "I drew this based on the descriptions I was finding that detailed what the landscape might look like around the city." He put the book down next to the giant map of Türkiye. The topography he'd drawn was almost an exact match for the area of the map where Kalli had drawn her dot.

Selene let out a whistle. "Good job, Professor. Spot on."

"This is it. We've found it." Excitement was obvious in Zoe's voice.

Kalli nodded. "Now we just need to get there before Eris does."

They agreed to head out first thing the next morning. Selene wandered off to gather supplies. Zoe grabbed her phone and closeted herself in a room to check in with her coworkers at Interpol, trying to get any updates on Eris's movements. That left Kalli and Sam.

The sun hadn't set yet, but she was still sore and exhausted from the fight the night before. Her ribs appeared to be on the mend, but Sam still looked like he could use some extra rest. Without a word, they turned and headed back into the room she'd chosen earlier.

The bleak walls and spartan decor left her pining for the lush hotel room on Lemnos. Thankfully the mattress was soft, and there were fresh linens on the bed. She should want to crawl right in there and pass out, but sleep wasn't exactly the first thing on her mind.

"We should probably get some rest," Sam said, standing awkwardly in the middle of the room.

Her stomach sank. "Sure, of course. That's probably for the best." She'd hoped for one last night before they rode off into battle again, but she would have to content herself with sleeping next to him and feeling his warmth. She crawled into the bed fully clothed, not bothering to locate her luggage and dig out pajamas.

Sam lay down next to her, his left hand barely brushing her right. She shifted, grabbing his hand in hers. His head turned, his eyes seeking hers in the fading light.

"Screw it," she said, leaning over and kissing him firmly on the mouth.

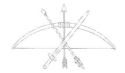

Chapter Twenty-One

S AM'S RIGHT HAND PLUNGED into her hair, holding her to him, deepening the kiss. "Oh, thank God," he said between kisses. "I've needed this." The split in his lip burned slightly and forced him to ease up. He switched to gentle pecks, planting them all over her face and neck.

Relief flooded into him. Finally, after what felt like forever, even if it had been only a few days, his hands were back on Kalli. A pained tug flashed across his ribs as he pulled her flush against his body, but he ignored it. Her life, her vitality, felt wonderful. It flowed into him, healing the bumps and cracks that Eris and her men had sown. His body would heal eventually. As long as he had Kalli, he could recover from almost anything.

He rolled onto his side, ignoring the pain that raced through his body from the bruises. His split lip tugged a little, and he ignored that too. Nothing was more important than being with her. Her very existence was what had kept him going during the days of torture and torment. The fact that he'd known she was out there, that he would go back to her at some point, was what had kept him from breaking.

Slowly, he drew his hands up her arms and to her neck, cupping it, holding her mouth to his as he kissed her fiercely. He ran his tongue over her upper lip, then nipped at her lower one, making her gasp. He took full advantage, diving into her mouth, his tongue mating with hers.

He skimmed his hands gently down her body, outlining her breasts without making a move to cup them. She groaned and arched into his hands, but he kept moving. He let his fingers breeze over her torso, his mind just barely conscious enough to remember her healing ribs. At long last, his fingers felt the bottom of her shirt, and he skated his eager fingers over the planes of her stomach.

Kalli was a warrior. There wasn't much that was soft about her, and that included her abs. Several ridges met his questing fingers as he tugged her shirt up slowly, revealing her barely visible six-pack. He'd never really thought of muscles on a woman being sexy, but on Kalli, they worked. She was everything he could have imagined and more.

With a small—somewhat painful—tug, Sam managed to get the shirt off her, revealing her sexy body adorned in pink lace. He had no idea why she'd brought sexy underwear on a mission to save the world, but he wasn't complaining. He ran his fingers over the lace, the rasp of the fabric driving him wild. By the way her nipples puckered, the move had an effect on her too.

"Sam," she breathed softly.

He satisfied them both by bringing his hands up to cup her breasts, feeling the warmth of her skin through the fabric. He heard her quickly indrawn breath and lifted his gaze to her face, watching her eyes as he flicked his thumbs over her nipples. Her nostrils flared, her tongue darting out to wet her lips.

It wasn't enough. His hands left her breasts, avoided her bruises, and grabbed for the waistband of her jeans. He popped the button and tried to pull them down her legs. Kalli lifted her hips and wriggled, distracting him for a moment, but between the two of them, they managed to get her pants off to reveal the matching pink-lace panties.

"Kalli, you're killing me," he said, his fingers tracing the lace.

Her hips bucked. "I'm killing you?" she panted.

Sam smiled. "More than you know." His shaft was rock hard and pushed against the barrier of his fly. He wanted to rip his clothes off and pound into her, but even if his body would have been up for that, he wouldn't let himself. He wanted to make tonight about her.

He bent his head, feathering kisses along the fading bruises on her sexy stomach before traveling to her legs. He traveled down one perfect thigh before switching and going back up the other one. He finally paused by her right hip, the scent of her driving him to the edge. His fingers rasped along the pink lace before he hooked one forefinger underneath and yanked, tugging her panties down her legs.

Her hands grabbed his arms, squeezing his biceps, teasing his shoulders. Sam rolled her carefully beneath him, and her hands moved to his back. He was still dressed, and her hands grabbed the bottom of his shirt, tugging it carefully over his head. Her fingers skated down his heated flesh, plucking at the waistband of his jeans until he lifted his hips just enough for Kalli to unzip his fly and push the pants down his legs. Impatiently, he finished shoving them off, flinging them over the edge of the bed with a small grunt. His battered body wasn't quite happy with what he was doing, but he couldn't bring himself to stop.

He paused to take in the sight of her splayed out on the bed beneath him, her brown hair draped over the pillow, her lips swollen from his kisses. He felt like he couldn't possibly get any luckier than he was right then and there, with his beautiful Amazon warrior letting him take the lead.

"I love you, Kalli. Whatever happens tomorrow, I love you." His hand gently skimmed down her cheek as he watched her, stomach clenched. Her eyes widened, and her mouth opened, but she didn't speak. He didn't need her to say the words back to him, but he'd needed to say them to her. He'd needed to tell her how he felt. She was his everything.

With a soft smile, he swooped in, kissing her senseless and preventing her from having to respond. Her breath was coming out in tiny pants against his cheek as he began trailing his tongue down her neck. He lowered his mouth to her collarbone and toward her breasts. He took the first one in his mouth, making the lacy fabric cling wetly to her skin as her nipple puckered. He swapped to the other side, giving the other breast the same treatment.

She grabbed the back of his head and held his mouth to her skin, her legs coming around his hips and crushing his shaft against her moist heat. He instantly went as hard as iron. Suddenly he couldn't wait anymore. He grabbed her hips and plunged deep inside, hearing her moan as he drove her higher and higher.

He met her gaze, watching her eyes flood with pleasure. With one last thrust of his hips, she came, her hips bucking violently and dragging him into bliss with her.

Sam collapsed, trying to keep his weight off her. She wrapped her arms around him and tugged him firmly against her, his weight pressing her more firmly into the mattress. Her hands idly skimmed up and down the damp skin of his back. The pain of his injuries slowly trickled back into his mind, but he couldn't bring himself to regret what they'd just shared.

With a reluctant heave, he carefully shifted his weight so he was lying next to her, his arm draped over her stomach. She curled into him slightly, not bothering to cover herself. He loved her self-confidence.

He was suddenly exhausted, his body aching slightly from the exertion. Even with the pain, it was as if his body could finally relax after all the uncertainty. With her by his side, he could sleep for days. Just as he was about to fall asleep, she tapped the tip of his nose ever so gently. He opened his eyes reluctantly.

Her beautiful blue eyes were staring intently into his. She took a deep breath. "I love you, Sam. I have no idea how you can love someone who's totally unaccustomed to being in romantic relationships, but I'm thankful that you do."

Joy rushed into him, leaving him slightly light-headed. He may not have a clue what the dawn would bring, but he knew that he and

Kalli would face it. Together. "How could I not love you? You're the most amazing woman I've ever met." Her eyes fluttered closed, but he tapped her chin to get her to open them again. "I mean it. You astonish me on a daily basis. Who else could calmly discuss battle strategy after talking to not one but two supernatural beings?"

Her lips curled into a smile. "Technically, you're talking to a supernatural being too."

He chuckled. "I guess I am."

"Can you imagine?" she asked, her voice trailing off as her hand traced gentle circles on his stomach.

"What's that?" he asked, stifling a huge yawn.

"The queen of the most man-hating group in the world has fallen in love." She kissed him gently.

He smiled slightly, tugging her closer to his side. "And I'm very glad she has." Together they drifted off into much needed oblivion.

⇥⇥⇥ ⇤⇤⇤

"Up and at 'em, lovebirds." Zoe came stomping into their room the next morning just as the sun started to slip through the dirty window. "No time to waste. We have a battle to fight and a civilization to save."

Kalli sat up with a groan, letting the sheet puddle on her lap as she rubbed her tired eyes. Sam made a squawking noise behind her, grabbing the thin fabric and tugging it back up around Kalli's naked body. She turned and gave him an exaggerated eye roll. "Prudishness is a very modern invention, you know. Trust me, it isn't something Zoe hasn't seen before."

Sam let out a huff. "Well, suit yourself then," he said, dropping the sheet back to the bed.

Zoe let out a low chuckle. "Don't worry, lover boy. She's not really my type. You, on the other hand . . ." She waggled her eyebrows, her eyes skimming his exposed chest.

Faint pink stained his cheeks adorably. Kalli couldn't help leaning over and giving him a quick peck on the lips. "Ignore her."

Zoe glanced at her watch. "I don't poach. Besides, no time for any more shenanigans. We're going to have to hoof it if we want to beat Eris to Themyscira."

All thoughts of tempting Sam into a quickie fled from Kalli's mind. "You found her."

"More or less. We have her last known location, and she's closing in, so chop-chop." With that, she turned and left the room, thankfully closing the door behind her.

Kalli sprang out of bed and reached for her clothes. Her mind began whirling, her thoughts sharpening into focus. She couldn't afford to be distracted from their goal. They needed to reach Themyscira first and stop Eris from wiping out the Amazons.

"I don't suppose you'd stay here?" she asked, turning to watch Sam as he tugged his clothes on much more slowly than she had. It was obvious he was still in pain. If he stayed in the house, she wouldn't have to worry about him as much if it came down to a fight.

Sam straightened, his pants half-on. "Not on your life. I may not be as strong or as fast as the rest of you, but I'm not worthless in a fight. Wherever you go, I go. Understood?"

As much as she'd been hoping he'd stay behind, she was equally relieved he hadn't taken her up on the offer. She would have missed him if she'd left him behind, probably distracting her almost as much as attempting to keep him safe would. She smiled and nodded. "Understood. Now get a move on, Professor. Zoe isn't going to wait much longer." With a wink, she left him to finish getting ready and went to find Zoe and Selene.

She located them outside, loading the van. They were doing their best to make the vehicle as defensible as possible, in case they ran into Eris and her men on the way. She had no idea how the rest of the Amazons would react when they saw their first car, but she didn't have time to worry about that. They weren't about to give up the utility of a vehicle for a bunch of horses.

"We almost ready?" she asked her friends.

Selene nodded. "Locked and loaded. The swords and shields are nice, but I managed to acquire a few weapons that were at least made in the last century," she said, gesturing to a handful of guns spread out on the seat of the vehicle.

Kalli's eyebrows rose, but she didn't comment. Selene might have questionable methods, but Eris was a black-market arms dealer. Kalli just hoped that a few guns would even make a difference.

"Everything else is ready to go. We're just waiting on . . ." Zoe trailed off as Sam came out the front door of the house, carrying his bags. "Nothing." She smiled.

Sam walked to the car, pausing when he saw the weapons. Kalli's stomach clenched as she waited for his reaction. The weapons were there to save their lives. If Sam wasn't okay with that, too bad.

"You ever handled one of these before?" Selene said, reaching for one of the Beretta pistols and handing it to him grip first.

Sam casually accepted the weapon, ejected the magazine, inspected it, and slid it back into place with a small click. "Don't worry about me. I've had training with firearms before. It never hurts to be prepared when your work involves going to some of the more war-torn parts of the world."

Selene nodded once, then turned to Kalli. "Looks like it's up to you and your feather."

They climbed in the van, Selene behind the wheel and Kalli in the passenger's seat, gently grasping the feather in her hand. She sent a small prayer up to Hermes that whatever magic he'd placed on the feather hadn't faded as Selene navigated toward the small dot she'd drawn on the map the night before.

The drive was both short and the longest journey of Kalli's life. She'd never thought she would be able to return to Themyscira after Hermes's veil had cloaked the city. She had no idea what to expect after being gone for so long. She just knew she had to do everything she could to protect her people from the threat they had no way to know was coming.

As they approached the spot on the map, the roads all seemed to vanish, and a vast nothingness spread out in front of them, an open area nestled among the hills and trees of the coast. Kalli opened her palm and concentrated on the feather.

At first nothing happened. Then suddenly, as if a movie backdrop had been dropped into place, a town appeared. Laid out in front of her was Themyscira.

She was home.

Chapter Twenty-Two

THE VILLAGE LOOKED EXACTLY as she remembered it, the stone buildings perhaps a little taller, the vegetation a bit more overgrown, but otherwise it appeared Themyscira hadn't changed much in more than twenty-five hundred years.

She sucked in a quick breath, her stomach clenching with nerves and excitement.

"Kalli?" Selene said, clearly unable to see what she was seeing.

Kalli nodded. "We're almost there."

A moment later, Selene gasped and slammed the brakes on the car, coming to a stop not ten feet from the closest building.

"Holy crap," Sam said, awe in his voice. "It came out of nowhere."

Kalli couldn't quite put a name to the emotions racing across her mind, but she clearly wasn't alone. Out of the corner of her eye, she saw Selene discreetly dabbing at her damp cheeks, and she could hear Zoe taking deep, calming breaths. It appeared that there were things that could choke up even battle-hardened warriors, and returning home was one of them.

"Where is everyone?" Sam asked.

It was a good question. There was no one to be seen. Kalli would have thought that a strange object barreling out of the veil into the Amazon haven would have attracted more attention.

Zoe was the first one to open her car door and get out. "Please tell me we're not already too late."

Kalli climbed out of the van and closed the door, and the other two followed suit. A faint sound of metal clanging against metal caught the wind. "I don't think so, but just to be safe, gear up."

The Amazons each grabbed a shield, a spear—which they tucked into a notch on the shield—and a sword that they strapped to their waists. They each also grabbed a gun. Sam, who wasn't trained with a sword, stuck with the Beretta.

"This way." Kalli led her party down the road, passing small houses on either side before coming up to the center square.

On the far side of the square was the largest building in town. While most of the houses along the main road were the same size as when she'd left, the Royal Hall was almost three times as large as when she'd been queen. Nyx had clearly been adding on while she'd been gone. The large stone building was more than just a house for the queen. It contained a large central hall used for festivities and war council meetings. It also held historical artifacts and treasures of their people, including the item she'd mentioned to Eris.

The clanging was getting louder. Kalli followed the noise around the side of the Royal Hall and to the back. As she'd suspected, the Amazons were training.

The field spread out as far as the eye could see. There were small groups of women everywhere, each group engaged in combat. The clash of swords banging shields and the sharp clang of sword hitting sword grew to a deafening clamor. It wasn't unusual for Amazons to spend time training and fighting, but there was something off about the way they were going about it. Kalli felt a desperation in the air mixed with hunger and a whiff of fear.

The women before her looked nothing like the ones she'd left behind. Their fighting had turned dirtier, their expressions meaner. Most of them were covered in scars, some of which appeared almost fresh. Blood spattered on the ground in large arcs, several swords still dripping with it.

Her stomach rolled, and she tried not to lose her breakfast. She had no idea what she'd walked in on, but she was determined to find out. Amazons had always practiced their fighting skills—it was part of their culture—but it wasn't part of their practice to wound unnecessarily. Doing so only had the side effect of weakening the victim, making them less fit for battle while they healed.

The cracking of a whip caught Kalli's attention, and she turned toward the source. Nyx was standing off to the side of the field, lashing a fighter who had dropped her sword. The victim's back was already covered with red slashes. Within seconds, Kalli was across the field, her hand snatching the whip before it cracked again at the poor woman's back.

Kalli barely felt the pain of the lash hitting her palm, and then she yanked it forcefully out of Nyx's grasp. She threw the whip to Selene, who snatched it out of the air, then carefully coiled it and hung it over her shoulder.

Nyx looked at her, brown eyes wide with shock and mouth hanging open. "Kalliope!" she sputtered.

The fighting around them slowly stopped as the Amazons became aware of the confrontation. Heads turned to see what was happening. Several Amazons approached them, forming a small huddle near Kalli, who was staring down Nyx. Kalli's fingers clenched on the hilt of her sword, her fingers twitching.

Resentment swelled, threatening to choke her. This woman, with her stringy black hair, big boobs, and taste for dominatrix-style clothing was the reason she'd spent the last twenty-five hundred years wandering the globe alone rather than living with her people. This was the woman who had stripped her of her throne and her dignity.

It would be so easy to take her revenge, to avenge the damage that had been done to the warriors around her. One swipe of Kalli's blade and Nyx would no longer be a problem. She would no longer be able to harm another person.

But now wasn't the time. She had bigger problems. Despite what Nyx had done, it didn't change the fact that Eris and her men were on their way there at that very moment.

Nyx shifted uneasily, and Kalli's eyes were drawn to the glitter of silver and sapphire that circled the top of her head. By tradition, the royal circlet was used only for ceremonial reasons and spent most of its time locked in the armory. Trust Nyx to turn an honored tradition into an everyday display of power. Only the ring had been intended for daily wear, but Nyx had never managed to acquire it. The thought brought a smile to Kalli's lips.

Swallowing down her personal feelings, she addressed her rival. "Nyx," Kalli said through gritted teeth.

Kalli's gaze scanned over Nyx's troops, assessing their well-being. They looked tired and worn down, like they had lived difficult lives. They appeared grittier and more muscular than she remembered.

"Is there someplace we can talk?" Kalli asked Nyx.

Nyx surveyed the small band behind Kalli, sneering at Zoe and Selene before almost laughing at Sam. "What could I possibly have to discuss with you?" Nyx said, her gaze scanning Kalli from head to toe, her eyes narrowing at her jeans and T-shirt.

"If you want to save our people from grave danger, you'll want to talk to me," Kalli said, trying to keep the impatience from her tone. They didn't have time for a pissing match.

Nyx threw her head back and laughed, a few of her simpering followers joining in. "I have the best trained warriors in the history of the Amazons. Nothing you say is of interest to me."

Kalli pulled the gun from the holster at her waist, took aim at a nearby training dummy, and squeezed off five tightly grouped shots in rapid succession, blowing a giant hole through the mannequin and the bronze armor it was wearing. "Still think you have nothing to fear?"

Nyx rolled her shoulders, glancing around at the other Amazons, her gaze landing on the whip Selene had over her shoulder. "Whatever you have to say to me, you can say in front of my people," Nyx said.

Kalli shrugged. "Suit yourself." She turned to address the warriors watching the confrontation. "All of you, listen to me. You are in danger from men bearing weapons you cannot hope to understand. Eris plans to return, and she does not come alone. She will bring dozens, if not hundreds, of the weapons I hold in my hand." Kalli displayed the pistol for all to see.

Nyx moved closer to Kalli, her voice getting louder. "And what of it? Why do I care that my faithful servant is returning to me? This should be a joyful occasion, not a reason to mourn." She smiled broadly and ignored the hushed murmur growing among the Amazons.

Hope flared in Kalli's chest. Maybe some of them would believe her.

Kalli rolled her eyes at Nyx. "Don't you mean the servant you banished because you thought she was a threat to you? Eris is bringing a force of armed men to attack our city. She means to end you, to take your power for her own."

Nyx just sneered. "Let them come," she said, walking in a large circle, keeping the attention of her troops. "We're the finest warriors of the age. No one can defeat us." There were several shouts of agreement from the gathered crowds.

Kalli just sighed. "The age has changed, while you have not. The weapons of this time have far surpassed what you can do with a bow and arrow." She was losing them. How could she possibly protect her people if they weren't able to grasp the danger they were in?

"Fine. Those who feel the Amazons are better off since Nyx took over as queen are free to stay here and practice, but those who wonder if I just might be telling the truth can follow me." Kalli held her right hand to the heavens, the queen's ring glinting on her finger and radiating with power.

Turning her back on her longtime enemy, Kalli started to stride off the battlefield. The clang of metal on metal stopped her in her tracks. Turning her head slightly, she saw that Nyx had drawn her sword and aimed for Kalli's neck. Thankfully Selene was faster on the draw and her sword had stopped Nyx's midswing. Even Sam had his pistol aimed in Nyx's direction. "I wouldn't do that if I were you," Kalli said offhandedly as she strode away.

"Look at your former queen," Nyx shouted at Kalli's retreating back. "Letting a man stand in front of her to defend her. That's the highest dishonor an Amazon can face."

A low murmur went through the crowd of women surrounding her. Kalli stopped in her tracks yet again, but before she could say a thing to defend herself, Sam beat her to the punch.

"Your true queen knows exactly what she's doing. She cares enough about her people and their survival that she'll use any means within her power to help save them. Even if that means trusting a man to help her." His deep voice resonated, seeming to bounce off the hills and ricochet back.

"Why would we take the word of one such as you?" asked a sneering woman with scraggly braids and a face covered in dirt.

"Then take mine," Zoe chimed in. "Your queen remains true to you. Did you not feel the power yesterday when she once again took the burden of the royal ring upon her finger?"

Several Amazons nodded, glancing around to see if others had felt it too. "Your queen has also spoken to the gods. It was Hermes who helped us see through the veil surrounding the city. And it was Harmonia who told her how to defeat Eris," Selene chimed in.

Kalli wanted to protest, seeing that Harmonia had told her nothing of the sort, but she held her tongue. At the mention of their mother's name, several of the Amazons had bowed their heads, some even saying a quick prayer to the skies. Kalli turned to face the crowd.

"I can't guarantee you victory, as no true leader could. I can promise you that I am not deceiving you. Eris and her troops are on their way as we speak, and they possess weapons such as you've never seen before."

"What is she after?" a nearby blonde woman asked, tentatively glancing in Nyx's direction before dropping her eyes to the ground.

Kalli's smile was bittersweet. "Melina, it's nice to see you again." The woman smiled quickly before once again dropping her gaze. Kalli addressed the group. "Eris is after Harmonia's gift. She seeks to steal the power of the Amazons for herself."

"We must stop her," another voice chimed in from the back of the crowd. "Harmonia's gift is what makes us who we are. Without it, we are nothing."

"Frona, you must never believe that," Kalli replied sharply, making the brunette in the back flinch. "The Amazons are powerful, strong, and fierce. Harmonia's gift enhances that, but it doesn't supply it. You are the source of your powers. Every one of you will need to search inside yourself, feel the source of your own strength, and bring it to bear against this threat, just as you always do."

"How do we know you're not just here to take the gift for yourself?" Nyx drawled, striding out of the crowd, once again challenging Kalli.

"If you think that, you really don't understand what it means to be the queen of the Amazons." Kalli's eyes found Nyx's piercing brown gaze. A swell of pity rose inside her. Even after ruling for thousands of years, Nyx still didn't understand what it meant to be a ruler, what it meant to lead the way and set the example. "Being the queen doesn't mean wanting the most power, the sharpest weapons, or even the biggest house." A few women let laughs escape before they were quickly muffled.

"Ruling is about being the best version of yourself. Not just for you but for the people you represent. It's about making the hard decisions and leading your people to the best of your ability, not so that you look good, but so that everyone flourishes together. It's also about forcing change when it becomes necessary." Kalli's eyes skimmed the crowds surrounding her, acknowledging every gaze she found, but seeking one in particular. Finally, she found Sam's beautiful face in the crowd. "The Amazons have always been a force to be reckoned with, but we aren't known for our flexibility. It's time to grow, to adapt, to accept that things have changed."

Without planning to, she took a handful of steps and crossed the distance between her and Sam. Leaning in, she kissed him passionately, her hand rising to grip the back of his head. She could feel his surprise, but his lips willingly parted beneath hers, his warmth infusing her with strength.

She broke away from her man and turned to face her troops once more. She expected censure or surprise, but most just smiled knowingly. "The world outside the veil is not one you would recognize any longer. I am a totally different person than I was when I was your queen. But if you'll let me, I'd like to help save your lives."

"I haven't lived this long just to die now," Frona yelled from the back of the group, making Kalli smile.

"Then let us begin," Kalli said. She turned her back on Nyx and walked back toward the square on the other side of the Royal Hall, with Selene, Zoe, and Sam falling in behind her. Most of the Amazons followed, though a handful stayed stubbornly behind, converging around Nyx. Kalli didn't want to leave anyone behind, but it was their choice, and she had to respect that.

Once everyone had joined her in the square, she turned to address her army. "They'll likely come through here." She pointed to the main road through the city. The road started right where they'd come through the mist, where they'd left their car, and led straight to the Royal Hall. "We're going to need to spread out. An all-out frontal attack isn't wise, since they have projectiles that can kill accurately from great distances." Kalli didn't bother to take the time to explain how guns worked. They were racing the clock, and Eris and her men could show up at any time.

"They'll probably be wearing armor, but it won't look like any armor you've seen before," Zoe chimed in, coming to stand next to her. "It'll probably look like they're wearing thick vests. You'll need to be very precise in where you aim and how you hit them."

"Will we get those?" Melina asked, pointing at the gun on Kalli's hip.

"We don't have enough to go around, and we don't have the time to train you how to use them," Selene said. "If we survive this, I'll get you stockpiles of them."

"I know I'm asking a lot of you, especially since I wasn't strong enough to fight for my role as your queen," Kalli said, her heart breaking as she looked around at the familiar faces of the women she'd fought shoulder to shoulder with so very long ago.

"That is a giant load of horse manure," a tall Amazon with long black braids said from Kalli's right side. "We've never held you responsible for what Nyx did to you. What Nyx did was unforgivable. That's not how an Amazon is supposed to act." A murmur of agreement went through the crowd, filling Kalli with a warm glow. She'd never expected to be welcomed back. It was beyond anything she could have hoped for.

She dabbed the corner of her eye before a lone tear could fall. "Enough sentiment. We can catch up more later. For now, we need to do what Amazons do best. We need to fight. We need to win." She looked around at the women, each one showing the same anticipation that was building inside of her. It had been a long time since she'd been in a battle. Amazons were built for battle; it was a normal part of their daily lives. While war clearly had its downsides, there was something about the makeup of Amazons that made them crave it. It was a sensation she hadn't felt in thousands of years, something she'd tucked away at the back of her mind, knowing it had no place in the modern world. But here, among her people and fighting an enemy they had no choice but to destroy, she could let her inner warrior loose.

"Go now. Gather your weapons and take positions. I imagine Eris won't be too far behind us."

The women scattered, gone almost before she could blink. Despite everything else she could say about Nyx, the one thing she couldn't fault her for was the fact that her troops looked battle ready and eager to engage.

Kalli watched them go, torn between pride and anguish. There was no way they were all going to make it through this alive. She was pitting women wielding swords and shields against trained mercenaries and a black-market arms dealer. The Amazons would have the physical advantage, being preternaturally strong and fast, but even they couldn't dodge bullets. It was a testament to their characters that they had done as she requested, no questions asked. They were willing to fight and die to protect their homeland.

A weight settled on her heart. This was the hardest part of being queen. Knowing that you had to be willing to send your people into a fight they may not come back from. It was her responsibility to make the hard calls, knowing that the sacrifice of a few could save the whole.

Warm arms circled her waist from behind. "You're doing the right thing," Sam said softly in her ear.

She nodded slowly. "I know that. But this part never gets any easier."

He spun her around to face him and planted a quick kiss on her lips. Her gaze traced the familiar lines of his face. It was torture not knowing whether they would both survive the coming fight.

If sending trained Amazon warriors into battle was difficult, the thought of sending Sam almost cut her off at the knees. After being alive for more than four thousand years, she had finally found her match. In a way, it finally made sense that the Amazons hadn't allowed themselves to fall in love. Sam had forever changed her for the better, pushing her to see the best in herself. He'd also become her greatest weakness. If anything happened to him, she had no idea what she would do.

She opened her mouth to speak, but he cut her off before she got out a single word. "No, I won't wait in the car."

Kalli laughed, swallowing down her fear. "Well, you can't blame me for trying." She had to believe they would both make it out of this alive.

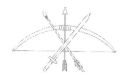

Chapter
Twenty-Three

S AM KNEW THAT THE anticipation of something was always far worse than the actual event. Just knowing that at any second they could be under siege from a militia of armed men had his teeth on edge. What on earth was a college professor doing in the middle of what was about to become a war zone?

His gaze landed on Kalli, who was standing tirelessly in the middle of the town square. That was what he was doing there, he reminded himself. As long as Kalli was fighting the good fight, so was he. He was in it up to his eyeballs with her, so there was no way he was leaving her to fend for herself, even if she did have dozens of trained fighters at her back.

To appease Kalli's worry, and because he was smart enough to know when he was outclassed, he'd agreed to stay to the back of the fight, standing near the Royal Hall, which he could use as cover, if necessary. He'd drawn the line at hiding inside.

Scanning the town, his academic eye took in the architecture of the buildings that were still standing after thousands of years. It was obvious where some had been repaired or added on to, but the majority of what he was seeing was truly ancient. He couldn't help wishing the battle would never come, or at least that it was already over. He couldn't wait to explore the town. Being here would unlock the hidden mysteries of the culture that had fascinated him for so long.

As he looked around, it occurred to him exactly what he wasn't seeing—the Amazons themselves. As soon as they'd run off to gather their weapons, he'd expected to see them return in force, forming a phalanx of battle-hardened warriors to face off against Eris and her men. He'd been surprised when he hadn't seen them again. If it were just him, he'd have been worried that they'd scampered off, protecting themselves and leaving Kalli and her band of merry warriors to fend for themselves. Kalli didn't seem worried, however, so he tried to follow her lead. She was a queen. She knew her people.

A sudden hum broke the quiet air, interrupting the silence that had fallen during their tense wait. It was a car engine, and since all the people who knew how to drive one were within his range of vision, his stomach clenched in fear. This was it.

Eris had arrived.

A mottled green military Humvee came bursting through the veil, appearing out of nowhere. It was followed by a second, and then a third. Unlike Selene, these drivers didn't politely stop at the edge of town. They barreled straight down the road, despite the fact that it was a rough dirt strip just wide enough for a few horses to ride abreast.

A great cry rose from the city, startling him. From his vantage point next to the Royal Hall, he saw Amazons pop out of hiding, emerging on rooftops and from behind buildings. They were armed with bows and arrows, not machine guns or pistols, but their aim was true, and no less deadly. One by one, the vehicles swerved drunkenly and slammed into buildings as arrow after arrow pierced the driver's-side windows. The remaining men inside the Humvees threw open the doors and crouched behind them to protect themselves against the onslaught of arrows as they returned fire.

The sudden noise of the automatic weapons was deafening compared to the relative silence of the town. Sam's stomach rolled, causing him to nearly lose his breakfast at the sight of Amazon after Amazon being cut down, their bodies riddled with bullets they had no way to defend against.

The armed men scattered like mice, ducking in and around the buildings, Amazons raining down a lethal onslaught of arrows and spears. Sam watched, horror-struck, as one man took an arrow to the left eye and another spun around in a circle from the force of a spear ramming into his side.

The Amazons fought the invaders and protected their home, beautiful in their terrifying ferocity. The men moved like trained mercenaries, barely missing a stride as the women came after them in wave after wave.

The biggest flaw in the plan to drive their giant vehicles straight down the main road of town was that it put the invaders at a disadvantage almost immediately. The Amazons had the high ground and kept them pinned down in the small area around their abandoned cars. One or two of the soldiers almost made it to the center square but were cut down by Zoe and Selene, who were alternating between their own guns and stabbing and slashing with finely honed metal swords. Sam managed to squeeze off a few shots, taking out the men who had almost made their way to Kalli.

Relief washed through him. As awful as the battle was, it seemed like they had it under control. They were winning the fight, beating back the men stupid enough to invade a village full of warriors on their home turf. He was about to come out of his hiding spot when he realized something.

Eris was nowhere to be seen.

There was no possible way that Eris would miss this fight. She had a bone to pick with the Amazons, and nothing would have kept her away from this place. Besides, she wanted the source of the Amazons' power, and she likely wouldn't trust anyone but herself to retrieve it.

The cracks and pops of gunfire were slowing as the Amazons managed to kill or subdue each of the men who had poured out of the vehicles. Maybe Eris had changed her mind, or perhaps she'd forgotten just how savage her people could be. A hush fell across the town. Only the moans of the injured broke the stillness.

Sam pushed away from the building, taking one step out into the open. Kalli's voice broke the relative calm. "No!" she commanded, holding up her hand and splaying out her fingers in a stop gesture.

His beautiful queen was still standing in exactly the same spot, dead center of the square, a large bronze shield on her left arm, a lethal-looking sword clutched in her right hand. It was the fear he saw in her eyes that had him frozen in place. A second later, he realized why.

A loud thrumming hit his ears as a fleet of Humvees broke through the veil, immediately separating, some going to the left, some to the right, and some straight down the road through town, smashing the crashed cars out of the way as they went. Within moments, the town square was completely surrounded.

Car doors flew open, and men jumped out and leveled their guns at the Amazons. Kalli, who remained motionless, received more than her fair share of attention. She didn't react, barely batting an eye at the men.

"Eris, is that you?" she called, her voice sounding merely curious and not in the least afraid. He had no idea how she managed to keep her cool under the watchful eye of at least six guns, but she barely looked ruffled. Sam, however, was clutching his gun tight enough that his knuckles were white, trying hard not to let his shaking hands drop his best form of protection.

One last door opened slowly, allowing the beautiful and deadly Amazon to emerge, her trim body encased in its usual black leather. Today she'd matched her skintight leather pants with a strapless leather corset, which couldn't have been comfortable in the baking heat. He had no idea how she intended to fight in her strange choice of attire, but perhaps she would let her men do the heavy lifting.

"My dear Kalli," Eris said, slowly crossing the hard dirt road toward the central grassy square where Kalli was standing with her weapons held loosely by her sides. "Here we are again. It's been such a long time since I've seen you."

Kalli rolled her eyes. "Longest forty-eight hours of my life," she said sarcastically.

"And where is your little pet?" Eris asked, ignoring Kalli's snide comments.

Crap. She meant him.

His muscles froze, each and every injury making itself known, screaming for attention he didn't have time to give them. He couldn't allow himself to be a victim again. He couldn't be responsible for Kalli doing something dumb just because he was in danger.

Before he could move, Eris's eyes darted around the town square and spotted him crouched by the Royal Hall. With a quick flick of her wrist, she gestured to the man closest to him. Before Sam could think about running, there was a gun barrel under his chin.

Sam walked slowly, trying to hide how much pain he was in. The man shoved him from behind, forcing him toward the square. He was hoping it just looked like he was uncomfortable because of the gun, but the way Eris's gray eyes skated over him from head to toe, she wasn't fooled.

The soldier marched Sam until he was standing in front of Eris. She smiled wickedly as she circled him, gazing at him from all angles. She trailed a long, manicured nail down his chest, jabbing it into his sore ribs and making him hiss in pain. His stomach rolled, and he drew in a deep breath, trying to remain upright. It wasn't a good time to pass out.

Kalli lurched toward them but pulled up before she reached them. Eris noticed the movement, her eyes widening along with her grin. "Yes, darling? Do you have something to say?"

It was a game of cat and mouse. Eris was toying with them, knowing full well that she had them outgunned.

Kalli refused to give in, her blue eyes hardening into glinting sapphires. "You don't want to do this, Eris."

Eris left Sam's side and crossed to Kalli, stopping just out of striking distance of her sword. "I really do. And just think, it's all thanks to you that this was possible."

Kalli's eyes narrowed. "What do you mean?"

Eris clucked her tongue in fake sympathy. "Haven't you wondered how I was able to locate Themyscira?" Eris went on before Kalli answered. "I followed you, of course. I knew I would never find it on my own—that damn veil and all—but you, my precious queen, have the ear of the gods. Only you could find a way back in, with a little divine assistance, of course. All I had to do was tag along."

Kalli's mouth dropped open, shock clearly visible even from where Sam stood twenty feet away. His heart was breaking for her. She'd done everything within her power to prevent Eris from getting to Themyscira and stealing the power of the Amazons. She'd fought tooth and nail to keep her people safe. To hear that she'd brought about the very thing she'd been trying to prevent must be devastating. Her gaze darted around the town, no doubt noticing all the Amazons being held at gunpoint, witness to her humiliation.

Zoe and Selene were the closest to Kalli, and he was pleased to see that the two of them looked more pissed at Eris than shocked. Whatever part Kalli had played in Eris's scheme, they were all equally guilty for helping. Zoe's hands opened and closed several times on the handle of her sword, and Selene tried to move closer, getting a gun jammed into her lower back for her trouble.

"Well, let's crack on, shall we?" Eris said sweetly, sauntering away toward the Royal Hall.

Kalli lunged slightly, as if to follow Eris, but was met by three very capable soldiers pointing guns at her.

"What's in this for you?" Kalli asked the men, her eyes gazing from one hard face to the other. "Did she promise you some of the power? Did she say she was going to share it with you?"

Two of the men stayed stoic, not bothering to react to her question. The man in the center, however, smiled cruelly. "She said you would try to talk to us, try to influence us. It's not going to work." He stepped closer, lifting his gun so the barrel rested under her chin.

"Whatever she promised you, she's lying," Zoe piped up from twenty feet away. "The artifact Eris is after is what gives the Amazons their power. It won't do anything for you."

"That may be," the blond man on the end said, shrugging. "But that still makes us the army of a god."

"Seriously?" Selene scoffed, drawing the men's attention to her. "She told you she was divine? Sorry to burst your bubble, fellas, but that's not how this works."

A few of the soldiers shifted uncomfortably, but they were too well trained to move. "Ignore them," a tall man with black hair said, glaring down each of the men in turn. "We follow orders, got that?"

Kalli opened her mouth to respond, but the doors to the Royal Hall swung open, drawing everyone's attention. Sam's heart sank as Eris slowly walked down the stairs from the hall, holding what appeared to be an ancient wooden shield in front of her. Carved into the wood was a giant version of the symbol of the Amazons, a bow lying horizontally, crossed by an arrow, a spear, and a sword. She'd found the gift.

Sam glanced around the town, his gaze flitting among the Amazons. Some looked confused, others awed, and a few looked angry and ready for round three. Every pair of eyes followed the redhead as she came closer.

"A shield made from the wood of an ash tree. It seems like a fitting artifact to have been created by the god of war and a wood nymph," Eris mused as she sauntered back across the grass, slowly approaching Kalli but carefully remaining out of reach.

Kalli stared at the shield, her eyes full of emotion. "Eris, please don't do this," she said, a pleading note entering her voice. "You really don't know what you're getting yourself into."

"Let's find out, shall we?" Eris asked with relish, slipping the shield onto her arm and holding it in front of her like she was fending off an army.

Nothing happened.

Eris frowned, staring down at the shield. Kalli smiled. "Can't figure it out?" she asked, her voice dripping honey.

Eris glared at Kalli as she pulled the shield off her arm. She used the long strap fastened to the back of the shield and slung it around her shoulders, letting it rest across her back, the strap landing between her corset-covered breasts.

Still nothing.

Maybe they would get out of this after all.

With a frustrated growl, Eris pulled a gun out of a holster on her waist and stalked over to Kalli, forcing her soldier out of the way so she could point her own gun at Kalli's face, right between her eyes. Sam's heart hammered against his ribs. He shifted, trying to get to Kalli, but the iron grip on his arm stopped him cold.

"Start talking," Eris demanded.

"The year was three thousand BCE, and a horny god fell for a beautiful wood nymph he stumbled upon in a forest," Kalli said.

Sam tried not to laugh out loud. Zoe and Selene sent each other quick grins. He admired Kalli's pluck, but this wasn't exactly the right time to be joking around.

Apparently Eris agreed, pulling the hammer back with a click and sending Sam's pulse skyrocketing. "Skip to the end."

He tugged futilely against his captors.

"Oh, but I can't," Kalli said. "There is no easy way out. There is no one magical thing. There is only the history, the story, the myth."

"What are you talking about?" Eris shouted, forcing Kalli's head back a few inches with the pressure of the gun.

Kalli smiled, not even acknowledging the gun shoved in her face. "You're looking for a magical artifact, an object that imbues the Amazons with the gifts and powers we've all enjoyed for so long."

Kalli turned her head, as much as she could, first meeting Sam's eyes before traveling to Zoe and Selene, then beyond to the rest of her warriors. "It doesn't exist."

Sam's stomach dropped. It didn't exist? They'd been racing all over the globe to stop Eris from stealing something that had never even existed? It didn't make sense.

"You're lying!" Eris yelled, once again jamming her gun into Kalli's forehead.

Kalli smiled, but it was bittersweet. "No, Eris, I'm not. The power of the Amazons is far too immense to be concentrated in a small piece of wood, however special that piece of wood might be. The power of the Amazons is in their unity, their sense of purpose, their sense of honor. The power of the Amazons comes from within all of us. Even you, no matter how far you may have fallen."

Eris spun away, ripping the shield off her back and throwing it with all her considerable strength across the square, where it hit the corner of the closest building, the dry wood splintering.

"Well, that's a damn shame. You don't find many five-thou-sand-year-old shields anymore," Kalli said, her eyes focused on where the shield had fallen. Sam's anthropologist heart broke at the sight of the damaged artifact.

Eris spun back around, once again getting into Kalli's face. "You lied to me."

Kalli shrugged. "I told you what you wanted to hear."

"Fine, then. You took this from me, and I'll repay you tenfold." Eris spun away from Kalli and strode over to him. Sam's stomach dropped, his heart racing. He barely had time to flinch before she had him by the collar, the cool metal of her gun jammed into his already aching ribs.

"No!" Kalli shouted, her composure dropping entirely.

"It's time to end this," Eris said.

Sam squeezed his eyes shut, bracing for the pain.

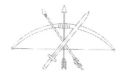

Chapter Twenty-Four

S CREAMS CAME OUT OF nowhere, a battle cry so fearsome that everyone in the square flinched at the sound.

Kalli didn't bother to turn to see the source of the commotion, her eyes fixed on Eris's gun jammed into Sam's side. Thankfully Eris was distracted by the uproar, and her guard dropped just enough.

Kalli launched herself in the air and did a quick forward flip, managing to make it over the heads of the line of soldiers who had their guns trained on her. She used the distraction to her advantage, spinning quickly to kick all three with one strong blow from her right foot, sending them sprawling face-first into the grass.

Eris's gaze left the charging line of Amazons—those who'd remained behind with Nyx—and focused on the more immediate threat of Kalli, who was now only inches away. Kalli's hand lashed out, rapidly knocking Eris's arm away from Sam's stomach, shoving him back a few steps in the process. He took the hint and got out of there, turning once to meet her eyes, a look of determination in his own.

She watched him go, relieved that he was safe and pissed that Eris had managed to get her hands on him again. This couldn't keep happening. Sam was too important.

The charging Amazons, with Nyx notably absent, caused enough chaos that fighting resumed. The sharp clang of metal on metal rang through the town, echoing off the stone buildings. Kalli's heart lurched as Sam pulled his gun and shot a soldier who tried to come after him. Out of the corner of her eye, she saw Zoe take out two armed men, confiscating their guns for her own use. Selene was on the other side, her guns popping loudly as she fired into the crowd of soldiers.

Kalli's distraction cost her dearly.

A small metallic snick reverberated far louder than it should have. Kalli's head whipped around just in time to see Eris finish cocking her gun as she leveled it at Kalli's chest.

"Say hi to Uncle Hades for me," Eris said. She squeezed the trigger.

The crack of the gun was deafening. Time slowed. Every fiber of Kalli's being focused in on the tiny metal lump that was about to kill her.

Kalli flew sideways as a body slammed into her right shoulder and sent them both to the ground. A pained male groan came from somewhere near her ear.

"Sam?" Without a second thought, she grabbed the gun still clenched in his trembling fingers and fired at Eris, hitting her center mass. There was no way Eris would be healing that wound. Kalli couldn't even bring herself to care that she'd just killed one of her own people.

Kalli was covered in blood, but she instantly knew it wasn't her own. "Sam!" Bile burned the back of her throat, and tears pricked her eyes. There was so much blood. How could anyone survive losing that much blood? He couldn't leave her, not when she'd just found him. She'd spent her entire life alone, and she wasn't going to do that again. Sam had to be all right. There was no other option.

She quickly rolled him onto his back, her hands frantically skimming over his body, looking for the source of the blood. She brushed his left shoulder, and he let out the most painful sound she'd ever heard.

"What on earth were you thinking?" she asked roughly as she ripped his shirt open from waist to neck with one tug.

He coughed quietly, moaning as he did. "She was going to shoot you," he whispered.

Kalli wanted to smack him upside the head and yank him into a bear hug all at the same time. She did neither, gently pulling the fabric of his shirt away from his bullet wound. The bullet wound looked like it went all the way through his shoulder. A pool of dark-red blood was spreading sluggishly beneath him.

"I'm immortal, you dolt," she choked out as she tried to hold back tears. She used his now torn shirt to mop up blood and put pressure on the injury.

"Who do you think you are, Superman? You're not bulletproof," he said weakly. His beautiful brown eyes were clouded with pain.

She sniffed, willing her tears not to fall as she hovered over his chest. "Clearly, neither are you. We need to get you to a hospital fast. You're not allowed to die on me."

"That makes two of us. I didn't think I'd make it in time. I was certain she was going to kill you. That's not an option. I love you too much for you to die." The hand of his noninjured arm came up to trace her face gently.

"I love you so much, Sam. I don't know if I could keep living if you died on me."

"Maybe you won't have to," a soft voice said from behind her—a voice she'd heard only once before in her entire life.

"Mom?" Kalli slowly turned until she caught a glimpse of the woman standing less than five feet away. Her mirror image in every way except attire. Where Kalli's jeans were covered in dirt and blood, Harmonia was clothed in a flowing brown satin gown that looked totally out of place in the middle of a battlefield. A battlefield that had gone eerily quiet.

Kalli's arms stayed exactly where they were—keeping pressure on Sam's wound—as she glanced around her. The battle was over. Eris's men were either dead or captured. Her Amazon warriors appeared weary but triumphant.

"Hello, darling," Harmonia said, smiling down at Kalli.

"Mom, not that I'm not happy to see you, but as you can see, I'm a little busy. What on earth are you doing here?" Kalli asked from her position on the ground, leaning over Sam.

Harmonia beamed at her, almost glowing as she did. "I came to deliver this," she said and held out a small glass vial.

Automatically Kalli grabbed the container, covering the glass with streaks of blood. There was a thick golden liquid inside that seemed to shimmer in the bright rays of the sun. She instinctively knew what it was even though she'd never seen it in person. "Nectar? The drink of the gods?"

Harmonia nodded, her brown curls bobbing slightly. "Of course."

"Where did you get it?"

Her mother blushed and lowered her gaze to somewhere around Kalli's knee. "I may have pilfered it from your aunt Hebe, the goddess of youth."

Ignoring her mom's kleptomaniac behavior, Kalli cocked her head. "I don't see how it will help anything if I drink this," she said doubtfully.

Harmonia chuckled, a wide smile spreading across her face once more.

Kalli couldn't see what was so funny about the situation. Sam was dying right in front of her eyes.

"Not you, dear. Sam."

Kalli sucked in a sharp breath, almost burning her nostrils with the hot air. Her mother couldn't seriously be offering what she thought she was offering. There was no way. She had to be mistaken.

Sam cleared his throat and tried to leverage himself off the ground. Kalli pushed him back into the dirt with one hand. "I couldn't possibly accept that. The nectar of the gods is what grants the Olympians their immortality. I'm no god."

Harmonia crouched next to him, staring him in the eye. "You may not be an Olympian, but you are a hero of legend. You helped thwart an attack on the Amazon homeland, and you saved their queen, my favorite daughter." She winked at Kalli. "The Amazons are my legacy, and they survive today because of your assistance. I'm in your debt. The least I can do to repay you is to enable you and Kalliope to stay together forever."

Sam's eyes sought Kalli's, uncertainty brewing in them. "Is that what you want?" he asked.

It wasn't even a question. "More than anything in the world."

The cloudiness cleared from Sam's face. "Bottoms up."

Joy rose inside her as Sam carefully unstopped the vial and swallowed the golden liquid in one shot.

"You'll never be rid of me now," he said weakly, then winked.

"Why would I ever want to be rid of you?" She placed a light kiss on his lips, pleased to see the color was already starting to come back into his cheeks. The blood had trickled to a stop. He was starting to heal, albeit slowly.

When she lifted her gaze again, Harmonia had vanished. Her people stood around her, battle weary yet somehow still smiling. They, like her, were covered in blood.

Kalli had killed more people that day than she would ever care to think about, and she'd watched Sam do the same. She tucked the pain of that realization deep inside to be dealt with later. Taking a life should never be an easy thing to come to terms with, even after thousands of years. The sharp anguish of slaughtering other living creatures was what kept a person from becoming a monster.

The important thing was that her people had survived.

She was eventually going to have to find and deal with Nyx for the way she'd been mistreating and abusing her fellow Amazons, but it could wait until another day. Tonight was a night for celebration—after the funeral rites for the dead, of course.

Kalli looked around at the tired, bloody faces she used to know so well. These were her people. She'd known these women for generations, their immortality giving them a bond that couldn't be rivaled by any human emotion.

Her gaze found Sam. Well, maybe one human emotion could be its equal. The love she felt for Sam was like nothing she'd ever felt before. Her heart ached to see the blood on his body. Her heart wept to see him safe, and it worried that he would always be in danger because of her.

She didn't fully understand it, this love she had for him. But she was willing to figure it out. She was the queen of the Amazons. It was her duty to lead them into the future, and the future meant embracing all parts of the modern world, including love.

"So there really is no gift?" Selene's voice broke the silence as she strolled over, her eyes quickly taking in Eris's body before swinging back to her queen.

Kalli shrugged. "It was a myth, propagated by my predecessors. It didn't feel right to disabuse our people of their source of hope. The idea that our mother had gifted us with an object that could give us limitless power was probably the only thing that kept our people charging into battle as fearlessly as they did."

"I think you underestimate your people," Zoe said. She also glanced briefly at Eris, but her gaze returned to the cleanup operations that were just beginning. Men were being hauled off to the small building used to hold their prisoners of war, many of them bleeding profusely and leaving a red trail in their wake.

Kalli watched as the Amazons began putting their city back to rights. Each and every one of them had just heard her tell Eris that Harmonia's gift didn't exist, that there was no magical object giving them powers. Yet here they all were, doing exactly what they would have done under any other circumstances. "Perhaps you're right," Kalli murmured.

"So what happens now?" Sam asked as he hesitantly stood, using her for balance. He gave Eris's body a wide berth. "Do you think they'll ever be the same?"

Kalli looked at the dozens of warriors who had been cut down by weapons they couldn't possibly understand. She saw the ring of giant Humvees, a method of transportation that the Amazons never could have imagined. And she saw Eris, one of their own who had betrayed them.

"No, they're never going to be the same," Kalli said. "But hopefully they can start to be better."

"Better?" Zoe asked quizzically.

Kalli nodded. It was time.

She crossed the town square and climbed to the top of the steps that led to the Royal Hall. A few of the closer women noticed what she was doing and paused, shooting each other confused looks. Kalli raised her arms, breathing in the familiar air and feeling the power of being back where she belonged.

"Amazons!" she shouted, her voice projecting through town as if amplified. Everything came to a halt, women stopping midtask to stare in her direction.

"There is nothing I can say that will remove the pain of this day. We lost fellow warriors, our friends. We lost them at the hand of one we used to call our own. There is nothing I can say to undo that type of betrayal. I can only hope that each of you will look inside yourselves and find the will and hope to continue. The power of the Amazons isn't in some magical shield. It isn't even in the physical strength that helped us defend our homeland from invaders. The real power of our people comes from our unity and strength of character.

"Yes, today will change us. How could it not? But it will not break us. The Amazons have been around for thousands of years, and we will continue to exist for thousands more. We will exist because we decide to, because we choose to."

Kalli looked around, capturing the eyes of each of her people in turn. "Several thousand years ago I asked Hermes to cast a veil upon our city, hiding us from the outside world. It was a decision that I felt was right at the time. Our numbers were dwindling, and the constant battles were bringing our very survival into question. Since that time, the world has changed drastically. There is still war, and men still do not always treat women as their equals." She glanced at Zoe and Selene, giving them a small nod of mutual understanding for all they had seen during their time on the outside. "But I believe that we can help change all that."

A murmur started among the gathered crowd. "What do you mean?" Melina asked from where she'd come to stand near the foot of the steps.

Kalli smiled, first at the woman brave enough to ask the question, then encompassing the entire group. "No leader is perfect, and I have made my fair share of mistakes. I still believe that the veil had a purpose, and I don't regret choosing to protect my people above all else. However, I believe it's time to move forward. I want to remove the veil."

A sharply indrawn breath had Kalli's head whipping to the left. She met Sam's surprised gaze and gave him an encouraging smile. "There is no reason for our people to hide any longer."

Kalli stopped talking, a clenching sensation around her midsection making her slightly queasy. She hoped she was doing the right thing.

A terrifying minute passed. No one moved or even spoke. Kalli was on the verge of trying to take back what she'd said when a movement caught her eye. Dead center in front of the steps, Zoe dropped to one knee, bowing her head. Selene followed.

The wave of movement started slowly but gained speed. Melina didn't hesitate, Frona and Ariadne quickly dropping to their knees too. The creak of leather and clang of metal sounded as one by one the Amazons knelt. In front, Zoe banged her sword into her shield, the sound reverberating across the square and echoing off the buildings. "Hail, Queen Kalliope!" she shouted and was answered by hundreds of voices.

"Hail, Queen Kalliope!"

Tears pricked her eyes, but she blinked them back. The tension faded from her belly as she looked across her homeland and her people. She could once again feel the heat of the sun against her skin and the breeze on her face. Her people supported her, and that meant more to her than anything.

Well, almost anything.

A slight movement caught her attention, and she saw Sam as he lifted his head. He'd knelt with the rest of them, but unlike the Amazons, he wasn't staring at the ground. He was staring at her with a huge, gorgeous smile on his face. He blew her a quick kiss and sent her a cheeky wink.

She would love him for the rest of their immortal lives.

"Amazons, rise!" Kalli shouted, lifting her sword in the air, the blue gem on her ring flashing in the sunlight.

As one, the Amazons stood, their shields lifting in unison, almost blinding Kalli with the reflected light. Hundreds of swords shot into the air, the warriors mimicking their queen's pose.

"Ares and Harmonia, we are your daughters, the Amazons. Heed our call." Kalli addressed her plea to the cloudless sky above. "Brave Hermes, hear us now. We ask for your assistance and favor. Too long have the Amazons been sitting on the sidelines. Too long have we been removed from the world. We beseech you now to help us undo what has been done. Remove the veil that protects this place and let us rejoin the world of men."

For the second time in as many days, power surged through her, starting from the ring and radiating outward. Wave after wave coursed across her skin, almost like she was being battered by gale-force winds. A brilliant blue glow emanated from the gem, so blinding Kalli was forced to look away. When that wasn't enough, she squeezed her eyes tightly shut, her hand almost melting from the heat.

A low rumbling started somewhere nearby, making it feel like the entire town was about to come down on top of them.

The pulsing wash of power continued for several minutes, Kalli's arm frozen in position, pointing at the sky. At long last and almost as rapidly as it started, the power fled, leaving a void as it retreated. Of its own accord, her arm fell to her side, and Kalli crumpled. A strong pair of arms grabbed her before she hit the hard stone stairs.

The last thing she noticed was that she could once again see the sea from the steps of the Royal Hall before the world went black.

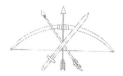

Chapter Twenty-Five

IT FELT LIKE SHE had a knife stabbing into her eye socket. Kalli slowly opened her eyes, but the sunlight pouring in the window didn't make her headache any less painful. She squeezed her eyes shut once more and brought her hand up to rub her forehead.

"Please tell me someone packed the aspirin," she said, her voice coming out as a harsh rasp.

Two small pills and a glass of water were placed gently in her hands, and she swallowed the medicine gratefully. Sitting up, she glanced around at the small, spartan room. The walls were stone, as was the floor. She was lying on a cot with a thin straw mattress that was nothing like her Sleep Number back at home but was probably the nicest mattress in Themyscira. The only other thing in the room was a small wooden chair, currently occupied by Sam.

"What happened?" she finally asked. She took in the clean shirt he was wearing, not a hint of blood in sight.

"Healed completely," he said. "You know, if we bottle that stuff, we could make a fortune."

He leaned down to give her a quick peck on the lips before pulling away, but she wasn't about to let him get away with that. She grabbed the back of his head and drew him into a much longer kiss, sinking into his warmth. Reluctantly, she let him go. As much as she would've loved to yank him down on the mattress and have her way with him, she needed information.

He pulled away, leaning back onto his chair. "More importantly, I think you changed the course of history," he said with a small smile. "I'm pretty sure I'm now out of a job. What use is there in digging through the dirt for hints about a mythical culture if they suddenly reappear out of thin air?" He chuckled lightly.

She smiled, knowing he wasn't really mad. It did, however, raise the question of whether he was planning on heading back to DC now that Eris had been stopped. "What if I could give you exclusive rights to study that culture? I happen to have the ear of the queen."

"That might work," he said, leaning down and giving her a quick kiss on the cheek. "So what happens now?"

She wasn't sure if he was asking about their relationship, his newfound immortality, or the future of the Amazon culture. She focused on the last part first. She knew that she was meant to lead these people, but she also knew she couldn't live in the past. The only way forward would be to lead her people, possibly kicking and screaming, into the twenty-first century.

"So it worked? The veil disappeared?"

Sam bobbed his head. "It did indeed. You can see clear to the sea on one side, mountains on the other sides. In case I failed to mention it before, you have a beautiful home, Kalli. Or should I say, Queen Kalliope?" His eyebrow cocked questioningly.

"For you, it will always be Kalli," she said, feeling her love for him glowing in her heart. "I'm glad you like it." It would make what she needed to ask of him that much easier.

He shifted slightly in his seat. "Zoe and Selene are out doing what they do, calling whoever it is they call. You were worried it will be a shock to the Amazons when they finally meet the modern world. Personally I'm not sure the modern world is ready to know that there's been a hidden society of badass warriors living right under their noses the whole time."

Kalli hadn't given that part much thought. Her main goal had been to do the right thing for her people. She hadn't considered how she would suddenly explain their presence to the world at large. One step at a time. She had something more important to figure out.

"Sam," she said tentatively. "You said you might be out of a job . . ." She didn't know how to ask what she wanted to. Her hand reached out instinctively and clasped his. He squeezed her fingers.

He laughed. "Yeah, I was kidding, though. My dean loves me, despite my strange choice of focus for my research."

Her heart sank. "Oh."

"It's a good thing too. If he didn't like me so much, he would never agree to let me move halfway across the world." He winked, and a grin split his face. "Did you think I was going to leave you that easily? I told you you'd never be rid of me," he said, reaching out to grab her chin.

Warmth flooded her belly as she nuzzled into his gentle touch. His newfound immortality aside, she hadn't wanted to assume he would be willing to upend his life to move to a remote village in the middle of nowhere.

"Dr. Samuel Treadwell, will you marry me?" she asked, her eyes seeking his.

"I thought you'd never ask."

She had no idea how they were going to work out the details, but none of that mattered. She was the happiest she'd ever been in her seemingly infinite existence, and it was all thanks to him.

"I guess we need to figure out how to throw a royal wedding Amazon style." Smiling with glee, she kissed him, knowing her life would never be the same and thanking the gods for it.

Thank you from Elizabeth

If you made it this far, THANK YOU for reading Amazon in Exile. I hope you enjoyed reading this book as much as I enjoyed writing it, and I hope you'll stick around to find out what happens to Selene and Zoe in books two and three.

Reviews and ratings are the life blood of independent authors. If you liked Amazon in Exile, I hope you'll consider leaving a review.

If you want to be the first to hear announcements and updates about future books, please consider joining my newsletter. As an added bonus, you'll get exclusive content (like a glimpse of how Kalli became queen of the Amazons or other fun related scenes).

http://www.elizabethsalo.com/newsletter/

Acknowledgements

This book would not have been possible without a host of people who believed in me and made it happen. Among those I should thank are my copy editor James Gallagher of Castle Walls Editing and my cover designer GraphicSoulArt. Not to be forgotten are my beta readers Pru Warren, Glori Medina, and Amanda Shaffer. And last, but certainly not least, my brainstorming partner/marketing director/social media coordinator/all-around go-to person Chris.

About the Author

Elizabeth Salo is a Michigan native who loves magic, myths, and mayhem. She writes paranormal romance, romantic suspense, and urban fantasy books and is a sucker for a strong female lead. She firmly believes she should have been born with superpowers, but since she wasn't, she'll have to make do with writing about people who do.

She currently lives in Michigan with her family and more fur babies (and feathered babies, and scaly babies...) than is probably wise.

http://www.elizabethsalo.com/

Also By

Wondering what Selene is up to and where she gets those wonderful toys? Stay tuned for:

Amazon in Darkness

Amazons of Themyscira Book Two

coming soon!